HEADCASE

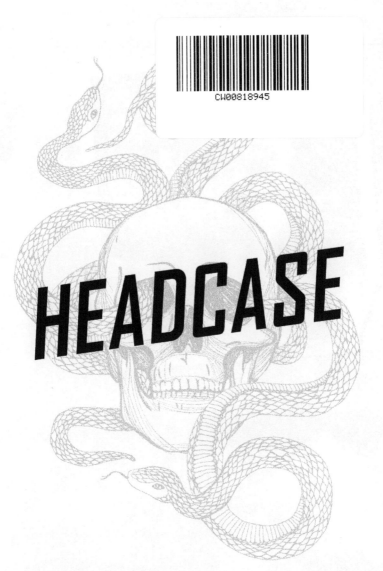

NECESSARY EVILS

HEADCASE

ONLEY JAMES

HEADCASE

NECESSARY EVILS BOOK FOUR

WWW.ONLEYJAMES.COM

Cover and Interior Design by We Got You Covered Book Design

WWW.WEGOTYOUCOVEREDBOOKDESIGN.COM

ISBN: 978-1-68489-141-2

TRIGGER WARNING

This book contains graphic depictions as well as frank talk about suicide and suicidal ideations.

They were perfect. Literally perfect. The two boys lay on the floor of the playroom, one pointing their feet north and the other south, their heads slotted beside one another, close enough for their dark brown hair to blend together, giving them the appearance that they were one unit.

Thomas hadn't been looking for two. Hell, he was never actively searching for new subjects—new children for his project—but, somehow, they found him. They came to him almost through some sort of divine will. He knew instantly they were his. His children, his subjects. Even knowing nothing else about them, he knew they would go home with him.

They appeared to be around five or six. Unlike when he'd found his other children, these two looked healthy, clean, and well-fed. Perhaps they'd lost their parents to an accident and there were no others to care for them. That seemed the only valid explanation for parents abandoning two children they'd clearly cared for. At least, physically.

"Identical twins," Thomas said, almost breathless. He could have never dared to hope for such a gift. Two children split from the same egg. Two halves of a whole. This would take his experiments to a new level. And he'd give the boys everything they needed to succeed, of course.

The woman beside him—Dr. Barbara Rice, the director of the group home—kept a close watch on the two children, her arms crossed over her ample chest. They knew they were being observed; there was no false mirror, no one-way glass. They simply stood outside the playroom where the two boys lay sprawled, staring up at the fake solar system overhead.

Dr. Rice clearly cared about this place and these children. Unlike many group homes Thomas had visited over the years, this one was bright and clean, as were the children. On his way in, every child he'd passed had appeared well cared for, even happy. But unlike the other children, Dr. Rice didn't smile when she looked at the two boys. She seemed unnerved by them.

"Mirror twins," Dr. Rice corrected. "Each one the perfect mirror image of the other, right down to their birthmarks."

The two weren't speaking out loud, but they would smile and laugh in tandem, as if one had told the other a joke. Even though they didn't look at each other, they seemed perfectly in sync. If one moved their left leg, the other moved their right. Same with their hand movements.

"Are they always like this?"

"Like what?" she asked, her tone implying she knew full well what he meant but was unwilling to say it out loud.

"Do they always communicate this way? That is what

they're doing, right? Communicating without speaking? It's not uncommon in identical twins. I imagine it's more so in mirror twins."

Dr. Rice looked at him in surprise. "Do you really believe that twins can communicate telepathically?"

"There have been studies," Thomas said carefully. "I do believe in science, but I think it would be hubris for me to declare that telepathy is impossible between children who grew from the same fertilized egg. Besides, look at them. They're clearly communicating. Don't you think?"

Dr. Rice watched in silence for a moment or two before giving a stilted nod. "Yes, they most definitely are communicating."

It became clear then. Dr. Rice, this woman who loved her job and took so much pride in her facility, was afraid. She seemed like a woman who wasn't easily rattled, but these two clearly spooked her. Interesting.

They didn't frighten Thomas. He had others at home who were equally unnerving, maybe even more so. He couldn't take his eyes off them as they continued their strange pantomime of a silent conversation. Would they like their new home? Their brothers? Their new curriculum? Thomas had decided he would take them even without knowing if they truly belonged with him. After all this time, he just knew. "History?"

She gave a weary sigh, shifting from one booted foot to the other. It was chilly outside, and she was dressed as if she'd entered the building and come straight to meet with him. She had on a long plaid skirt, a red turtleneck, a blazer, and brown leather boots that disappeared under the hem of her skirt.

She reached for the file on the table beside her, but she didn't open it, just hugged it against her chest as if she could absorb the information through osmosis. "According to the case worker who brought them here, they were adopted at just six months old from an adoption agency in Hungary."

"International adoption? Were the parents a poor fit for adopting here in the States or were they only looking to adopt infants?" Thomas questioned.

"Hard to say. I've not met the parents, but the mother is a corporate lawyer for a large corporation and the father is a dermatologist."

Thomas frowned. "Was there abuse in the home?"

Dr. Rice shook her head. "Not to our knowledge. They came to us clean and well cared for. The social worker—Rachel—said the mother spent most of the meeting talking about how it was better for the boys to be with someone else. She said, even as babies, they cried all the time, were often inconsolable, and that it was clear they 'didn't like her.'"

"Her babies didn't like her?"

Dr. Rice nodded. "She said they never interacted with her or her husband. That they abhorred all attempts at affection. That they embarrassed her often by refusing any attempts to bond with her. They never hugged her or asked for help."

She sounded like a narcissist to Thomas. But what did he know? He was raising a household of psychopaths. None of them were particularly affectionate unless it was part of the curriculum. One of the biggest components to making what Thomas did work was teaching those without any ability to feel to pass in society. Sometimes, that meant teaching them how to fake being polite, civil, charming, funny, even how to hug each other or shake hands. It was all new to them.

"So, this was a vanity thing?"

Dr. Rice grimaced. "She said they didn't smile, rarely spoke, and that the other mothers constantly judged her behind her back while pretending to be sympathetic to her plight."

"Her plight?"

"Yes, being a mother to sons who hated her."

Thomas's stomach sank. "And how did they go from living in suburbia to living in a group home?"

She hesitated, but he wasn't sure if it was because it was something truly awful or just because she was having second thoughts about inviting him in. What they were doing was highly illegal. Handing over these boys to Thomas essentially meant making them disappear from this life and reappear a few months later as two entirely new people. It meant acknowledging that these children would become research subjects, even though that came with the perks of being raised by a billionaire.

Thomas was good to his sons. And they were his sons. For all of his grand plans to train these children to do what was in their very nature to do, he still loved his children. He wanted them to succeed, wanted them to exceed all expectations and limitations society often placed on people like them.

Dr. Rice finally spoke. "They tried to separate them. It didn't…go well."

"Separate them?" Thomas echoed.

Dr. Rice's lip curled in disgust. "Yes. The parents got divorced, blamed the stress of trying to raise two boys with severe mental issues—their words, not mine. Said before the adoption, they were a perfect couple. When they divorced, they decided they would each take a twin and move far away from each other like it was the fucking *Parent Trap.*" She must have realized what she said because she darted her gaze to him. "Sorry."

Thomas shook his head, waving a hand dismissively. "Don't be sorry. That's a terrible thing to do to children, twins or not."

Dr. Rice made a derisive sound. "She called it an equal division of assets."

"Christ," Thomas muttered. Maybe the mother was the psychopath? "What happened once they separated the boys?"

Dr. Rice tilted her head, leaning in closer to the window. "They…went feral."

"Feral?" Thomas parroted.

Dr. Rice nodded again, watching the two boys lying together, still occasionally laughing or making funny faces like any typical six year old might. "Within an hour or two, the boys became inconsolable. After around twenty-four hours, they grew violent."

"How violent?" Thomas asked, also leaning in.

"Biting, kicking, scratching. Within two days, they'd stopped speaking, stopped eating. They would scream for hours, urinate on the floors, kick holes in the walls, scratch at their parents. Often at the same time their sibling was engaging in the same behavior."

Thomas processed that information. "I'm assuming the state intervened in one or both cases?"

Dr. Rice frowned. "The parents decided to put each of them on a seventy-two hour psych hold. When that hold was up, the state—for whatever reason—said they weren't a danger to themselves or others and ordered they be released."

Thomas frowned. "Yet, they're here."

"The parents refused to take them back."

Refused? "An adoption is a legally binding contract. You cannot simply refuse to take custody of your children."

"You can when you're an attorney, it seems. The woman claimed she was given fraudulent information regarding the children's pasts. Said the adoption agency failed to disclose that the children had been terribly neglected for the first six months of their lives, leading to a severe attachment disorder. She had the adoption overturned."

Thomas took a deep breath and let it out. Children weren't disposable. They weren't props to be moved around on a set. He knew his outrage smacked of hypocrisy. It wasn't like he was some saint, taking in the needy. He also had an agenda, an ulterior motive, but that didn't mean he'd treat these boys as such. It didn't mean he wouldn't love and care for them, even if they were incapable of returning that affection.

"The acting out only started when they were separated?"

"Before that, they were still distant, but the parents

were workaholics who left them to be raised primarily by a nanny. There's no way of truly knowing whether they could have grown to have some attachment to the family eventually. But while the boys were being held on their psych hold, the mother found out she was pregnant, and she and her husband decided to give their relationship another try…without the boys. She thought they might be a danger to the baby."

Thomas arched a brow. "Was there any validity to the theory?"

Dr. Rice shrugged. "They have been perfectly polite here. They do as they're asked. They share their toys, pick up after themselves. They are both incredibly gifted, though in completely opposite ways. As long as we make no attempt to separate them, they appear perfectly content. They just aren't particularly affectionate."

Dr. Rice's implication was clear. She wouldn't allow Thomas to take one without the other. Not that he ever would. That would simply be cruel, and Thomas was many things but not cruel.

"Why am I here, Dr. Rice? I'm sure you understand what I'm looking for. You clearly have powerful connections if you know what I do, if you've been told of my research."

Dr. Rice turned to Thomas, giving a heavy sigh. "While they are intelligent, polite, and respectful, they are also most definitely…void."

"Void?"

She glanced back at them. "There's nothing there. When you look at them, they study you. They profile you. And more than that…they do it as a team. They can communicate telepathically. I never really believed that was something twins could truly do, not until them. But there's no doubt they're speaking to each other."

As if on cue, the two boys began to laugh, like one had told a funny joke. They paid no attention to Thomas and Dr. Rice behind the glass, but it felt as if that laugh was for their benefit, like they could hear their conversation and found them amusing. It was unsettling to say the least.

Thomas watched them carefully. "No violent outbursts towards the staff? No bedwetting? Arson? Cruelty towards small children or animals?"

She shrugged, then shook her head. "Not that we've witnessed. But I do have to warn you. There's something else."

A trickle of unease shivered along Thomas's spine. "Something else?"

She nodded. "They don't seem to have any interest in harming the staff or other children…but they do seem to enjoy harming each other. But only each other."

Thomas startled. "What?"

Dr. Rice stared at the two boys for a long moment before dragging her gaze back to Thomas. "You see the splint on the one boy's finger?"

Thomas followed her eyes. "You're saying the other did that."

She nodded, swallowing audibly.

"CIPA?" he asked.

Congenital insensitivity to pain with anhidrosis was rare and came with a handful of issues that would make even the most attentive parent paranoid that their child was going to jump from a roof or sit on a hot stove. A child who can't feel pain literally has zero sense of self-preservation.

"No," Dr. Rice said, shaking her head emphatically. "You're not understanding me. They do feel pain…" She shivered. "They just really enjoy it."

ONE

ZANE

"Are you at the office? Why's it so quiet?"

Zane huffed out a sigh, pinching the bridge of his nose. Zane Scott didn't have an office. He didn't even have a cubicle. Because he didn't have a job. Not a real one, anyway. Not that his mother knew that. "No, Ma. I'm working from home today."

And every day.

"Do they have you working on any exciting stories? I told all the ladies in my bridge club about my reporter son. They're very excited to read your first story."

So was Zane. He just had to come up with one. "Ma, please stop telling people about my job. Being an investigative journalist requires a lot of research. It'll be a while before my first major story hits the papers."

His mother sniffed. Then there was the sound of her taking a big gulp of something. Gin, no doubt. It was noon, after all. "I'm allowed to brag about my son. We weren't sure you'd ever make something of yourself. Poor grades. Skipping school. Your brother had sports and debate team and a 5.3 GPA, but you… We thought we'd end up supporting you forever."

Zane knew that. Anybody who knew his mother knew that, too. This wasn't a new conversation.

"Thanks, Ma," Zane said with an eye roll.

She made a disgusted noise. "A writer. Ugh. Might as well be a fitness instructor. At least they have a shot at working with celebrities."

Zane did work with celebrities. Just not in a way his mother would want to brag about.

"Yeah, Ma. I know," he said, seeing the bend in the conversation coming but unable to hit the brakes before it derailed.

"Don't 'I know' me," his mother said. "When we lost your brother, we thought we'd lost any chance…"

No matter how much Zane tried to steel himself for this point in their conversations, it hurt no less. His brother, Gage, had been the heir, and Zane was most definitely the spare. The one they'd tucked into the closet and ignored on the assumption that their original was just too fucking perfect to die. Guess Gage showed them. All of them.

Zane stared down at the pic of a movie star sneaking out of a famous singer's apartment, glancing up at the clock. "Yeah, I know, Ma. I'm just saying, I'm up to my eyeballs in research and I'm on company time. I'll call you and Dad this weekend, okay?"

"Okay, doll. But don't call on Friday. We're having dinner at the Silvers'. And on Sunday, we're having dinner at the Country Club. You know what? I'll call you. Okay?"

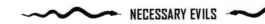

Zane sighed internally. "Yeah, sure, Ma. Love you."

His mother blew kisses into the phone. "Talk soon."

Zane didn't know why he said 'love you' every time they ended a call. His mother had never once said it back. Not when he was five, not when he was eleven, not when he was twenty-one, standing beside his brother's casket. And not now.

The cold, hard truth was his parents didn't love him. He and Gage had been accessories to them. Only Gage had been the designer brand and Zane the cheap knock-off. Which was why he lied to his mother about his glamorous job as an investigative journalist. Writing borderline slanderous articles for the tabloids and blogging about true crime stories was nothing his mother could brag about over brunch.

He pushed the thought away, refusing to give her any more real estate in his head. *Shake it off, Scott.* What he did wasn't pretty, but it paid the bills. Just as he opened his laptop, the door rocketed open, Blake falling through, like the wind had blown him in off the street. Except, Blake was that wind. A big, bearded tornado with copper skin and inky black hair just a smidge too long.

"Took you long enough," Zane grumbled.

Blake frowned at him. "You know what the lines are like at McKabe's this time of day. You want it fast or you want it good?"

Zane sighed. He didn't know why he was taking out his frustration with his mom on Blake. He was pretty much Zane's only friend.

When Zane didn't answer, Blake frowned. "What happened to you? Why are you suddenly so grumpy?" Blake gestured to the wall before them. "I thought you wanted to talk me through all of this."

"Let's just eat," Zane muttered, unwrapping his tuna sandwich and taking a bite, closing his eyes and enjoying a tiny sliver of peace.

Blake made an *aha* noise. "Shit. Your mom called, huh?" Zane stared at him warily. "Yeah, she definitely called. Nobody but Bev can make you look like you just watched your cat get mauled by a bear."

Zane winced. "You have such a way with words."

Blake scoffed. "You're the writer. I just take pictures. Why do you still take her calls? You could just stop answering. Hell, I cut my mom off years ago. Best decision I ever made. It hurt, but it's like gangrene. Sometimes, you gotta cut off the infected limb before that shit spreads. Your mom…she's spreading."

Zane's lips twitched with the barest hint of a smile. His mom really was like deadly bacteria. But she was his mom. "Your mom's a two-time felon who runs with one of the most violent biker gangs in the US territories."

Blake fell into the swivel chair in front of Zane's desk, spinning it a few times before he peeled back the paper on his pastrami sandwich. "And your mom is a gin-swilling narcissist who spends her days sucking the hopes and dreams out of people like a dementor. The only difference in our moms, man, is capital. One's rich, one's poor. They're both shitty people."

Blake was right. He was one hundred percent right. But Zane still wouldn't cut his mom off. He didn't know if that made him a masochist or weak. His mom would say the latter.

Zane sighed, glancing up at the wall covered in string and multicolored pins. In the center, he'd tacked a map of the city, highlighting certain areas in a garish yellow. Thomas Mulvaney's properties. Zane had taped the man's picture to the top.

He'd reserved the sides of the map for the key players in Mulvaney's life, starting with his seven children.

"Run me through this," Blake said around his pastrami sandwich.

Zane finished his tuna sandwich in four large bites, then pointed to the silver-haired man in an expensive navy blue suit. "You know Thomas Mulvaney."

"Everybody does," Blake said, chewing obnoxiously.

"These are his kids." He pointed to each. "The professor, the doctor, the architect, the designer, the gambler, the model…and last but not least, the loner."

Blake scoffed. "Yeah, man. I photograph celebrities for a living. Tell me the ones I don't know."

Zane pointed at a photo taped next to Mulvaney's youngest, the model. Adam. "The pretty freckle-faced one who looks like he should sell skin care? He's engaged to the model. His name's Noah. Noah Holt. Name sound familiar?"

Blake shook his head. "Should it?"

"Son of Wayne Holt. Suspected child molester and murderer. He died under 'mysterious circumstances.'"

"Good fucking riddance," Blake muttered.

Zane agreed. But it was only one small piece of the puzzle. He pointed to a man in a tweed coat. "That one there—that's Lucas Blackwell, a former FBI profiler who had a mental breakdown."

"It is a stressful job," Blake reasoned. "I wouldn't want to deal with all that stuff."

Zane picked up the baseball on his desk and tossed it into the air. "He told his superiors he solved cases using psychic powers, then he pointed to another FBI agent as the perp in a dozen abduction cases."

Blake barked out a laugh. "Shit. Did he get carted off to the funny farm?"

Zane nodded. "Thirty-day psych hold. Then they sent him to teach at a small liberal arts college where he met the genius professor and they fell in love, got married, and had two babies."

"So, they're living the American dream. What am I missing?" Blake asked.

"The former colleague—the one he accused of abducting and killing a dozen women? Well, he too disappeared under mysterious circumstances."

Blake's gaze shot to his and he sat up straighter in his chair. Yeah, now Zane had his attention. "Okay, I admit, that's a little weird."

Zane nodded, pointing to the redhead. "And this one, the doctor? Yeah, this is his husband. He's a mechanic."

Blake gazed at the picture of the dark-haired man, shrugging. "That's it? Your big reveal is that the doctor married a blue-collar guy? Some people like a man who knows how to use their hands. Hell, if I could find a woman who knew a carburetor from a car battery, I'd probably marry her."

Zane rolled his eyes. "That's not the suspicious part. He owns that auto shop down the road. The one where there's a dozen kids running in and out at all hours of the night."

Blake shook his head. "So, what are you saying, man?"

Zane continued to toss the ball in the air. "I don't know what I'm saying. Maybe the doc is a dope supplier and the kids are runners? Maybe it's a chop shop."

"Why would the son of a billionaire need to run drugs or chop cars? Hell, why would a doctor have to do that? I think you're reading into shit. Your mom's got you chasing ghosts, man."

Zane shook his head. "Well, get this. The mechanic? His sister disappeared a decade ago, then turned up dead in the river, missing a kidney. No explanation given. Nobody even investigated."

Blake frowned, staring hard at the picture of the man in question. "We live in a shitty neighborhood, man. People wind up in the river all the time. And not to put too fine a point on it, but she's not white. We all know only rich white ladies get all the attention."

Zane had thought of that. "Okay, but you don't think it's weird that three of Thomas Mulvaney's sons ended up with men who lost somebody close to them under shady circumstances?" Zane asked.

Blake shook his head, threading his fingers behind his

neck as he stared up at the board. "Not really, man. No. My Aunt Carol's husband beat her to death with a toaster. Christabel, in accounting—somebody killed her cousin with a machete back in Haiti. Beach's dad got shot and killed in a liquor store holdup. We live in a violent world. The only difference between us and Thomas Mulvaney is that nobody gives a fuck about our lives."

"I'm telling you, there's something suspicious about this fucking family." Zane jumped to his feet. "See these red pins? Those are dead bodies found in the area over the last two years. Look at how many they found in or around Thomas Mulvaney's properties?"

Blake smiled at him like he was hilarious. "The dude owns most of the city, bro. It would be harder to drop a body on a piece of property not owned by him."

Zane shook his head, frustration burning through him. Blake was right, but there was something there. Zane's gut was never wrong. "I need to keep digging. I need to get closer."

Blake side-eyed him. "No, you need to stop playing Truman Capote and write the copy for the picture I took or you won't be able to afford the rent on this hideous roach motel you call home. Do you want to ask Bev for money because you lost yet another job?"

Zane hadn't lost jobs. He'd left jobs. Writing articles for tabloids wasn't a job. It was a backup plan. If Zane wanted the world to take him seriously as a journalist, he needed to crack a huge story. A story so big even his mother couldn't find a reason to negate his success.

"Don't you want to be something more than just paparazzi?" Zane asked.

Blake scoffed. "I make a lot of money taking pics of celebrities. Enough to afford my camera equipment that lets me take the pictures I really want to take. The ones that will win me awards someday."

Blake was a good guy. He was smart, talented, funny. But he didn't have the instincts for this. "There's something here. I know there is. Believing in an altruistic billionaire is like believing in the tooth fairy or Santa Claus. They don't exist."

"That's a bit classist, no?" Blake asked.

Zane thrust his jaw forward. "Not if I'm right."

Blake crumpled the wrapper of his sandwich. "Okay, let's just say Thomas Mulvaney is the devil. He's some—what?—high-ranking criminal mastermind. What are you going to do about it? You think you'll live long enough to even write the article? Pretty sure he once had Obama on speed dial."

Zane pointed to a grouping of red pins. "Yes. I need to write it. Because of them."

Blake frowned. "Them?"

Zane nodded. "These men were all killed in a fire on one of Mulvaney's properties."

"And?" Blake said.

"And they were a congressman, a priest, a teacher, and a police officer. People with pull. People who had families who miss them."

"That's not a story. That's the start of a bad joke. The story of those men has been told. They were pedophiles. Serial abusers. Nobody misses them. Not even their families. If it turned out Thomas Mulvaney killed them, the city would probably throw him a goddamn parade."

Zane shook his head. "I just need to get closer."

"Closer to what?" Blake asked, exasperated.

"To Thomas Mulvaney."

Getting to Thomas Mulvaney was the key to cracking this story, whatever it was. He needed clues. He needed a trail to follow. There was a difference between suspecting somebody was a criminal mastermind and proving it. To take down the Mulvaney clan, he'd need iron-clad evidence, and for that, Zane would need to get into Thomas Mulvaney's inner circle.

If Zane could just meet him, convince him he was some altruistic bleeding heart, maybe it would give him just the tiniest peek behind the Mulvaney family's curtains. But Zane had nothing in common with a one percenter like Mulvaney. Zane had been born middle-class and, through his father's hard work and perseverance, he'd risen to upper-middle class. Mulvaney probably spent Zane's rent payment on a tie clip.

"If you were to get to him, how would you do it?" Zane asked.

Nobody knew better than Blake how to get to people who didn't want to be gotten. He'd seen the man hang upside down from a tree to get a shot of a celebrity.

Blake sighed, pulling out his phone. "You'll never make it past the front door. Hell, you won't make it through a backdoor. The best you can hope for is to slip through a basement window, metaphorically speaking."

"What would Thomas Mulvaney's basement window be?" Zane asked.

Blake shrugged. "Look at his social media. The man spends his life attending galas for shit like saving alpacas. He takes pictures with little bald-headed cancer kids. If you want to get to him, that's how you do it."

"Please, tell me you're not saying I need to crash a fundraiser for cancer kids." Zane had some principles.

Blake turned his phone towards Zane. "How about a press awards dinner? Seems he's receiving some kind of award tonight."

"How do you know that?" Zane asked.

Blake rolled his eyes. "It's called the internet, Zane. We all have access to it now, you know?"

Zane huffed. "How do I sneak into a press awards dinner? I don't think I can just stroll in."

Blake shook his head. "All those major events are bar-coded now. You have to scan your phone at the door." He hopped to his feet. "Thanks for lunch, but I gotta go. Oh, and Beach needs that copy in an hour."

Beach. That was who he needed. She was their editor, and the definition of the word ballbuster had her picture beside it. He pulled out his phone and scrolled to her name, pressing send just as the door closed behind Blake.

She answered on the third ring. "Do you have my ad copy?"

He probably should have called after he finished writing that up. "Not yet. I need a favor."

Beach scoffed. "No copy, no favor."

"It's a little favor. Just a teeny tiny one."

Beach sighed. "What is it?"

"I just need to get into the press awards dinner tonight."

"Are you nuts?"

"I can have the copy to you in literally twenty minutes," Zane bartered. "Please? This could be a huge story."

"Zane, I am a forty-year-old woman who spends my days playing *Let's Make a Deal* with every publicist in the city to keep their celebrity clients either in or out of the public eye, depending on what benefits us all most financially. The only stories I care about are trashy ones. So, unless you're going to bring me a story where you find Barbara Walters giving a handjob to Matt Lauer under the table at that dinner, I'm not helping you."

Zane's lip curled at the all too vivid picture she painted. "Thomas Mulvaney can be plenty juicy if you'd just help me find something."

Beach groaned. "Are you still on about this? Leave it alone. Nobody cares about corrupt billionaires."

"Please, Beach. Please? You don't even have to do anything, I'll just swap a couple of name cards when I get there."

Beach scoffed. "You're not even invited. There is no card swapping when your card doesn't exist."

"It's an awards show for the press. Nobody will give a shit if I crash their little party. Surely, somebody at the paper was invited. We are technically press, right? Just put me in as a sub. I'll be whoever you want me to be. Please?"

"You know what? Fine. But you better find a goddamn story so juicy you'll be sticky for a week."

"Thank you. Thank you. Thank you. You won't be disappointed."

"I've heard that from almost every man in my life and it's never true," she muttered.

Zane heard a lighter flicking, and then Beach inhaled. "I thought you quit smoking?"

"What are you? My mother? Mind your business, nosey."

"I only care about your health."

"Fuck this up and it will be your health in question. And Zane?"

"Yeah?"

"Listen carefully because I mean this. I swear to all the gods and saints, if you get caught stalking Thomas Mulvaney, I'm going to pretend I don't know who the fuck you are. I will smile and wave as they cart you off in handcuffs."

Zane snickered. "Handcuffs? For crashing a press dinner? Somehow, I highly doubt that."

Beach made a *we'll see* noise. "Do you even have anything to wear that won't make you look like a cater-waiter?"

No. No, he didn't. He wasn't even sure he owned a tie that didn't have a stain on it. "That's hurtful."

She snorted. "Cry me a river."

Zane grinned. "Just text me who I'm supposed to be."

"Yeah, yeah," she muttered.

"Thanks. You're the best," he said sweetly.

"Eat shit," she said, voice equally saccharine.

TWO

ASA

I made it. Aiden says fuck you.

Asa Mulvaney stared down at the text from his twin brother, Avi. As if Asa didn't know Avi had made it to Aiden's safely. There was never a time when they didn't know where the other one was or what they were doing. Not without putting effort into breaking the connection.

Asa didn't say any of that. Just typed back: **Tell him fuck you right back.**

There was no malice in their exchange. Asa enjoyed spending time with all his brothers, though given the complicated history between his father and Aiden, it felt weird calling Aiden his brother. At the moment, it was harder to call Thomas his father.

Thomas was the reason for Asa's suffering. He was the reason for his agitation, for this sudden need to kill something with his bare hands. Asa usually killed for pleasure. Sure, it was necessary. There was no killing without cause in the Mulvaney family. That was the cardinal rule, and breaking it would result in a bullet to the head. But there was no shortage of people who needed to get dead.

A jarring laugh pierced the inaudible murmur of unending conversation around him. A bullet to the head would be preferable to his current surroundings. But his father was hellbent on torturing Asa, it seemed. In addition to exiling his brother to bum-fuck nowhere, he'd sent Asa to the press awards dinner to accept his bullshit honorary award and to make an acceptance speech in his name.

Asa had done neither.

It was all taking too long. He drained his whiskey, gaze scanning the throng of people in their black-tie finery. How the fuck was it barely seven o'clock? Had his father also mastered the art of slowing time for maximum irritation? The sound of silverware scraping against china and glasses clinking together, combined with the nauseating scent of rubber chicken and the spill mats behind the bar, was all too much.

Especially without Avi.

People found their closeness odd. There were rumors, quiet whispers behind hands, blind items implying they were far closer than two brothers ever should be. It wasn't true. What they had went beyond physical. It wasn't something sexual or even mental. It was…universal. They were created to function as a unit. Not to be separated. They were two halves of a whole, and they hadn't spent more than a night or two apart in over twenty years.

His father said he wasn't doing it to be cruel—that it was imperative that one could function without the other, just in case. In case of what? There was no Asa without Avi, and vice versa. If one was killed, they might as well put the other down immediately. But his father didn't want to hear it. Didn't want to believe it. So, now, they were forced to endure this ridiculous experiment under the guise of helpfulness. Avi just had to be the one to help Aiden with a kill across the country. It was bullshit. They all knew it.

He tugged at his collar, loosening his bowtie before sliding it free. He signaled for another whiskey as he contemplated just leaving. He'd already missed his father's award, leaving some random woman to accept it for him. Something Asa would no doubt hear about tomorrow.

He gave a frustrated growl, startling the middle-aged woman attempting to retrieve her wine from the man behind the bar. He gave what he hoped was an apologetic smile, but she scurried away. Asa had a hard time keeping his mask in place when agitation burned through him like fire ants beneath his skin.

He just needed a body. Anybody. He didn't know if he wanted to fuck someone or kill them, but the longer he sat there drinking, the less it mattered. If his father had given him a target tonight, some deserving piece of shit who needed to suffer before he died, that would at least have given him an outlet. Asa without an outlet was dangerous. It made him more reckless than usual, and Asa was already pretty reckless.

"You look like a supervillain."

Asa glanced over to see a man leaning against the bar in a white button down and black pants. He thought he was a server until he noticed the Chuck Taylors. He certainly didn't look at him like a server. He looked at him with an interest that Asa found surprising given how far his mask had slipped.

The stranger wasn't hot in the traditional sense. He wasn't Asa's type at all. Asa most often stuck to hot fuckboy types, who were only looking for a few good pics for social media and didn't cry too hard when he didn't stick around for breakfast.

This stranger looked very ordinary. No, not ordinary. He didn't look varnished. There were no veneers, no spray tans, no colored contacts and bleached tips. He had an angular face, and plush lips, and soft curls that fell into his eyes when he tilted his head to look at Asa like he was now.

He was heroin-chic pretty. Rock star pretty. Just this side of too thin, but put him in a pair of leather pants and a fur-coat and girls would throw their panties at him before the house went dark. Somehow, it worked. The dark curls, thick brows, and whiskey-colored eyes framed by black-framed glasses just…worked.

Or maybe Asa just knew a victim when he saw one. He turned his bar stool towards the stranger, giving him an obvious once-over, his lips curving into a smirk. "Oh, yeah. How so?"

The man took the question as an invitation, sliding onto the stool beside him, gesturing to the bartender before leaning in like he was going to tell him a secret. "Well, you've got this broody, sexy thing going on, but beneath that…you look like a predator." He sat back, nodding to

Asa's hands, his voice losing the low throaty rasp he'd had seconds ago. "Also, you look like you're about to strangle somebody with your bowtie."

Asa glanced down to see he'd wrapped the ends of his tie around his fingers, fashioning it into a garrote of sorts. "Seems anybody with any sense would know to stay away from a predator."

The man gave him a flash of perfect white teeth in a there and gone smile. "Well, to hear my mom tell it, I don't have the sense God gave a turnip. But I'll keep my eye on you. Just in case."

Asa arched his brow. "Yeah, you do that."

The bartender arrived, and they ordered their drinks. "You're one of the Mulvaney twins, right?"

There it was. The problem with being a Mulvaney was that everybody knew you were a Mulvaney. "Yes. Asa. And you are?"

The man held out his hand. "Zane Scott."

Asa took his hand, surprised when Zane squeezed it. His skin was warm and soft. Asa didn't want to let go, but he did. "You have a reporter's name, Zane Scott. Are you a reporter?"

The corner of the man's mouth curled upward in a half-smile as he looked around the room. "A reporter? In here?"

Smartass. "Is that a yes?"

"No. Not yet, anyway. Right now, I'm just a blogger waiting for my big break."

The bartender returned with their drinks, and Asa took a long swallow of his whiskey while he watched Zane tip the wine glass to his lips. Asa's brain was a mess of booze and bad decisions. He couldn't stop himself from picturing his hand around Zane's delicate throat, forcing his cock between those perfect lips until he gagged.

But he was a reporter. That alone should have had him saying goodnight. The rules on reporters—and wannabe reporters—were very clear in the Mulvaney house. Don't talk to reporters. Don't react to reporters. And while his father had never uttered the words 'don't fuck reporters,' Asa assumed it was implied.

Asa leaned in closer. "You look like Clark Kent in those glasses," he said, pushing them up the bridge of Zane's nose, noting the way his nostrils flared at Asa's touch.

Asa's dick noticed, too.

Once more, Zane gave him another blink-and-you'd-miss-it smile. "I wouldn't look like Clark Kent in any incarnation of the DC universe. More like Lois Lane."

Zane was right. He was no superhero type. But that was fine with Asa. He wasn't looking for a fair fight. Once more, that urge to drag Zane off and make him his overtook him. Would he let him drag him off to the bathroom and fuck him in a stall? Would he go to his knees for Asa? Asa tamped down the urge to find out.

He met Zane's gaze. "Superheroes are overrated. The villains are always more fun."

"Villains like you?" Zane countered, taking another sip of his wine.

Asa reached out a hand and wrapped one of Zane's curls around his finger. "Your hair is really pretty. All of you is really pretty. Even if you dress like a server."

Zane didn't move away, his expression bemused. "I can't figure out whether you're flirting with me or making fun of me."

Asa grinned. "I'm propositioning you, Lois Lane. But I highly encourage you to say no."

Zane leaned forward, bracing his elbow on the bar, his chin on his fist. "Oh? Interesting."

"Is it?" Asa asked.

Unease dripped along Asa's spine like cold water. There was something there. This shrewd intelligence behind Zane's eyes that let Asa know he had an agenda. Maybe Zane was the predator.

Zane tilted his head, gazing up at him. "Are you at least going to tell me why?"

Yeah, Zane Scott was full of shit. This flirty, innocent thing was all bullshit. He had a fucking agenda. But Asa had one, too. He wanted to play with him. He wanted to punish him. He wanted to fuck him.

Asa looked him dead in the eye. "Because I *am* a predator, and you're looking a lot like prey."

Zane's eyes widened. "Oh."

Asa sighed. "Don't listen to me. I'm drunk. I'm reckless when I'm drunk."

"I thought the Mulvaney twins were always reckless."

Asa chuckled. "Yeah, but that's the thing. I'm down a twin. It's just me. And drunk me…without supervision… he's the real supervillain."

"Color me intrigued."

I'll color you in your own blood. "Listen, by the end of the night, I'm going to fight someone or fuck them. Preferably both."

Zane's pupils dilated, his body swaying closer. "Is that what sober Asa would do?"

Sober Asa would go home and call a sex worker, who would sign an NDA so he could live out his sick, twisted fantasies in a controlled environment. "Sober Asa would take you out to the parking lot, bend you over the hood of his Maserati, make you come hard enough to forget your own name, and then probably never call you again."

Zane's lips parted. "Oh," he said again.

"Would you say no?" Asa countered.

Zane appeared to think about it, then shook his head slowly, a smile forming on his lips. "No."

"Exactly," Asa said, like that was a problem.

"So, we won't be doing that?" Zane asked, sounding amused.

"No, I'm drunk Asa. Well, moderately tipsy Asa." He drained his whiskey. "You don't want to meet drunk Asa."

Zane snickered. "Drunk Asa is worse than fucking me in a public parking garage and never speaking to me again?"

Those warning bells in Asa's head were now screaming like sirens. Police sirens. No sane person would poke Asa like this knowing how close he was to snapping. Zane clearly wanted to force him to do something he couldn't take back.

Asa *wanted* to do something he couldn't take back. He leaned in close. Zane smelled clean, like soap. Asa pressed his lips to his ear, fighting the urge to bite down until Zane cried out. "You're playing a very dangerous game. Are you willing to see it all the way through?"

Zane's voice grew raspy, his tone full of promise as he feigned innocence. "I don't know what you mean?"

"I mean, you shouldn't taunt a supervillain when you smell like prey." Asa's cock thickened behind his zipper at Zane's surprised exhalation. "Yeah, you're definitely prey. I bet your heart is pounding so fast right now." He curled his hand around the back of his neck, his thumb caressing the skin there before landing on his artery. Zane's pulse was jackrabbit fast. "Yeah, there it is. You know you'll lose. Still want to play?"

"How do I know when you haven't told me the game?" Zane asked, swallowing audibly.

"But I have. The game is predator versus prey," he said, letting his lips brush against the shell of his ear, not at all concerned about the surrounding crowd. "I feel like hunting."

"You wanna chase me through the parking lot?" Zane's voice was no longer teasing but eager, breathless, like he could taste the danger on the air.

Asa pulled back enough to look him in the eye. "The parking lot? No. That's no fun. There are far too many witnesses. Somebody might stop me."

"Then let's go to your place," Zane countered, his gaze never wavering.

Asa's cock throbbed. "To be clear, if you agree to go home with me, I will strip you naked, set you loose in my house, then I will run you down and fuck you where you fall. And there won't be a single soul to save you."

Zane's voice was no longer teasing but raw. "Who said I want to be saved? But I have a warning for you, too."

Asa gave a low rumble of approval. "And what's that?"

"I will fight back."

Asa's grin was feral. "You fucking better."

THREE

ZANE

Zane could hear his brother's voice in his head. *You've lost your goddamn mind.* Gage was always the voice in his head. His subconscious. His Jiminy Cricket. The ghost in his machine. Ghost Gage was right, though. Zane had lost his mind. Was he really willing to go to bed with Asa Mulvaney for a story? No, not go to bed—get hunted, stalked, and fucked by Asa Mulvaney. All on the off chance he might find something that could clue him in on what exactly Thomas Mulvaney did in his free time?

Yeah, he most definitely was.

Zane could pretend this was all in the spirit of getting a story, but the cold hard truth was Asa Mulvaney was the sexiest man Zane had ever seen up close and the idea of being held down and fucked senseless sounded like exactly what he needed tonight. Or any night, really. It had been a long time since anybody had looked at Zane like he was worthy of being hunted.

If he snooped around a little afterward, so be it.

Asa had offered to take Zane to his place in the limo, but he wanted to drive his own car. He wanted a viable escape option if this went from kinky sex to felony assault. Asa hadn't batted an eyelash when Zane said he preferred to drive. He'd handed over his address with a smirk, brushing his lips against Zane's cheek in a way that shouldn't have made his dick hard.

The farther from town Zane drove, the more he contemplated turning around and going home. Asa lived on a large piece of property thirty minutes outside the city in a home he'd designed. His brother lived there, too, but they also kept an apartment in the city. Zane had thought Asa would take him to his apartment, where there were neighbors and a doorman. People who knew Zane had ever been there.

Zane sang along to Bon Jovi while he contemplated his life choices. His hands shook whenever he unclenched them from the steering wheel. He didn't want to die in a house that had appeared on the cover of Architectural Digest. But he also didn't fucking turn around. Why wouldn't he turn around?

Because he'd lost his fucking mind.

He'd told Asa Mulvaney he could strip him naked and chase him. No, hunt him. Asa said he'd fuck him where he fell. That shouldn't have been hot, right? There was something fundamentally wrong with Zane. Being stalked and claimed by Asa shouldn't have been the hottest thing he'd ever heard. But it was. It really fucking was. He turned up the air conditioning until there was practically frost on the windows. Flop sweat wasn't sexy. Neither was dry mouth. He took a sip of water from the bottle he'd left there earlier, grimacing at the lukewarm temperature.

When he pulled into the winding drive, he sat in his car for ten whole minutes, trying to quell the shaking of his insides. The limo wasn't there, but the Maserati Asa had mentioned earlier was front and center. The Maserati Asa had said he wanted to bend Zane over. His dick throbbed behind his zipper. Christ. Zane wasn't afraid. He was fucking horny. It wasn't fear that had him trembling but adrenaline.

When he made it to the front door, it swung open before he could knock. Asa stood there, his hands in the pockets of tailored black pants that clung to thick thighs. He was barefoot and bare-chested, looking perfectly at ease as he studied Zane.

Holy Mary, mother of fuck. No one human should be this hot up-close. He'd swept his thick dark hair out of his face, like he'd raked his fingers through it a hundred times, the bright lights of the foyer highlighting perfect cheekbones and dark blue eyes that tracked him as he moved.

The ink was a surprise. Asa had a huge black snake tattooed on his left pectoral muscle and a tiger on the right. Both of his arms were a swirl of black and red ink. Below the snake was a revolver wrapped in flowers. *Jesus.* Was that a metaphor for something?

Did Zane even care? His fingers itched to feel the ridges of his abdominal muscles. He wanted to trace his tattoos with his tongue.

"I wasn't sure you were going to come in," Asa said, his amusement obvious.

“Me neither,” Zane admitted.

“Having second thoughts?” he asked, his voice a warm rasp that burned through Zane like hard liquor.

Zane gave a wobbly smile. “How many times can you panic and still call it second thoughts? I’m at least at third or fourth thoughts by now.”

Asa struck fast, his hand suddenly gripping Zane’s shirt, dragging him inside and pinning him against the now closed door. He stepped between Zane’s open legs, letting him feel how hard he was. “Are you afraid of me?” he teased.

Zane swallowed audibly. “Would I be risking cool points if I said yes?”

Asa gave a husky chuckle that was like something out of some dirty novel, then leaned in to run his tongue along the corded tendon of Zane’s neck in a move that should not have been hot. “I prefer honesty over bravery.”

Zane gave a nervous laugh. “Okay, how’s this for honest? I don’t want to die for this orgasm.”

Asa’s thumb tugged on Zane’s chin, his tongue dipping inside to slide over Zane’s before disappearing again. “You’ll still be alive when I’m done with you. Promise.” Zane’s lids fluttered as Asa’s mouth slanted over his in a deeper kiss. “Last chance to change your mind.”

Zane’s heart hammered against his ribs, and he was almost positive he couldn’t feel his feet. “I’m good,” he said, trying for casual but sounding one step above strangled.

Asa grinned, like he found Zane’s terror adorable. “First things first. I’m negative. You?”

Zane blinked, his brain trying to catch up with the

abrupt change of topic. Nobody had ever asked him that point blank before. "Yeah…" he managed, clearing his throat before putting more confidence behind it. "Yeah."

Asa nodded. "This isn't without risk. I'm trusting that you're being honest with me. I'll use a condom if you want, but I can't promise my cum will be the only body fluids we exchange tonight."

Christ.

Gage's voice screamed in Zane's head now. *Get the fuck out of there.* This was insane. Zane wasn't an experimental guy. He was a missionary-sex guy. An in-bed-by-ten guy. An always-followed-the-rules guy. But now, he was a reporter, and reporters did whatever they needed to get the story. They were willing to die for it.

That was what he told himself anyway, that this was all about a story and not about some deep-seated need to be taken and owned by the most beautiful man he'd ever seen. He almost didn't recognize his own voice when he said, "You don't have to use a condom. Just don't leave me so battered I need to go to the hospital."

Asa's pupils blew wide at Zane's words, something very close to a snarl falling from his lips, then Zane was being devoured. Asa smelled like spice and tasted like expensive whiskey, and when he ground their hips together, the sounds Zane made were completely out of his control.

Asa's hands tore at Zane's ill-fitting shirt, sending buttons scattering across wood floors, yanking the material from his shoulders. He bit and licked and sucked at Zane's bruised lips as he worked open his belt and pants with little finesse.

Like he needed him naked, like he couldn't wait to be buried inside him. God, what would that feel like? Would it sting and burn? Would it be a blunt, throbbing pain?

When he was naked, Asa's arms curled around him, his hands squeezing his ass, then teasing his fingers between, spreading him open. Zane groaned. He'd never been so hard in his life and they hadn't even left the doorway yet.

"I don't mean to tell you how to play your own game, but if you don't want me to come right here in the foyer, we should probably slow down."

A growl tore from Asa's lips. A literal fucking growl. Like a goddamn werewolf. He dropped his hands, stepping away from Zane, and for a split second, he thought he'd ruined everything.

Asa gave Zane a full, appreciative once-over, a slow, wolfish smile spreading across his face.

"Run."

Zane bolted for the stairs bisecting the center of the room, banking left when he reached the first landing. Asa's chuckle echoed all around him like something out of a carnival funhouse. He realized too late that the second floor left him with too many options. It was a hallway of closed doors.

Maybe it was Zane's fight-or-flight instincts, but he could hear Asa's bare feet beating up the staircase, could hear his own ragged breaths as he moved from one door to another, trying again and again to get just one to open. But they were locked. They were all fucking locked.

Shit. Shit. Shit.

Asa took him to the ground without warning, both of

them rolling before Asa pinned him beneath him. He was still wearing those dress pants. They both scrambled for purchase, but Asa had the upper hand. He was bigger, stronger. But Zane was smarter. He went limp. Asa's disappointment was evident. He thought Zane was quitting.

Asa loosened his grip, and Zane struck, hitting him hard enough in the nose for blood to spray over his face, warm and sticky. Asa snarled as blood poured from his nose into his mouth, but he was grinning. Zane kicked him in the thigh and then wiggled free, having no choice but to run for the stairs leading to the next floor.

He was at a dead run, Asa hot on his heels. At the top of the stairs was a door. He threw it open, grateful it gave without effort. Until he was inside. There was a large bed, an iron frame. Paddles. Chains. Cuffs. Strange instruments Zane had never seen before.

His breath left him in a gasp as Asa hit him with the full force of a linebacker, taking him to the ground once again. Zane put his hands out just in time to keep his face from slamming into the floor.

He'd fallen right into Asa's trap. He'd herded him directly into his play room? Sex dungeon?

Torture chamber.

Asa flipped him over, pinning his wrists over his head, his legs locking around Zane's. They were both breathing hard, sucking in harsh breaths that made Zane feel like somebody had tried to dry clean his lungs. There was an odd sense of satisfaction in seeing blood dripping from Asa's nose.

"You done?" Asa asked.

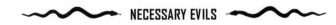

Zane drove his knee into Asa's diaphragm, ducking from his grasp. He got to his feet, but Asa reached out a hand, wrapping it around his ankle and yanking hard. This time, Zane's face connected to the floor, his eye socket feeling like it exploded, stunning him just long enough to lose the small leverage he'd created.

Asa was on him then, pinning him down with one hand as he undid his pants with the other, shoving them just far enough out of the way for Zane to feel how truly big Asa was. He threaded his fingers into Zane's hair, yanking his head back until he hissed. "You lose."

Zane gave a soft laugh. "Do I, though?"

Asa bit down on Zane's earlobe hard enough to pierce it. Maybe it was the adrenaline, maybe it was fear, but what should have signaled pain to his brain instead flooded his system with dopamine, making him moan.

"Don't fucking move or I will chain you to the bed."

Zane blinked in confusion as Asa's weight disappeared briefly, but it was back almost before Zane could register his absence. Asa's knees forced his thighs apart. Then two slick fingers were slipping between his cheeks, forcing their way inside his body. He grunted from the shock of the invasion, but his cock was painfully hard, leaking onto the floor below.

"Fuck, you're tight," Asa rasped, his fingers brutally efficient at working him open. Then they disappeared, replaced by the blunt head of Asa's cock driving into him, stealing the breath from his lungs.

It was painful, his body burning as it tried to rearrange itself to accommodate him. Asa didn't wait for Zane to adjust. His hand gripped the back of his neck, pinning him to the floor as he fucked into him, used him, grunting as he drove into him hard enough for tears to leak from Zane's eyes. It was monstrous, barbaric, and selfish, even. But Zane had never felt more wanted in his life.

The pain in his ass was nothing compared to the endorphins. There was a heady feeling in knowing it was Zane who made a man like Asa Mulvaney this needy, this hungry, this fucking reckless. And it was reckless and painful and just this side of too much, but he couldn't stop himself from canting his hips, addicted to the stretch and burn of Asa using him.

Asa suddenly gave a harsh shout, his head dropping to sink his teeth into Zane's shoulder hard enough to draw blood as he emptied himself inside him. He could feel his cock throbbing as he came. Zane deflated against the floor, breathing heavily as Asa's hips spasmed against his in tiny, aborted thrusts.

Then it was over.

Except, it wasn't. Zane found himself on his back. One of his legs caught over Asa's elbow as he practically bent him in half to drive back into him. "I thought..." Zane muttered.

Asa grinned down at him. "What? That I'd leave you like this? Nah, Lois Lane. Now, it's your turn. Though, I don't know how much more I have left in the tank, because your hole is sloppy with my cum and it feels too fucking good."

Asa captured his mouth in a bloody kiss, rolling his hips as he fucked into Zane with an almost pained expression on his face. He shifted, changing his angle, glancing that tiny bundle of nerves. Zane couldn't stop the helpless moan that fell from his lips. Asa grinned. "Yeah? Right there. Is that the spot?"

Zane tried to speak but couldn't, instead making another embarrassing sound.

"Yeah, that's the spot," Asa said, sounding all too pleased with himself.

He planted his hand, taking Zane's leaking cock in his fist, jerking him in time with his slow, targeted thrusts until it felt like a spring tightening inside him, driving him towards that ultimate release. Zane's hands shot out, wrapping around Asa's back, desperate for something to cling to. He couldn't breathe. "Harder. Oh, fuck. Harder, please."

Asa chuckled but complied, slinging his hips, until Zane couldn't stop the needy whines, the desperate pleas falling from his lips or his blunt nails dragging along Asa's skin until they both grunted, one from mind-numbing pleasure and the other from pain.

Zane's orgasm punched from his body, his entire brain freezing as something akin to bliss flooded his system and, for just a few seconds, the world went dark. When he blinked his eyes back open, Asa was pulling free, falling onto his back beside him.

"Damn, Lois. I did not think you would be this much fun. No offense."

Zane was too cum-drunk to even take offense. "You really need to come up with a better nickname for me than Lois."

Asa rolled onto his side, propping his head on his fist. "Why? This is a one-night stand. Good thing, too. 'Cause

I might call you something soft. Like sugar britches or sweet cheeks."

Zane snorted. "Those are your go-to fluffy terms of endearment?"

"What can I say? I'm a romantic at heart."

"Mm, well, do you think you could point me toward your bathroom and maybe get me some water? I'm way more out of shape than I ever imagined."

Asa's face suddenly loomed over him, barely an inch away. "Now, that's just not true, sugar britches. You put up one helluva fight." He jumped to his feet, and Zane finally got to see what a completely naked Asa Mulvaney looked like. God really gave with both hands with him. And there were two of them? Jesus.

He shook the thought away, eyes going wide. There were huge, jagged scratches down Asa's back, some deep enough to bleed. "Uh, did I do that?"

Asa glanced over his shoulder, realizing what Zane was looking at. "Mm. I must have been doing something right."

More than something. Everything. Zane yawned hard enough for his jaw to crack.

Asa smirked, pointing to a door on the left. "Bathroom's right there."

Zane smiled. "Your sex dungeon has a bathroom?"

"Yeah, every good dungeon should, no?" Asa said.

Zane shook his head. Once inside, he looked at his reflection in the mirror. There were already bruises forming, including swelling around his eye he just knew would be black and blue tomorrow. *That shouldn't make you happy.*

Zane rolled his eyes at his brother's voice. *Shut up.*

He cleaned up and slowly made his way downstairs. Muscles he didn't even know he had ached. It was awkward to wander around a house this large without a stitch of clothing on.

"My other phone is dead," he heard Asa say, clearly not talking to him.

Zane froze. Other phone? Who has two phones? Nobody up to anything good. Zane's heart rate sped up as he craned his head, attempting to get eyes on Asa. He could make out the top of his head. He now wore a pair of jeans and a black t-shirt.

Great, so now Zane was the only one naked. He stayed where he was, eavesdropping as best he could without moving closer.

"No. No fucking way. Not tonight. It's bad enough Dad made me go to that dumb fucking press—" Asa's voice cut off as if listening. "No, I didn't get his stupid award. He doesn't need another fucking trophy. I'm not leaving the house for…that. I have company. Get Archer to help you." Once more, silence, then he said, "I have a life, too, you know. Where's Adam? Or August? Shit, where's Freckles?"

Freckles? Maybe sugar britches wasn't so bad.

"Fuck. Fine, but you owe me so big. Text me—Fuck, you can't text me on this phone. Double fuck. I need to find a pen. Who uses pens anymore when there's texting?"

Asa's voice faded as he made his way deeper into the house. Zane padded down to the first floor, grabbing his underwear from the pile of clothing at the foot of the stairs, slipping them on before following Asa's now muffled voice. He peeked his head around the door of what turned out to be a study just as Asa dropped a pen onto the desk and pulled a yellow sticky note from the top of the square. "Got it. Give me an hour. Yeah, an hour."

"Everything okay?" Zane asked, knocking gently on the open door.

Asa looked up, his fury fading into a polite smile. "Family emergency."

"Oh, I'm sorry. I'll just get my things," Zane said, pointing to the door.

"No, it's cool," Asa said, his gaze raking over Zane. "Just grab a water from the fridge. Take your time getting dressed. The door will lock automatically behind you."

Zane stood there, dazed, as Asa walked back to the foyer where a tray held his keys and wallet. He palmed his wallet into his back pocket, glancing up to see Zane watching him with wide eyes.

Asa moved quickly, crossing back to Zane, once more crowding him up against a door, capturing his mouth in a kiss that lingered. "Fuck, you look hot. I was really hoping to spend the night inside you."

Zane sucked in a breath at Asa's casual comment.

"Yeah, that whole scandalized maiden thing is so hot," Asa teased.

"I'm not a scandalized maiden," Zane muttered, heat blooming beneath his skin.

"Uh-huh. Well, in that case, don't get any ideas. There are more cameras planted around this house than the Pentagon."

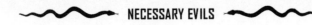

"So, you recorded us doing…on camera doing…" Zane trailed off.

Asa frowned. "Don't worry, sugar. I don't keep trophies. I'll erase them once I'm home."

With that, he was gone, door slamming shut behind him. Zane had a split second to decide. Fuck. He opened the door to the study, running to the desk to grab the stack of little yellow papers. He snatched a pencil from the cup on his desk, rubbing it over the paper, adrenaline flooding his system as GPS coordinates appeared.

What kind of family emergency required a burner phone and GPS coordinates? The kind that might win him a fucking Pulitzer.

Or get you shot.

Was he really fucking doing this?

Yeah, he was definitely doing this. He snatched the sticky note, quickly making his way back to his clothes. Once dressed, he took one last look around before running to his car, grateful he hadn't taken Asa up on his limo offer.

A tremor of trepidation shivered over him. Would Asa look at the cameras later? Would he see Zane snooping? Would he know he wasn't just borrowing a piece of paper? Did it even matter?

Zane punched the coordinates into his phone, frowning when he saw it was in the middle of nowhere. Gage's voice whispered that this was a trap. That Asa was luring him away from the house to kill him. But it was Zane who was the one doing something shady. Not Asa.

At least, not yet.

FOUR

ASA

"Why exactly"—Asa swung his ax with a grunt—"can't your husband help with this?"

He picked up the neatly severed hand and chucked it into an industrial strength trash bag before standing up to take a breather. Dismantling bodies was hard work. Dismantling the corpse of a four-hundred-pound leather-clad biker was damn near impossible.

Jericho gave Asa an incredulous look. "Can you imagine Freckles out here wielding an ax in his Ferragamos?"

Asa snorted. Freckles—aka his brother, Atticus—used to unalive and dismember people all the time before he fell in love with a guy who was far more comfortable with the work than he was. Some people thought it was Atticus's vow as a physician to do no harm, but Asa thought Jericho was probably right. It was probably about the shoes. His brother was a label whore and a neat freak.

Asa sighed, glaring at the mostly intact corpse. "Still, it hardly seems fair. You shouldn't always have to do the dirty work."

Jericho brought his ax down, amputating the man's leg just below the knee. "I enjoy the dirty work. Besides, I knew what I was getting into. The day I said 'I do' was the day your brother said he won't. As in, he won't be killing anybody else unless I've exhausted all other options. If I called and asked him out here for this, I wouldn't get laid for a month."

Asa grimaced, bringing the blade down again, this time separating the shoulder from the torso, hissing as beads of sweat rolled down his back and into the open wounds left by his little reporter.

"You good?" Jericho asked at Asa's pained sound.

"Yeah, fine," he said dismissively. "I would have thought Dad would have made murder part of the Mulvaney wedding vows. For better or worse. To kill and dismember? Forever and ever, amen."

Jericho shook his head. "We didn't consult him on our wedding vows."

Asa looked around the tiny cabin. Calling it rustic would have been generous. It was essentially a large empty room with a sturdy wooden table, a kitchen sink set into a wooden slab, and a bathroom in the corner that was only recently inhabitable. That was it.

"Didn't Atticus buy you this murder cabin—where you two first tortured and killed somebody together—as an anniversary present? Doesn't that sort of imply the blood and guts part of your marriage?"

Jericho chuckled, severing the man's other leg below the

knee. "No. He bought me the cabin where we first hooked up after *I'd* tortured and killed a man. He just ate a granola bar. Besides, a cabin in the middle of nowhere stocked with a lake full of flesh-eating fish is the gift that keeps on giving in this family. And he still kills with me on date nights."

Asa snickered, watching Jericho heave the man's meaty calf into another garbage bag. "How'd you even get this guy out here?"

Jericho shrugged. "You promise a piece of shit like this a bag full of guns and money and he's more than happy to drive his ass right to your front door."

Asa wiped his brow with his forearm. "Okay, but did it not occur to you that you'd need help to get him out of here?"

Jericho shot Asa a look like he was stupid. "Of course, it did. August was on the roster. He was en route when he got a call from Lucas and had to turn around."

Asa frowned. "Why? What's wrong with Lucas? Another psychic vision?"

Asa never thought they would have a psychic in their midst, but Lucas was the real deal and had proven to be invaluable. Unfortunately, those visions often came with a pretty severe emotional side effect.

Jericho shook his head. "Adelyn sneezed and Arabella had a runny nose. August had to go talk Lucas off a ledge before he called the CDC or sent the cops after the college daycare for giving the girls the plague."

If anybody had told him five years ago that August would be the first of them to have kids, Asa would have laughed himself sick. His older brother was the most twisted and depraved of them all. He loved killing more than Asa or Avi. More than that, he loved torturing them. Reveled in it, even. And now, he had babies. Tiny human babies, who gazed up at him with huge green eyes, implicitly trusting his maniac brother to care for them.

And he did.

Hell, they all did. The girls had a veritable army at their disposal between the Mulvaneys and Jericho's boys. Not that they'd need an army. They'd been on this planet for less than six months and were already proving to take after August. The thought of babies with his brother's spooky high IQ was a terrifying prospect. Still, family was family, and Asa would protect the little snot faucets with his life.

"Aren't all babies just naturally drippy? Can't Lucas, like, psychically tell if there's something actually wrong with the little crotch goblins?"

Jericho shrugged. "Babies are scary, man. And these babies are only a few months old."

"Yeah, they're babies being raised by a psychic and a serial killer," Asa reminded, eyes widening as something occurred to him. "Oh, God. And the serial killer is the voice of reason."

Jericho grinned. "You know he hates when you call him that."

Asa rolled his eyes. "Yeah, well, I hate my brothers becoming domesticated."

Jericho took off another arm, tossing it in the bag, giving Asa a smirk. "Domesticated?"

Asa nodded. "Yeah, Noah practically neutered Adam.

They have a fucking dog. A dog Noah treats better than an actual human. Atticus obsesses over that dumb cat of yours—"

Jericho pointed the ax at him. "That cat is his. One hundred percent. Every time I come home, that fuzzy little shit is sleeping on my fucking pillow now."

Asa continued his diatribe as if Jericho hadn't broken in. "And now, August and Lucas are *literally* breeding."

"So what?"

"So what?" Asa repeated, exasperated. "Soon, Dad's going to get ideas. He'll want us all to find mates so he can find new ways to test and study us. And if that happens, we're fucked. The holidays will be a goddamn bloodbath."

Jericho dropped his ax on the tarp, then leaned against the counter. "Speaking of fucked…did your hookup give you that?"

Asa reached up and touched his swollen nose, wincing. Yeah, he wasn't going there.

"Nah. Where's Felix?" he asked. "Why isn't he here?"

Jericho gave him a hard stare, like he knew there was a reason he was changing the subject but unsure if he should probe any further. Felix would have been no help in this situation. While Jericho's brother was feisty and lethal, he was also the definition of dainty.

Asa just didn't want to talk about Zane. Thoughts of their encounter had been bleeding through since he'd left, making for some awkward boners. It had been the definition of animalistic. Running after him, getting him on the ground, holding him down while he fucked him, bred him, claimed him. His prize. His prisoner. His captive.

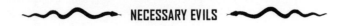

Fuck.

The sounds Zane had made while Asa was inside him, the heat of his body, the way he'd begged, panted, wanted it harder. God, he'd been so perfect. So hot. So tight. He'd loved Asa's dick so much he'd fucking mauled him like a goddamn tiger.

"What do you mean? My brother is with your twin," Jericho said, dragging Asa's thoughts from Zane.

Asa paused mid-swing. "But my twin is with *our* brother."

Jericho smirked. "Yeah, I know. Avi insisted Felix needed to be there. Just in case any work emergencies arose."

Asa blinked at him. "My brother is a fashion designer. What constitutes a fashion emergency?"

Jericho glanced at the corpse before them. "I'd say this guy but, somehow, I don't think that's what your brother had in mind."

Asa shook his head. "Fuck, man. You don't think Avi and Felix are…you know—"

Jericho lifted a hand, interrupting him. "Felix hates Avi. I hear about it day and night. 'Avi made me carry a dozen lattes for a meeting and then canceled the meeting. Avi made me take a work phone home with me because 'fashion never sleeps.' Avi made me sew sequins on the ass of a velour tracksuit for a throw-back photo shoot and ruined my manicure.'"

That didn't sound like complaining to Asa. "But he's still there. I'm telling you, this is some kind of fucked up foreplay for them. Every time Felix loses it on Avi, he doesn't stop smiling for hours. It's like his spank bank material."

Jericho grimaced. "Okay, I don't want to know that your brother jerks off thinking about mine."

"It's just biological, man," Asa teased around a laugh.

Jericho glowered at him. "Seriously. Shut up unless you want me to talk about what your father might get off thinking about."

Asa shrugged. "I'm not gonna be all dramatic about it like your husband. Who my father sticks his dick in is his business."

"Even if he's sticking his dick in somebody who has your last name?" Jericho countered.

Asa waved a hand, dropping his ax next to Jericho's on the tarp to grab a bottle of water. "They're not blood related, and Aiden was practically an adult when my dad randomly adopted him. To be honest, I wouldn't even care if they were blood related. I'm a psychopath. We're a family of murderers. Incest is our moral high gro—"

Jericho frowned, holding up a finger, cutting Asa off. He'd heard it, too. It was faint, the sound of crunching gravel beneath the kitchen window, like somebody lost their footing. Jericho grabbed his Glock off the counter and shot out the door.

Asa didn't follow, just opened the cap on his water and chugged it down. Jericho didn't need any help from him. There was a sharp cry, and then Jericho said, "Stop fighting me."

"You have a gun in my ribcage, asshole," a man responded.

Asa's stomach churned. He knew that voice.

"You're about to have a bullet there," Jericho retorted, shoving Zane through the cabin door, where he fell in a heap next to biker-guy.

Zane tried to get to his feet, but Jericho pointed the gun at his head. "Stay down."

Zane stayed on his knees, his hands raised in the air. Christ, he looked good on his knees. Asa should have used his mouth, too. Bet he would have sounded so hot gagging on his cock. Asa's dick hardened behind his zipper. Oof, yeah. Not the time.

"Who the fuck are you?" Jericho demanded.

Zane looked Asa in the eye. "Ask him."

Jericho frowned at Asa. "You know this guy?"

Asa ignored Jericho, studying Zane as he tried to put the pieces together. "Do any of us really know anybody?"

"Asa." Jericho said his name like a warning.

"Fine. He's just some guy I hate fucked on my floor an hour ago."

"Wow," Zane said. "I'm flattered."

"Did you follow me? How could you have followed me? You had time to change clothes. There's no tracker on my car 'cause I left it at the garage."

Zane huffed out a breath through his nose, his expression mutinous, as if he was the wounded party here. "I didn't follow you. You wrote the fucking location down on a sticky note."

Jericho's eyes went wide. "Seriously, man?"

"You can't kill me. I live-streamed your entire conversation. I bet the cops are already on their way to arrest your whole fucked up family," Zane spit, scowling at Asa like he really was a supervillain.

Asa and Jericho both rolled their eyes.

"No, you didn't. This cabin's in a dead zone. Nice try, though," Asa said.

Zane's shoulders deflated, defeated. Asa would have thought there would be more histrionics. Finding out you fucked a guy who came from a family of murderers seemed like it would be life altering news.

But Zane didn't look shocked. Disgusted. Furious. But not shocked.

Asa hunkered down in front of him. "Is this why you went home with me, Lois Lane? Were you hoping to use me to get to my family?"

Zane sneered at Asa. "I don't know what you're complaining about. I let you use me first. If you're gonna kill me, just do it. Preferably not with the same ax you used to chop up that guy."

Asa's lips twitched in an aborted smile. Zane was much more comfortable when faced with death than he'd been when Asa had him crowded up against a door. That was interesting. "Damn, that's cold, Lois Lane. Maybe *you're* the psychopath."

Zane thrust his jaw forward in a look that shouldn't have been cute but somehow was. "I'm a crime reporter. You think this is my first dead body?"

"You fucked a crime reporter?" Jericho shouted. "Are you kidding me? Your father is going to kill us both."

"I'll take care of this," Asa said.

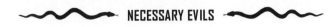

"Take care of it, how?" Jericho asked. "Do you know how much he heard?"

Asa's temper flared, and he wasn't sure if he was more pissed at himself or at Zane for putting him in this situation. "I said I'll handle it," he snapped.

Asa went to his go-bag, pulling out duct tape and tossing it to Jericho. "Bind him. Wrists and ankles."

Jericho sighed, still furious, but he shoved Zane to the ground, sitting on his thighs, so he could yank his arms behind him. Asa had him in that position not that long ago. With his wrists bound, Jericho jerked him to his knees, binding his ankles.

"Just fucking kill me already," Zane muttered.

Jericho's eyes went wide at Zane's cavalier attitude towards his impending demise. "Suicidal ideations aside, he's not wrong. The safest course of action is to put a bullet in his head and throw him in the lake with that dude."

Asa stared at him, incredulous. "Do you know what my father would do to both of us if we killed an innocent guy? We might as well throw ourselves in right after him. We cannot break the code. It's the only unforgivable rule."

"How very Harry Potter of you," Zane muttered.

Asa flicked his gaze to Zane. "Pipe down, Lois Lane. Nobody's talking to you."

"If you're trying to convince me you're the good guys and I've got this all wrong, it's not going to fucking work. I've just spent the last twenty minutes watching you hack this guy to pieces while casually discussing about ten different felonies. You're fucking—"

Asa picked the taser up off the counter and jabbed it into Zane's chest. Whatever he was going to say became a garbled mess before he crumpled at his feet for the second time in five minutes. Well, that was unexpected. Who passed out from a stun gun? Did Zane have a heart condition? Why the fuck did he care? He squatted beside him and pushed two fingers against his pulse, relieved when he felt the reassuring thud.

"How the fuck are you going to fix this?" Jericho asked again.

"Just help me get him in the back of the van."

"What about him?" Jericho asked, jerking his thumb towards the pile of body parts.

"The pieces are small enough for us to fit them in the wheelbarrow now. We'll wheel him down to the lake and then you can handle the rest of the cleanup from there, right?"

Jericho gave him a hard look but finally nodded. "Yeah. Yeah, I can do that."

"Okay, good. And whatever you do, don't tell my father."

"You fucking tased me!"

Asa flicked his gaze upwards from the book on his lap. "Morning, sunshine," he said, his voice full of fake cheer. "I was getting worried. Most people don't pass out from a stun gun, you know."

"Am I supposed to apologize?" Zane snapped, his head on a swivel as he tried to take in his situation. "Where the fuck am I?"

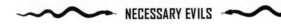

Asa supposed it was a lot to take in. He looked down at himself where he lounged fully dressed in his empty bathtub. "My bathroom. Well, one of my bathrooms. I'll leave you to guess which one."

"You can't just fucking kidnap me. People will notice."

Asa saved his page in the book before stepping free of the tub to sit on the edge. "I'm going to be very honest with you. If I hadn't just fucked you, I would have let my brother-in-law put a bullet in your head and made sure my father never found out. But that seemed…ungentlemanly with the claw marks you left still bleeding."

Zane's eyes bulged, his pretty face almost purple with fury. "You're deranged."

Asa had to admit, he loved the fight in this one. He also found it amusing to see him chained to his radiator with fuzzy pink handcuffs. "Sticks and stones, sugar britches. Sticks and stones. I could say the same about you."

"I'm sorry. How am I the crazy one in this scenario?"

"You went home with a stranger. Played a very dangerous game. Fucked me without a condom. That's pretty crazy."

"You kidnapped me," Zane snapped.

Asa tilted his head, folding his arms across his chest. "How did you see this playing out, Lois Lane?"

"I thought, if I was lucky, I'd get some dirt on your father. I didn't expect to find out you're all a bunch of goddamn serial killers," Zane snapped, his chest heaving.

"Exactly. You used me, sugar. Had sex with me under false pretenses. So, who's the real wounded party here?"

"Me!" Zane snarled, incredulous, as he fought against the bindings.

Asa snagged the cashews he'd been snacking on, tossing one in the air and catching it in his mouth. "Keep telling yourself that, Lois Lane."

Zane glowered at him, but his gaze kept dropping to the cashews.

When was the last time Zane ate? "You hungry?"

Zane narrowed his eyes at him. "Fuck you."

Asa sauntered closer, hunkering down beside him. "I mean, I'm game if you are. You're a real wildcat in bed." He curled his hands into claws. "Or on the floor, I suppose."

Zane's booted foot caught Asa right in the diaphragm, driving him into the bathroom door. It took a moment for the air to return to his lungs. Still, he grinned. "I'm getting mixed signals here. Are you saying you don't want me to fuck you again?"

"I'd rather fuck a cactus," Zane said, voice sullen.

Something warmed inside Asa, a smirk forming on his lips. "You're lying." He advanced again, this time sitting squarely on Zane's knees so he couldn't use them as a weapon. "What's wrong? Did you like having sex with me? Is that why you're so mad? 'Cause you loved having a murderer inside you? Hell, some of me is still inside you, I bet."

Asa leaned forward, licking across the seam of Zane's lips, giving a pleased rumble when they opened beneath his, slipping his tongue inside. Fuck, he loved kissing him. There was a sharp pain, then the taste of copper flooded his mouth. He leaned back to give Zane a stern look, but it died when he saw the red smeared across his lips. "Fuck, you look good in my blood."

"Let me out of these cuffs and I'll happily fucking bathe in it, you psycho," Zane snarled, once more testing the strength of his cuffs.

The restraints might have looked frilly, but they were police grade handcuffs. Zane wasn't going anywhere until Asa let him.

"Nah, I think I'm going to leave you as you are for now. But, if you're a good boy, I'll let you have some of these." He rattled the cashews. "But if you bite me, you're going to go hungry."

Zane huffed out a breath through his nostrils. "Whatever," he finally muttered, opening his mouth obediently.

Shit.

Was this what cowboys felt like when they broke colts? Breaking Zane was a prospect that made Asa's blood pump a little faster. How long had it been since he'd felt any kind of excitement like this?

He fished a few salted cashews from the container, feeding each one to him slowly. After that, he opened the bottle of water, letting Zane see him break the seal before holding it to his lips, watching his throat convulse with each swallow. When he'd drained the bottle, Asa smiled, wiping a droplet from Zane's lips. "There. That wasn't so bad. Was it, sugar?"

Zane continued to shoot daggers at him, but his voice was wary. "You can't keep me here forever. People will notice."

Asa gave him a patient smile. "I'm not planning on

keeping you here forever, just until I convince you it's better to have the Mulvaneys with you rather than against you."

"Good fucking luck. The second you let me go, I'll tell the world about you and your brothers and send you a copy of my prize-winning story for you to hang in your cell, you fucking piece of shit."

Asa leaned in close, pushing a lock of Zane's hair from his face. "I really hope you change your mind. I like your brains so much better on the inside."

"Fuck you."

Asa grinned. "You keep offering yourself up to me and I'm going to think you mean it." Zane sagged against his restraints, suddenly looking far more fragile than he had minutes ago. "I'll be back in an hour, just in case you need to use the bathroom."

"I am not using the bathroom in front of you," he called as Asa closed the door.

Asa didn't respond, just chuckled as he shut the door behind him.

That laugh died as he realized his phone—his real phone—was ringing, his father's picture flashing on the screen. *God fucking dammit.* Had Jericho ratted him out that quickly? There really was no honor among thieves…or killers. Whatever. Fuck.

He watched it until it stopped ringing, then collapsed onto the bed, only for a text to appear on the screen. **Don't ignore me. I can do this all night.**

Shit.

When it started ringing again, he growled, then picked it

up, keeping his voice upbeat. "Hey, Pops. What's going on?"

Thomas hesitated. "What's wrong with you? Why do you sound like that?"

"Like what?" Asa asked, wincing as his voice rose another octave.

Thomas scoffed. "Like you're ten and I just caught you in a lie about what you and Kenny Baker were actually doing in your closet."

Asa grinned. He'd forgotten about that. "Uh…no reason. I'm just waiting for you to yell at me for skipping out on your award dinner."

"Oh, I'm not going to yell at you about that," Thomas said in a voice that implied there was something much worse to come. "But you are going to do me a favor."

"What kind of favor?" Asa asked suspiciously.

"I need you to look into something for me," Thomas said.

Asa frowned. "What do you mean…look into?"

"I mean, a friend asked me to look into something." *Friend* said in that tone always implied a person in the know about their extracurricular activities. "A mystery of sorts."

Asa frowned. "Um, I don't solve crimes, Dad. I just clean up the mess."

"You do whatever I tell you to do, Asa," Thomas said sharply. "I know you're acting out because Avi is with Aiden, but I need you to act like an adult."

An adult doesn't take orders from his father. But Asa didn't say that. "What's this mystery?"

Thomas sighed, sounding relieved. "Five suicides at the university in the last two months."

Asa shook his head, even though Thomas couldn't see it. "Yeah, so? Suicides often trigger a chain reaction. I don't think that's a mystery to anybody."

Thomas's voice grew terse again. "That's only part of it. Five years ago, it happened, too. Five suicides in two months. Then nothing."

That piqued Asa's interest a bit more. "Okay, weirder, but hardly proof of anything."

"These kids weren't considered 'at risk.' They were popular, had good grades. The parents are reeling from this, and some are pulling kids from school."

"Low risk kids still off themselves, Dad."

"There have been rumors circulating around campus that the students were playing a game," Thomas said.

Asa frowned. "A game where the prize is death?"

"That's what I want *you* to find out, Asa."

"Why me and not Calliope?"

"Because one: Calliope can only do so much from behind a computer screen and two: she didn't directly disobey me so she could go get laid." How the fuck would he know that? As if he could read Asa's mind, he said, "Never forget, I have spies everywhere. *Everywhere.* I'll text you the info I have. Let me know what you find. And Asa?"

"Yeah?"

"Don't you dare try to pass this off on one of your brothers."

Asa glanced at his closed bathroom door. None of his brothers had any kind of knowledge he might need. "Yeah, okay, Dad. I'll let you know what I find."

FIVE

ZANE

Zane's whole body ached like he'd worked out every muscle at once. The result of the taser, no doubt.

Or the kinky sex, you fucking perv.

Zane huffed out a breath. "Or that," he muttered, rattling the chains like a ghost in a Dickens novel, grimacing as his shoulders protested. They hurt the worst. That he blamed on the handcuffs. Jesus. The handcuffs. He was wearing handcuffs. Because Asa had handcuffed him to a fucking radiator. Because he was a murderer and Zane was a klutz. This had to be the worst date ever.

This is what happens when you don't have a backup plan.

"Fuck off," Zane grunted, voice strained as he leaned all his weight back against the restraints, hoping his body weight might cause them to give. When they held firm, Zane lost it, jerking his arms against the unyielding metal until his wrists were raw. "This is bullshit!" he shouted before sagging against the wall.

Well, that was useless and childish.

"Seriously, fuck off."

I'm in your head, asshole.

Zane started singing loudly and off-key, attempting to drown out the voice of his dead brother. Some small part of him hoped he was also annoying the shit out of Asa, too. Wherever he was. Were they back at his grand country estate? Had he taken him somewhere else? Some secret far away property where nobody would ever find him?

He closed his eyes. He needed to chill. He just needed to wait it out. Blake would get his text and go to that godforsaken house of horrors in the woods, and, eventually, the cops would find him. And then, he could show them the video he took. He hadn't been lying about that. He had a video of Asa and the other man, Jericho, basically confessing to a handful of murders while casually dismembering a corpse. There wasn't a lawyer in the world who could fight video evidence.

Zane had texted Blake the coordinates before he'd headed to the cabin. He'd told him if he didn't hear from him by morning to send the cops. At the time, it had seemed like overkill. Laughable even. Now it wasn't nearly enough for Blake to piece together what had happened to him.

He'd considered getting Blake to meet him, but he would have just talked him out of going, would have advised him to check out the location at a different time, when there was less risk. He would have told him he was acting recklessly.

And if you had listened, you wouldn't be chained to a radiator by your one-night stand.

I wouldn't have found out that the Mulvaney family was a

group of body-hacking lunatics, either.

Holy shit. He couldn't believe this was happening. This would definitely win him accolades. All the journalism awards. If he lived. God, he really hoped he lived. He fucking deserved this. Fuck. If he died, his parents would be furious. Two dead children. How embarrassing. His mom would have to find a new group of friends and pretend she'd never had children. Maybe it was better that way.

The door opened and Asa strolled in.

"My bladder is fine," Zane snarked, too tired to even give Asa a proper glare.

He grinned at Zane, giving him a thorough once-over. "I'm happy to hear it. But that's not why I'm here."

Zane had to look like shit. He'd changed his clothes in the car, throwing on jeans and a faded t-shirt from his high school marching band days. He always kept a bag in the back with the basics. Working for the tabloids meant always being ready. If somebody got the jump on your story, you didn't have a career left afterwards. He hadn't had time to clean up, though. His hair was curly from sweat, and he was certain he was as covered in grime as his clothes.

Asa wore jeans that clung to his ass and thighs and a shirt that left little to the imagination. When he moved just right, Zane could glimpse a bit of skin and the deep vee of his hips. His hair was wet and his feet were bare. Nobody should look that good. It really wasn't fucking fair.

"So, why are you here? Did you change your mind? Are you here to kill me?" he asked warily.

Asa studied him for a long moment, then sat on the side

of the tub like he'd done earlier, crossing his arms over his chest. "It seems I'm in need of a detective. And while you don't exactly fit the bill, you're probably way more qualified than me."

Zane blinked at him. "You can't be fucking serious."

Asa crowded into his space and, for a split second, Zane was sure Asa was going to kiss him again. His stomach fluttered nervously. But he was actually unlocking his handcuffs.

"Sure, I can. Dead serious, even. See what I did there?" he asked, acknowledging his own bad joke.

Asa didn't move, just took Zane's wrists in his hands and worked the blood back into his fingers. Zane fought the urge to moan. Everything hurt but Asa's hands were the good hurt, like the weird satisfaction from pressing on a bruise. And he was bruised, inside and out.

Yeah, because of Asa.

Zane yanked his hands free, earning another grin from Asa, who didn't return to the tub but sat across from him on the floor with his back against the door. Zane rolled his shoulders with a grimace. He couldn't believe this was the same man he'd let hunt him through a house just a couple of hours ago. Was it a couple of hours ago or had more time passed? He didn't even know. "No, thanks. I'll take my chances."

Asa chuckled. "You haven't even heard my proposal."

Zane scoffed. "The last time I heard you out, I ended up face down in your playroom."

Asa's responding grin was salacious. "Yeah, you did. But let's not veer down that memory lane just yet." He looked him over. "I might get distracted."

Zane sneered. "You really think I'd ever let you touch me again?"

The smile slid from Asa's face, his hunger making Zane's mouth dry. "Sugar, I think I could have you on your knees begging for my cock in less than twenty minutes, if that's what I wanted. But, first, let's talk about our deal. And your lack of options."

Zane gave Asa a smug smile. "I have more options than you think. I sent my friend the coordinates to your cabin before I went there. By now, the cops are probably swarming the place."

He'd thought that might spook Asa, but he just waved it off. "Maybe you did, maybe you didn't, but my family is exceptionally good at what we do, and by the time anybody makes it back out there, my brother-in-law will have that place clean enough to eat off the floors. They'll find nothing except a small little hunting cabin my family legally owns." Whatever. Zane still had the video. "And if you're sitting there thinking you can just show them the video you took, it's long gone, as is anything you might have sent to the cloud. Money buys a fantastic IT department."

God fucking dammit. His lip curled in disgust at himself and at Asa. He racked his brain, trying to think of any other viable offer. How long would it take Blake to convince police something nefarious had happened to him? How long would it take to hunt him down? Blake didn't even know which Mulvaney he'd left with.

"What's your offer?" he finally muttered.

Asa spread his legs out, his thighs falling open, his bare feet now slotted between Zane's legs. "It's a good one. I think you'll like it. It's far more generous than you deserve."

Zane rolled his eyes. "Get on with it."

Asa's foot was distractingly close to Zane's upper thigh. He had to force himself to concentrate on Asa's words.

"You and I work together to find answers for my family. In exchange, I answer any question you want about me and my family. At the end of our time together, if I haven't convinced you that my family does far more good than harm, I'll let you go and you can try to convince the world that we're all a bunch of psychopathic murderers."

"You are a bunch of psychopathic murderers," Zane said, exasperated. Why did Asa not get that?

"We kill bad men. And women," he added hastily. "We're equal opportunity vigilantes."

"You're fucking crazy." There was no heat behind his words, only a strange sense of awe.

"So I've heard."

Zane shook his head, rejecting the very idea that Asa could be serious about this deal. "Yeah, right. I'm supposed to believe that you'll just let me blow up your family."

"Yes."

Zane snorted. "I'll end up with a bullet in my head before I even make it back to my apartment."

Asa crawled closer until he was once more in Zane's space, this time kneeling between his splayed knees. "Look me in the eye and tell me I'm lying," Asa demanded.

Zane's gaze flicked to his without hesitation, face

flushing as he realized how easily he'd submitted to Asa's order. He saw it, too, but was apparently smart enough not to mention it.

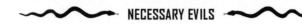

Zane hated to admit it, but he believed Asa. He was one hundred percent cocky enough to gamble his entire family's future on his ability to charm the fucking pants off of Zane. "You're insane," he said again.

"What about this surprises you?" Asa asked, sounding genuinely curious.

All of it. Zane had seen Asa chopping up that body—had listened to him talk about killing—but none of it seemed real. It was too much of a mind fuck. He'd fucked a mass murderer. Or a serial killer. How was this his life? "And what do you get out of this?"

Asa shook his head. "I told you. Help. A friend of my father's reached out asking for his help with a problem. My father dumped it in my lap. I don't solve crimes or do research. Lucas and Noah are the investigators. My father is judge and jury. My brothers and I, we're just the executioners. But my father is trying to drive home a point. I'm being punished. But I'm also being studied. He wants to see how I do without my brother."

"Without your brother?" Zane echoed, frowning. "What does that mean?"

"Avi and I haven't been apart since we were little. We don't do well apart," Asa admitted.

Zane frowned. *They don't do well apart?* They had jobs. Relationships. Lives. Zane had heard of twins being unusually close—especially identical twins—but never two so close they had to be forcibly separated. That was…weird.

No weirder than being chained to the fucking radiator.

Shut up.

Jesus. Zane was just as fucking crazy as Asa. At least Avi was alive. Zane spent his days talking to a brother who didn't exist and, worse, his brother talked back. He might as well be talking to a six-foot rabbit like in *Donnie Darko.*

Zane shook his head. "You can't mean you're never apart. You guys travel the world, date celebrities, have fancy jobs. Surely, you've been apart before."

Asa narrowed his eyes with a slight smile. "You know an awful lot about us, Lois."

"Yeah, I'm a journalist." *Sort of.* "Answer the question."

Asa sighed, his hands dropping to his sides, his fingertips brushing Zane's jean-clad thighs. "We've spent nights in our own places. But we always see each other the next day. Being apart is painful. Like, psychically painful. The longer we're apart, the harder it is for us to keep it together, mentally."

Jesus. If this was Asa keeping it together, what the fuck was he like when he unraveled? Zane's brain helpfully provided a mental image of thousands of dead corpses piled sky-high. He hated being in his head sometimes.

Zane sighed. "What's this big mystery?"

Asa's blue eyes glittered with triumph. "There have been five suicides at the local college."

Zane's reaction was visceral. He lurched for the toilet, dry heaving the meager contents of his stomach, retching until his stomach muscles hurt as much as the rest of him. When he finally stopped, a wet hand towel appeared beside his face. He wiped his mouth and sagged back against the wall.

"You good, Lois?" Asa asked.

Zane didn't look at him. "That's not a mystery. It's a tragedy. A common one."

Asa studied him, like he wanted to probe his reaction further, but finally nodded. "That's actually what I said. My father said his friend isn't so sure. Apparently, five years ago, there were another five suicides."

Zane's whole body flushed ice cold and, for a split second, he thought he might pass out. "What school?"

"Henley."

Zane tipped his head back, pressing the cold rag against his eyes. His brother hadn't gone to Henley. He'd gone to the private college across town. But it seemed like a strange coincidence. His brother's death had also been part of a suicide cluster. "What—why doesn't this person think they were suicides?"

"There have been rumors. They were low risk. There have been whispers about a game," Asa said cautiously.

A game. Zane wanted to be shocked, but there really was nothing shocking after tonight. "It wouldn't be the first time some internet game turned fatal. What else do we know?"

"We?" Asa asked.

Zane rolled his eyes. "What fucking choice do I have?"

Asa shrugged. "That's fair. Where do we start?"

Zane thought about it for a moment. If Asa was going to let him out of the bathroom, he'd have ample opportunities to signal for help if it seemed Asa wasn't really holding up his end of their deal. "What's the likelihood of us being able to interview your father's friend?"

Asa sighed, scooting in close once more. "Slim to none. My father's friends, the ones in the know anyway, tend to want to remain anonymous. At least, to everyone but my father. But I have a friend who owes the Mulvaneys a favor. He goes to school at Henley. I figure maybe we can start with him."

Zane arched his brow. "You have friends?"

Asa smirked. "No. I have friends who owe me favors. Not quite the same thing. A different kind of friends with benefits. If we hurry, we might catch them before they leave work."

Asa stood, so Zane did, too. Once they were on their feet, Asa looked him over with interest. "Do you want to shower? I have nothing that would fit you, but at least your scent wouldn't be so strong."

Zane's eyes went wide. "Wow. Fuck you. I smell like this because I went running through the woods, got tased, and then held hostage in a bathroom."

Asa crowded him up against the wall, pressing his face against Zane's throat and inhaling deeply. "That's not why you smell like that. I mean, yeah, you smell like sweat and a little like fresh dirt. But more than that. You smell like fear. You smell like me, like us. And believe me, I'm not complaining. But it's distracting as hell."

Zane's traitorous dick hardened as much from Asa's words as from the feel of his breath against his skin. That shouldn't have been hot. Fuck. This was a bad idea for a thousand different reasons. Mainly because being a murderer should have been a deal breaker for his libido. The way Asa spoke should have disgusted him, knowing what he now knew. His touch should have repulsed him.

Asa touched Zane like he belonged to him, like he had a claim, like them falling into bed again was a foregone conclusion. That should have infuriated him, and it did, a little. But the truth was, he liked it. He enjoyed having the undivided attention of someone like Asa. No, not someone like Asa. Just Asa.

Zane blamed his mother and his fucked up childhood. It wasn't normal to be horny for a man who kidnapped you. It wasn't normal to want to kill somebody and fuck them. None of this was okay. But he knew he wouldn't say no. He knew he'd do whatever Asa asked, at least for now.

Still, he tilted his body away from Asa's lips so he could look him in the eye. "If I get a chance to run, I'll take it."

Asa's laugh was downright diabolical. He gripped Zane's chin in his hand, his gaze dropping to Zane's lips. "I hope you do, sugar. But just remember what I'll do to you if I catch you."

Somehow, Zane didn't think he was threatening his life.

SIX

ASA

"Are you giving me the silent treatment already, sugar britches? That doesn't bode well for our future."

Zane didn't answer, just continued to glower, as he stared straight ahead out the windshield of Asa's black SUV. He'd been silent since Asa had insisted on watching him shower. It wasn't like he was trying to get off—though, he easily could have. There was something very appealing about a naked and soapy Zane. But, truthfully, Asa just didn't trust him not to find a way out while he wasn't looking. Zane should be flattered. Asa found most people to be stupid.

The joke was on Asa, though. Zane no longer smelled like sweat and sex and cum; he now smelled like Asa's soap and shampoo and, somehow, that was so much worse. Adam liked to joke that Asa and Avi were more animal than human, but he wasn't wrong. Asa truly preferred to trust his baser instincts. When he stripped away all the window dressing of polite society, Asa was just a hunter and he had the instincts of one.

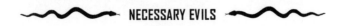

Which was why sitting across from a sulky Zane was driving him nuts. He wanted to bury his face against his neck, rub all over him, let the world know that he was his, whether he liked it or not. But that was insane. Because Zane wasn't his. Zane was a total stranger. A total stranger hell-bent on destroying Asa's family. That should have been a massive deterrent. But it wasn't. Not even a little.

What would Avi think of Zane? Would he see it, too? Would he welcome him into their little cozy den of two? It was only a matter of time before it became a den of four. His twin might not see it, but Felix was already marking his own territory when it came to Avi. He'd been cockblocking his brother for months. Not that Asa would ever tell him that. It was just too much fun, watching Avi be outwitted at every turn and not even notice.

Or, at least, it had been. Until his little reporter threw a wrench in his plans. "Come on, don't be mad, Lois. I was just trying to ensure I didn't lose you before the fun even started. Don't act like you aren't curious about this. I bet you've never met an unanswered question."

Zane turned his furious gaze to Asa. "You watched me shower."

Asa lowered his voice, giving him a confused look. "We exchanged DNA. I came inside you. My blood and skin is still under your fingernails. I thought we were long past being shy."

"Consent can be revoked at any time," Zane muttered, turning his whole body away like a sulky toddler.

Asa should not have found that as cute as he did. "Maybe

in sex, sugar, not so much in kidnapping. A lack of consent is a key element. Though…I'd be okay with exploring your consent boundaries once I convince you not to throw me in prison. I think we could have a lot of fun together. Besides, I found your spare glasses for you, didn't I? At least you're not blind."

Zane snorted but said nothing more.

Asa liked the wire-rimmed frames more than the thick black ones from earlier, but he kept his opinion to himself, fairly certain Zane would have rolled down the window and chucked them out just to spite him. They pulled onto the sprawling campus, Asa following the GPS to find the coffee shop tucked away in the farthest corner, directing the car into the shadows of the empty parking lot.

"Who are these guys?" Zane asked. "Are they dangerous?"

"One of them is a psychopath. The other once killed somebody. But in the grand scheme of things, these two don't even ping at a one on the danger scale."

"Where do you ping on that danger scale?" Zane asked.

"Scale of one to ten?" Asa asked, considering the question. "Twelve, maybe?"

Zane shivered but fell quiet again.

Asa had brought his Range Rover so there would be plenty of room for their guests, but it had also put too much space between him and Zane. While he found his scent distracting, he also wanted to bathe in it. He shook the thought away, attempting to put himself in game mode. Though, usually, game mode involved far more carnage than this.

The shop was closed, but the boys Asa looked for were

still inside. They would just have to wait for them out back by Dimitri's car. It couldn't be too much longer. As soon as he stepped free of the Rover, he heard the door lock behind him. Asa snickered. Zane was as petty as he was pretty. Asa walked around to the passenger side and rapped his knuckle against the window. Zane continued to ignore him until Asa pressed the key fob in his hand, disengaging the lock and pulling the car door open.

Zane offered no help in Asa's endeavor, forcing him to unlatch his seatbelt and pull him from the car like an unruly child, only contributing when Asa laced their fingers together. Zane pulled his hand free. Asa laughed. "You can't stay mad at me forever, sugar."

"Watch me," Zane muttered.

"Now you want me to watch you?" Asa asked, wrapping an arm around Zane's bicep to guide him along to where Dimitri's Toyota sat in the gravel behind the shop.

Zane's lip curled. "I hate you."

Asa laughed again. "I can feel how much you want that to be true. But it's not, and that's what's making you truly crazy. It's alright. I won't tell."

When they reached Dimitri's Camry, Asa turned Zane and forcibly leaned him against the back driver's side door before moving to stand beside him. "I feel like you're wasting a prime opportunity to ask me about my family."

Zane shifted and, for a minute, Asa thought maybe he would continue to ignore him. Finally, he asked, "Your whole family kills people?"

"Our whole family has killed people, but they don't

actively participate in killing. My father oversees the operation. Noah killed the pedophile who shared him with a bunch of strangers. Lucas killed his colleague who was massacring vulnerable women. Jericho… No, yeah, Jericho kills because he likes making people pay for their sins, just like the rest of us."

"How is it possible that you all are killers?" Zane asked, some of the stoniness leaving his voice.

"Because we're all psychopaths. It's why my father adopted us."

Zane turned to him, incredulous. "All of you? I mean, I know I said it earlier but I didn't really think you were all actually clinically insane."

"We're not insane, Lois. We're…evolved. Our lack of empathy allows us to do what needs to be done."

"And what's that?" Zane asked, his tone implying Asa was full of shit.

"Take out the trash."

Zane opened his mouth to say something but, before he could, the door banged open and slammed closed again and Dimitri appeared with a boy tossed over his shoulder.

"What's wrong? What's happening? Why did you stop?" the boy asked. "I'm getting dizzy."

Dimitri carefully set the boy—Arlo—on his feet before turning him to face Asa and Zane. Arlo gasped, backing directly into Dimitri, who put an arm around him to steady him. It was nice to see he'd made such an indelible impression on the boys. It would make this much easier.

"What are you doing here?" Dimitri asked, not sounding

particularly concerned by his sudden appearance. But then, Dimitri was a psychopath, too. The lack of fear made situations like this less ominous.

"We need a favor," Asa said.

Dimitri squinted, peering into the darkness. "Which one are you?"

Asa stepped out of the shadows. "Asa. This is Zane. We need your help."

"What kind of help?" Dimitri asked warily.

"Does it matter?" Asa asked, the question weighted.

Dimitri gave a heavy sigh. "Have you cleared this with my mom? I really can't afford to get on her bitch list again."

Asa grinned. Dimitri was the son of their resident hacker, Calliope. Asa understood not wanting to get on her bad side. She sounded deceptively perky, but knowing now that she'd raised a psychopath of her own made Asa view her in a whole new light.

"My dad cleared it with your mom. All parental units are in the loop. Let's go get some food. I'm starving."

Arlo glanced over his shoulder at Dimitri. "Are we really doing this?"

"What choice do we have?" Dimitri asked.

Asa nodded, happy at least one person tonight wasn't going to give him shit about his excellent plan. "Exactly. Glad we're all on the same page. We'll take my car. It's right over there."

Asa snaked an arm around Zane's waist. He didn't fight him at least, but he didn't look enthusiastic either. He could practically hear the other two wondering about their dynamic.

"What do you think their deal is?" Asa heard Arlo ask quietly.

"I think it's none of our business," Dimitri whispered back.

Dimitri was smart. He had good instincts. When he was a little older, it might be a good idea to bring him into the fold. If it turned out August's daughters weren't psychopaths, they could still be raised as killers, but it would be years before that happened. Jericho's crew was young and deadly, but they lacked training and were very emotion driven. It would be nice to have Dimitri on the crew.

The crew.

Jesus.

Murder was the family business and business was good. Did his father think of the future? About what would happen to the next generation? Had he realized that being a psychopath wasn't a prerequisite to being a good killer?

Asa snapped back to the present when he heard Arlo mutter, "So much for getting fucked tonight."

Asa glanced back to see Dimitri wrap an arm around Arlo's shoulders, their fingers still intertwined. "Oh, we might still get fucked tonight, but not in the way either of us was hoping."

"Christ, you two are giving me a toothache with all the cuteness," Asa said, giving Zane's waist a squeeze.

"Then go kidnap two other people," Arlo quipped.

"Oh, don't tempt him. He loves holding people against their will," Zane muttered, still pouting.

"Don't be sassy, Lois Lane," Asa said, dropping his hand

and sliding it into Zane's back pocket. "They might think you don't like me."

Zane wiggled out of Asa's grip. "I don't like you."

Asa scoffed, giving him a look. "The scratches down my back say otherwise, sugar britches."

"Gross," Arlo groaned, earning a laugh from Asa.

When they reached the Rover, Asa gestured to the backseat. "Chop-chop, young lovers. There's fuckery afoot."

The two of them climbed up into the bench seat, squeezing together in the center. Up front, Asa walked Zane around and forcibly settled him into the passenger seat before buckling his seatbelt. When he glanced in the rearview mirror, Arlo looked like he'd seen a ghost. "Jesus, relax, you two. I just need some information. I'm not here to rip off your toenails with pliers."

"Well, that adds a whole new layer of horror to this," Arlo muttered.

"Don't worry, baby. I will keep your toenails safely where they belong," Dimitri promised.

"That is both gross and romantic," Arlo said, a smile spreading across his face.

"That's me. Grossly romantic," Dimitri promised, leaning down to drop a kiss on his forehead. "And for the record, there's nobody else I'd rather be kidnapped with."

Arlo looked up at him with soft eyes. "Aw, me neither. I love you."

"I love you, too," Dimitri promised.

"And I love noise canceling headphones," Zane said around a groan, glaring at Asa. "Can you put some music on or something?"

Asa winked at him. "Anything for you, darling."

Zane sighed in exasperation. "I really, really fucking hate you."

The diner was a dive, one of those 24/7 places that smelled like stale coffee and pancakes. It was busy enough for them to not draw much attention but not so busy they couldn't hear each other speak. They chose a booth at the very back near the kitchen.

When an elderly server with hot pink hair wandered over, the others were momentarily rendered speechless. She had to be seventy, but her hair was the color of bubble gum and held back in a thick ponytail with blue butterflies nesting in the top. She looked bored and arched one thin dark brow at them as if daring them to remark on her wild appearance. They did not.

"What can I get ya?" she asked.

They all looked at Asa, as if asking if they were actually going to eat. He wasn't lying when he said he was starving. Between his extracurriculars with Zane and his body dumping with Jericho, he was famished. He ordered a huge omelet with a side of pancakes and coffee.

Arlo ordered pancakes as well, and Dimitri ordered a burger. When they got to Zane, Asa leaned into his space, his hand curving over his thigh, lips pressing against his ear so only he could hear him say, "You're not going on a hunger strike, sugar. Order, or I'll order for you and make you eat every bite of whatever's put in front of you. Your choice."

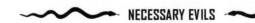

Zane cleared his throat. "Can I get the bacon waffle, please?"

The server narrowed her eyes at them suspiciously but nodded. "Sure thing."

When she was gone, Zane's fist wrapped around Asa's middle finger, turning so he could nuzzle his cheek against Asa's in a way that made his dick take notice. He hissed as Zane wrenched his finger back hard.

"Touch me again without my permission and I'll break your fucking hand. Got it?" Zane growled.

That shouldn't have been a turn on, right? This shouldn't be fun for Asa, but it was. He hadn't once thought about the giant gaping hole of Avi's absence since meeting Zane. Somehow, Zane had become his sole focus in just the span of a few hours. That had to be some kind of black magic.

Asa yanked his hand free, giving Zane a wan smile. "Whatever you say, honeybunch."

Across the table, Arlo stared at Zane for a long moment before asking, "Were you in an accident or something? What happened to you?"

Dimitri gave Asa a knowing look before nudging Arlo, shaking his head. Asa watched as the two seemed to have a silent conversation that ended in Arlo's eyes going wide with understanding. He blushed, then looked at Zane's bruises and bite marks with much more interest.

"So…why are we here?" Arlo asked. "Unless we're just here to witness whatever the hell is going on between you two weirdos?"

Dating a psychopath clearly made people bold. "We're looking into something that happened at Henley and thought you might have some information."

Dimitri and Arlo looked at each other. "What kind of something?"

"A string of suicides over the last couple of months."

Arlo's face immediately grew stormy. "Yeah, those were sad."

"Not sad, weird," Dimitri corrected, taking a swig of his soda.

"Weird how?" Asa asked.

"Okay, like, we've had the occasional unaliving around here, right? But, usually they follow a pattern. So, even if, say, a quarterback jumps off a building and an unpopular kid follows suit, it makes sense from a psychological standpoint. You know what I mean? There's a sort of follower/followee relationship, you know?" Dimitri asked.

Asa frowned, nodding. He didn't really know but he was hoping his point would become clear if he kept talking.

"But this recent string… They're not in the same social circles, but they're all on the same social tier," Dimitri said.

"Social tier?" Zane echoed.

"Yeah. The first suicide nine weeks ago was Xander Hamilton. I only remember that because, you know, Alexander Hamilton. But he was super popular. Swim team captain. Straight As. Captain of the debate team. Super shocking, but maybe an outlier. The low risk kid who killed himself. But then, the next death happened and it didn't make sense."

"How?" Asa asked.

"The second boy—I can't remember his name—was in a frat with my friend, Jason. Rich daddy. Tons of friends. Cocky asshole. As far as I know, the two didn't know each other. They didn't run in the same social circle. But they were on the same social tier. Both at the top of their respective friend groups. Now, I'm not saying popular kids don't off themselves, but two popular kids? Three? Five? That's fucking weird," Dimitri finished, eyes going wide as his plate was set in front of him.

They took a couple of moments to prep their food. Asa watched as Zane drowned his bacon waffle in maple syrup, only returning his attention back to Dimitri when Zane took his first bite.

"I admit, I don't know a whole lot about the mental process behind suicide," Asa said as he chewed.

"A single suicide has the ability to touch around a hundred and thirty-five people. Exposure to a peer's suicide can increase suicidal ideations, but it doesn't, on its own, cause an increase in suicide in a low-risk person," Zane said, looking a little green around the gills.

"What?" Arlo asked, his fork halfway to his lips.

"He's saying just being around a person who took their own life isn't enough to cause a person to copycat unless they were already considering killing themselves in the first place," Dimitri said, looking to Zane to confirm.

Zane nodded. "Yeah, that. Suicide only increases the chance of someone who already had ideations following through with it. You're saying none of these kids were considered at risk?"

Dimitri shrugged. "I just know that it was really scandalous. Lots of whispering behind hands and popular girls holding candlelight vigils."

"Yeah, there are tons of little mini-shrines all over campus now," Arlo said with a shiver. "It's…kind of creepy."

"Have you heard any whispers about a game?" Zane asked, voice strained.

Asa frowned. Zane was sweating, his skin unnaturally pale. First him vomiting when Asa even brought up the word suicide, then his almost savant-like statistics, and now, he was once more looking like he wasn't going to be able to keep down his breakfast.

Arlo and Dimitri exchanged glances before Arlo said, "You think these suicides are part of the game?"

"The game?" Asa repeated. "What game is this?"

Arlo bit down on his bottom lip, chewing thoughtfully before he said, "I mean, I don't really know. There have just been rumors on campus about a bunch of kids playing some kind of online game. Like, they earn points for doing dangerous shit. There's supposed to be some kind of monetary reward."

"That didn't strike either of you as weird?" Zane asked.

Arlo raised a brow. "We don't even know those people. Besides, there's always some kind of dumb internet thing going viral. Our school was in the paper last year because a frat was using a rating scale for the girls they slept with. People ate Tide Pods and laid down in busy streets for

TikToks. Like, college boys suck."

Asa wouldn't argue with that. He and Avi had been pretty insufferable during their college days. Nothing like rating their bedmates, though. His father would have killed them himself if either of them had humiliated him like that. "I need you to find a way to get us information on that game and whether it's still going on."

"Do you know if this is the first time this game has hit campus?" Zane asked. "Have they played it at other schools?"

Arlo looked at Zane, startled. "Are you okay? You don't look so good."

Zane's gaze darted to Asa. "I need to use the bathroom. Now."

Asa didn't question him, just moved, watching as he lurched for the bathroom just to the left of the kitchen door.

"Is he okay?" Arlo asked again.

"I'm not sure, to be honest," Asa said. "I need you to get me literally anything you can. Either text me, or send it to your mom so she can get it to me. Seriously, don't fuck me on this. My father's on my ass."

Dimitri gave him a sympathetic look. "I get it. It's been six months and my mom's still pissed about one tiny murder."

Asa gave him a nod and tossed a hundred dollars cash on the table. "Can you two catch an Uber back to your car? I need to go take care of this."

They looked at each other and then him, nodding. "Yeah, sure. I hope your friend feels better," Arlo said, expression earnest.

"Me too," Asa said.

SEVEN

ZANE

Zane kneeled by a toilet for the second time that night. This time, in a shitty roadside diner. His stomach was now gnawingly empty, burning from hunger or maybe just acid, his muscles cramping like he'd been kicked by a horse. When was the last time he'd eaten? When Blake had brought his sandwich? Was that only yesterday? He fell back against the stall door, begging his brain not to think too hard about the tiles beneath him.

This story was proving hazardous to his health. *Asa Mulvaney* was proving hazardous to his fucking health… and his sanity. Sweat beaded along his forehead, ran into his eyes, rolled down his spine until his t-shirt clung to him. He definitely hadn't predicted this was how last night would go. He'd anticipated boredom. Charming Thomas Mulvaney into friendship and slowly ferreting out all his dirty little secrets had sounded intriguing in theory but would probably have been boring in reality.

When Thomas never showed, Zane almost left—was in

the process of leaving—when he'd seen Asa at the bar. Why hadn't he just kept walking and tried again? Instead, he'd decided to try to seduce a different Mulvaney. He'd been so smug about it, too. Until he was in the car driving to his house. Zane had gone looking for a news story and had somehow cast himself in the world's gayest action movie.

Action movie? Try porn movie. And not even vanilla porn. The kinky niche stuff you have to dig for on the internet. The borderline illegal kind.

Ugh. "Not now," Zane said out loud to…to nobody. Because his brother wasn't there.

Mom would say God was punishing you.

Zane could hear the smug humor in Gage's voice. It was how Gage said everything. Like the whole world was funny and beneath him. He was right about their mother, though. She would say that. She would shake her head and wave her hand while swilling down another martini and complaining about their family's terribly bad luck. Only his mother could make being an upper middle class lady an albatross.

He wiped the perspiration off his forehead. Who was he kidding? He was feeling sorry for himself, too. Nothing like one life changing event to realize he was barely hanging on by a thread. He'd thought he was strong, resourceful, that he had it all figured out. But one tiny crack—okay, massive crack—and Zane was fracturing into a thousand mentally unstable pieces.

Was it possible to have a mid-life crisis in his mid-twenties? If so, this was it. He was unraveling. He'd spent his whole life with one goal: being a crime journalist. He'd thought it would be the best way to put his love of true crime into something good for the world, by telling victims' stories. So noble. So altruistic.

But no. Because he wanted fame, too. Needed it, even. Not money, not celebrity, just fame, because fame might garner just a crumb of his mother's affection. His desperate laugh echoed around the empty bathroom. He didn't even like her and, still, he was willing to die to impress her.

Zane really was a fucking masochist.

And Asa was a sadist. A literal sadist. Zane hadn't had to work at all to feel wanted by him. He still didn't. There was a weird thrill that came from knowing even the slightest amount of interest would earn Zane more of Asa's unwavering attention, like waving a red cape in front of a bull.

Yeah, a bull who murders people. Why doesn't that bother you anymore? It only took five hours to smash your moral compass?

Zane closed his eyes, their encounter flashing through his memory. The feel of Asa stretching him, his breath against his skin, the way he almost purred in Zane's ear as he'd fucked him, holding him tight enough to leave bruises, fucking him hard enough to make him forget how fucking lonely he was.

Asa had said Zane smelled like prey. If any other man had ever uttered something like that, Zane would have rolled his eyes hard enough to sprain them. But Asa meant it. He lived it. If they'd done it outdoors, Zane didn't have to stretch his imagination to know Asa could find him. Asa *would* find him. It was beyond unhealthy how much that turned him on.

Zane was supposed to advocate for victims, tell their stories, get them justice, and instead, he was trying really hard not to fuck the perpetrator. *Fuck him again, you mean?* Zane shook his head. He'd never gone condom free with another man in his life. Not that there had been all that many, but still. The intensity of their connection had felt… holy? Ritualistic almost. Certainly more animalistic than human. But it had soothed the neediness in Zane, the desperate need to feel like just one fucking person saw him.

And now, he was kneeling in a shitty little bathroom in a greasy spoon diner after almost puking on the table in front of two psychopaths and a barista. But why? Zane had been reading books on true crime since he was ten years old. He'd read *Helter Skelter* in fifth grade. He'd seen gruesome crime scene photos, read victim impact statements, and crime reports more horrific than anything Stephen King could manage. So, why was this case getting to him?

Because some part of you now wonders if I killed myself over some fucking game.

Did you? It would be just like you to think gambling your life was something to be done for sport, leaving me behind to pick up the fucking pieces. Again. Always. Mom and Dad had no idea who you really were.

He dug the heels of his hands into his eyes until fireworks danced behind his eyelids. If he didn't stop talking to himself, he was going to be the one who ended up locked up, not the Mulvaneys. He didn't even care, that was the kicker. For weeks, he'd eaten, slept, and breathed all things Mulvaney and was sure he'd uncovered some giant conspiracy.

Surprise. You did.

Maybe. But it didn't matter. Being right didn't matter. Asa Mulvaney had told him with his own sexy-as-fuck mouth that he was a stone cold killer, that his entire family murdered people…and it didn't fucking matter. The world would never know about it. Asa would kill him before he let the story get out, and if he didn't, his family would. And none of it mattered.

There was no story big enough, no reward or achievement impressive enough, for his mother to give a fuck about him or say that she loved him. For his father to look up from his World War II books long enough to realize one of his sons had actually survived. At Zane's age, he'd imagined it would hurt less, being this alone. But really, he was just a lot better at ignoring the big, gaping hole Gage had left behind.

I fucking hate you for this, you fucking asshole.

He didn't, though. Not really. It wasn't Gage's fault his parents coddled him. Gage was just as uncomfortable being the chosen one as Zane had been as the invisible one. Their lives were equally hell, just for different reasons. Gage had only wanted to experience life. He'd never met a reckless idea he hadn't immediately wanted to try. He reminded Zane of Asa in that way.

As if on cue, the heavy door to the restroom creaked open like something out of a horror movie. "Lois?"

"I didn't escape out a window if that's what you're worried about," he muttered.

"You okay?" Asa asked, his voice closer than it had been

a moment ago.

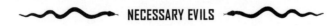

Zane could feel his face contorting with exasperation. "No, I'm puking my guts out in a dirty diner bathroom. I'm definitely not okay."

Asa sighed. "This is my fault," he said, with the same tone a parent uses when their child gets sick eating too much sugar.

"No shit," Zane snapped.

He was right outside the stall now. "I should have taken better care of you."

A shock of awareness rocketed through Zane, his heart rate skyrocketing, leaving him breathless. "What?"

"What we did earlier…it can cause an adrenaline surge. When that chemical drops, it can leave you feeling a lot of different ways. Sad. Sick. Drained," he said, his voice somewhere between condescending and educational. "Usually, I only play with pros, but I should have told Jericho to fuck off so I could take better care of you. It was irresponsible."

Zane hated the way something inside him shriveled at Asa's casual dismissal of his downward spiral. Of course, it was all just chemical. What a polite psychopath Asa was. Zane shook his head, immediately regretting it when the room spun. What was wrong with him? Asa was a hookup. Why was Zane so upset that he was treating him like one? Well, aside from the kidnapping.

Jesus. How was this his life now?

He forced himself to his feet, too tired to make his response as scathing as he'd hoped. "While the idea of fucking you does make me sick, that's not what this is."

He swung the stall door open to find Asa directly in his path, their faces not even an inch apart. "Well, you're making jokes, so you must be feeling a little better."

"You think I'm kidding," Zane quipped, walking to the sink and washing his hands for far longer than necessary.

He pretended not to notice as Asa studied him in the mirror. "I think you wish you were kidding, if that matters? But yeah, I think you liked fucking me and you're mad about it. I don't think you're mad enough to vomit over it, so I can only assume it's sub drop."

"Sub drop?"

"Yeah, that's what it's called. Sub drop."

Sub. As in submissive. As in Zane was submissive to Asa's dominance? Consenting to being held down and used was pretty submissive. Zane was learning far too much about himself tonight.

Asa stepped behind him until he was close enough to curve his hands around Zane's narrow hips, the warmth of his fingers causing goosebumps to erupt along his skin. "I wasn't lying. I really did plan on spending the night with you."

That wasn't what he said earlier. He'd said, '*I really wanted to spend the night inside you.*' Inside him. Fuck. What would have happened if he'd stayed? Zane could feel his cock hardening. If Asa's hand slid any farther around his waist, he'd feel it, too. He bent forward to splash some water on his face and realized his mistake as Asa's erection pressed against his ass. Was he just always ready to go?

Asa took Zane's position as an invitation. "I like you like this," he mused, sliding a hand up under Zane's t-shirt, his fingers running along the knobs of his spine. "Bent over for me. I like being able to see your face. You look so fucking hot when you're underneath me. The sounds you made… Fuck."

Zane wanted to pretend he hated it, but he didn't. He fucking didn't. His nipples were hard. His dick was hard. Every atom of his body was aware of Asa. Part of him wanted to grind against him so badly, entice him into taking over, into forcing Zane to do something he desperately wished he didn't want. There was a sound like velcro ripping, then the door burst open.

Zane bolted upright, glancing in the mirror, grateful when the man just walked to the urinal without giving them another look.

"Let's go," Asa murmured, nodding towards the door.

It wasn't until they were back in the SUV that Zane finally asked, "What do we do now? What happened to Arlo and Dimitri?"

Asa took his eyes off the road to glance at him. "I sent them home in an Uber. We're going home, too. It's too late to question anybody else tonight. And you need sleep."

Hearing the word *sleep* had Zane yawning hard enough for his jaw to crack. He was so goddamn tired. Still, he glowered at Asa. "You going to chain me up to the radiator again? Sounds super cozy."

Asa gave him a heated glance. "No, I was going to handcuff you to my headboard. My bed is much more comfortable."

Zane's stomach flip-flopped, but he scoffed. "No thanks. I'd rather snuggle a radiator than you."

Asa laughed a genuine honest-to-God laugh. "You're so full of shit. A therapist would have a field day with you. I know one if you need one."

"Yeah, well, if you're his star client, I'll pass."

"I'm the picture of mental health," Asa said.

"Is that picture posted beside John Wayne Gacy?" Zane asked, pulling a face.

Asa chuckled. "Yeah, maybe. But it doesn't change the fact that you desperately need sleep."

Zane opened his mouth to argue but then stopped. Why was he fighting this? Asa clearly wasn't going to let him go so he could sleep at his own place. Did he want to sleep chained to a radiator? No. Did he want to sleep next to Asa?

Yes.

No.

Liar.

"You'd better keep your hands to yourself," Zane finally said, letting his temple rest against the cold glass of the window.

"I can keep my hands to myself, Lois. But you seem to forget that you approached me. You came to my house. You consented twice. You said we could play without a condom. Now, I'm not saying I don't like a little non-consensual role play, but even that—hell, especially that—requires written consent. If you want me, you're going to have to come and get me."

"Don't hold your breath."

Asa turned to face him as they pulled up to a red light on a nearly deserted street, leaning into his space, tone conspiratorial. "Okay, Lois. I hear you. But when you change your mind—when you wake up so fucking horny you can't bear to go another minute without me touching you, I'll be here. And I'll pretend not to notice how quickly you caved."

Zane swallowed the sudden lump in his throat, crossing his arms over his lap. "On second thought, I changed my mind."

A slow grin spread across Asa's face. "Oh, yeah?"

Zane gave him a slow smile of his own. "Yeah. You should definitely hold your breath."

EIGHT

ASA

Asa fought back a smile the whole way out of the city. Beside him, Zane fumed—arms crossed, cheeks flushed, jaw thrust forward. Fuck, he was sexy. Every time Asa glanced over at that pouty fucking mouth, his dick got a little harder. He wanted to do dirty, dirty things to that mouth. He wanted Zane on his knees for him, putting those plush lips to good use. He wanted to watch tears roll down Zane's cheeks as he gagged on his cock, making eye contact while he came down his throat.

Asa took a deep breath and let it out, earning another furious side eye from Zane. Yeah, Asa needed to stop that line of thinking or he was going to pull over and test the limits of both of their restraint, and it would be all his father's fault.

Part of him wanted to snap just so Thomas could see what came of his meddling. So he could look at the consequences of his actions and say, "This is what happens when you take my brother away." His father would tell him Avi not being there had nothing to do with whatever heinous acts Asa ended up committing, but it just wasn't true. Not even a day apart from his twin and Asa wanted to do things to Zane that would probably violate the Geneva convention.

He missed Avi, and that metaphysical pain would only deepen and fester like a splinter under his skin. By tomorrow, there was no telling how bad it would be. But that was tomorrow Asa's problem. Or later today Asa's problem. Zane needed sleep. His eyes were glassy, and the bruise from where his face hit Asa's floor was turning a purple black. At this rate, he might have to carry him. The thought held a certain appeal.

"How is it you know so much about suicide statistics?" Asa asked finally, more to keep himself from fantasizing about defiling every part of his passenger.

Zane's head snapped to him so fast Asa was surprised he didn't hear his neck snap. Zane's reasons were clearly personal. The hurt and frustration bleeding from his honeyed gaze made that obvious. He'd lost somebody to suicide, and he was mad at whoever had done it but also furious with Asa for bringing it up.

Zane was a complicated man.

Asa shouldn't find it as compelling as he did. But most people bored him. When one was raised in a household full of psychopaths, being around people who society considered normal was often painful. Psychopaths really didn't have time for bullshitting and small talk. Sure, they played the part to hide their secrets, but there was no such thing as dinner conversation in the Mulvaney household.

They passed potatoes over talk of severed heads and torture techniques. Compared to the outside world, they were the fucking Addams family. Hell, they were the Manson family.

What would Zane think of the real Mulvaneys? Would they horrify him? Asa didn't think so. For all Zane's pearl-clutching, he'd knelt a foot away from a dissected corpse and hadn't so much as flinched. He wasn't squeamish about death, just murderers. And judging by how soft and hazy his face got when Asa had him bent over in front of that mirror a few minutes ago, even Asa being a killer didn't seem to bother Zane's dick too much.

"Who was it?" Asa asked.

"Who was who?" Zane said dully, turning to stare out the window.

"Who was the person who unalived themselves? They were clearly important to you."

Zane turned his gaze forward again, and Asa watched his Adam's apple bob as he swallowed hard. "My brother."

Asa sucked in a breath. There wasn't much he feared in this world, but being without Avi was the highest on his list. Being without his brother would feel like he'd lost a literal part of himself. "Twins?"

Zane shook his head. "He was older but only by seven months."

"Seven months?" That math didn't add up.

Zane's words were thick, like he had to force them from his throat. "They called us Irish twins. My mom got pregnant with me five weeks after Gage was born. I was not planned, clearly."

There was definitely more to that story. "How old was he when he died?"

"Twenty-one."

Asa did the math. Zane couldn't be more than twenty-five or twenty-six. "Where did he go to school?"

"Where your brother teaches."

Had they had any suicide clusters at August's school? He'd need to ask about it tomorrow. Was that why Zane had suddenly looked so ill? "And now, you're wondering about the timeline and whether there really is a game and whether your brother might have played it."

Zane gave a stilted nod. "My brother was an adrenaline junkie. He liked fast cars and jumping off cliffs and free climbing. Anything dangerous. When he died, they said he wasn't a thrill seeker but that he'd had a death wish. But it wasn't true. Gage loved life. He just hated our parents. But I never thought he hated them badly enough to kill himself… Badly enough to leave me behind with them."

The last part of the statement was muttered under his breath, like he hadn't meant to say it. Or, at least, like he hadn't meant for Asa to hear it.

They pulled into the long, curved drive, and Asa threw the SUV in park. "Is this too hard for you?"

Zane snapped his gaze to him once again. "What?"

"Is this going to be too much for you?"

Zane shook his head in confusion. "Why? Are you—the guy who handcuffed me to a radiator—now concerned about my mental well-being?"

That was fair. "Yes."

"And if it is? Then what? Then you kill me?"

That was also fair. Zane made a lot of good points. "No. I'm not going to kill you. But if you can't handle helping me on this case, then we'll…figure something out."

Zane blinked at him, mouth gaping, before he said, "Figure something out? Like what?"

"I don't know," Asa said honestly, hopping out of the SUV and walking around to open Zane's door. He helped him out and escorted him to the door. The door where he'd stripped him naked just hours ago. Fuck. Maybe this was why Asa had never brought anybody he wasn't paying to his house before.

He placed a hand on Zane's lower back, leading him inside and directly up the stairs, into his large bedroom.

Zane gazed longingly at Asa's king-size bed as he continued to gently guide him into the bathroom. He handed him a towel, a pair of joggers, and one of his t-shirts. "Go shower."

Zane frowned, glaring at the bathroom door. "Now, you trust me to shower alone?"

Asa grinned. "No, but now, the house is in lockdown. You can run anywhere you want, but you won't get out unless I let you out. If you want to exhaust yourself trying, be my guest. Or you can take a hot shower, then slide into a bed with a thread count so high you'll think literal fucking angels stitched them. Choice is yours, Lois."

Zane didn't answer him, instead marching to the shower, yanking the water to scalding. He started pulling off his clothes before Asa even left the room, clearly too tired to care whether he was there or not. Or maybe some part of him wanted Asa to watch. Which was good because he had to visibly tear his gaze away from Zane's naked body.

He left him to clean up, choosing to rinse off in the shower down the hall, before retreating to the kitchen and making Zane some toast. He needed to have some food in his stomach or he was going to wake up even sicker tomorrow. He poured him a glass of juice, too, and carried his offerings upstairs.

Zane was coming out of the bathroom just as Asa entered. He hadn't bothered with the shirt, just Asa's much too big joggers that clung for dear life to Zane's narrow hips.

"What's that?" Zane asked, eyes narrowed at the toast.

"Food. You need to eat something."

Zane made a face, shaking his head.

"Please, don't make me make you eat it. Just...behave."

Anger flashed in Zane's eyes, but it died just as quickly. He crossed the room and stuffed the two pieces of toast in his mouth in one go, chewing angrily before swallowing, then reached for the orange juice and slammed it back like it was a shot.

Asa gaped at him for a solid thirty seconds before saying, "I'm not going to lie, I'm a little turned on right now."

Zane rolled his eyes. "Where am I sleeping?"

"Pick a side."

Zane's brows knitted together. "You don't have a side of the bed that you prefer?" he asked, clearly suspicious.

Asa frowned back at Zane. "What? No. Who does that?"

"*Everybody* does that," Zane said, exasperated. "Except

psychopaths."

Asa tilted his head and raised his brows, a smug smile spreading over his face. "See? You have your answer. Pick a side."

Zane picked the side closest to the bathroom.

Asa snagged the pink fuzzy cuffs from the chair in the corner of his room. "Get comfortable." It was clear Zane wanted to fight, but he was just too fucking tired. He rolled onto his side, facing Asa's half of the bed. Asa couldn't help but smile. "I definitely thought I'd be the last thing you wanted to look at tonight."

Zane scoffed. "Don't flatter yourself. I just don't think I'll get much sleep with my back turned to a psychopath."

Asa leaned into Zane's space, inhaling the scent of spicy soap and clean skin as he slipped one cuff around Zane's wrist and the other to the bars of the metal headboard.

When he finished, their faces were barely an inch apart. Fuck. Asa wished he could just take what he wanted with impunity, wished Zane would just consent to being his. His to own, his to fuck, his to care for. "You comfortable?"

"You serious?" Zane countered, though with no real malice.

Asa gave a humorless laugh, then stood, undressing as he locked eyes with Zane. Zane's eyes struggled and failed to stay on his face, his gaze sliding lower to Asa's hard cock, his tongue darting out to wet his lower lip before he dragged his gaze away from Asa entirely.

Yeah, he wanted Asa, too. This was going to be torture. Zane was too proud to give in, and Asa had given him an ultimatum, all but guaranteeing he would never get laid by him again. Was this what relationships felt like?

He slid under the covers, rolling to face Zane. He didn't have total trust in Zane either. Asa might be the psychopath, but Zane was clearly pissed, and nobody knew better than Asa what people could do when they felt backed into a corner. And Asa had done exactly that. But nothing could be done about it now, so Asa closed his eyes and pretended to sleep.

Zane did not pretend to sleep. He shifted restlessly for the next hour, causing Asa to keep a wary eye on him before finally asking, "Can't sleep?"

"No, I'm sleeping with a metal ring around my wrist, chained to a bed next to a man I despise."

Asa smirked. "You would have ended up chained to this bed tonight one way or the other, if that makes you feel any better."

"Yeah, okay," Zane said, voice dripping with disbelief.

Asa scooted closer, closing the distance between them to push Zane's hair out of his face."It's true. I can't help it. There's just a part of me that likes you helpless, that likes you completely at my mercy. There's a part of you that likes it, too. If you'd just stop fighting it."

"Do you talk like this to every guy you sleep with?" Zane asked.

"I don't sleep with anybody. People fall into two distinct categories. Those I have boring vanilla sex with and sex workers I pay when I need to…release all this aggression. Neither of those groups have ever warranted an invite to spend the night."

"But you said I would have stayed the night."

Asa caressed his knuckles along Zane's cheekbone. "Mm, you were the exception to the rule."

Zane stared at him, seemingly too curious to pull away from Asa's unwanted touch. "Why is that?"

Asa could have lied, but he didn't want to. "Because you let me play with you. *Really* play with you. No holds barred. By the time I came inside you, I'd already thought of a hundred different ways I wanted to defile you the next time. Does that scare you?"

"I don't know," Zane answered, studying Asa's face like he could somehow gauge the truth of his words. When Asa slipped his hand beneath Zane's pillow, he flinched. "What are you doing?"

Asa pushed the button on the cuffs that caused them to release in an emergency, freeing Zane's wrists, then dropping the cuffs between them. "There. You're free. You really can't leave, though; this house is Fort Knox." Zane stared at him in disbelief. "You're welcome to try, like I said. If you want to sleep elsewhere, there are a dozen bedrooms. Pick whichever one you like."

Zane blinked at him. "Just like that?"

Asa's chest was inexplicably tight, but he forced himself to keep his tone light. "Yep, just like that."

Zane frowned hard. "What if I call the cops and tell them you're holding me hostage?" Zane countered, almost like he wanted the cuffs back on.

Did he? "What if you did?" Asa asked.

Zane shook his head in wonder. "You get off on this,

don't you? The danger. You like knowing I could destroy you if I wanted. That's twisted."

Zane was trying to provoke him. Why? All he'd done since stumbling upon Asa in that cabin was demand to be free. Now, he was free, yet he was still there. Why? Because he wanted to be. He wanted to be there with Asa and he was pissed about it.

Asa raised a brow. "As twisted as how upset you are that I uncuffed you?"

Zane thrust his jaw forward. "I am not."

Asa dipped his head until their lips were almost touching. "Oh, you are. Because when I was forcing you to stay in bed with me, you could convince yourself it wasn't your choice. But now, you have to either admit that you want to be here, with me, or go sleep alone somewhere else. And we both know where you want to be."

"Fuck you," Zane muttered.

Asa couldn't stop himself from wrapping a hand around Zane's throat and squeezing just enough for Zane's pupils to dilate. "You want this so badly. I bet if I slid my hand under these covers right now, I'd find you're rock hard." He bit down gently on Zane's lower lip. "You like this, like being my sole focus. It's okay. I like that you like it. If you don't want to admit it, if your pride is too great, then I can take the choice away from you, if that's what you want. Slide that cuff back on your wrist and I'll give you what you want."

"And what do I want?" Zane asked.

"For me to hold you down and fuck you, use you in any way I choose, while you pretend you don't want it.

While you pretend I've forced your hand and you're only doing it because you have no choice. That you're only enjoying it because it's a natural biological response and not because having your choices taken away sometimes feels so fucking good."

Zane swallowed audibly. "You're deranged."

Asa sighed. "Okay. Have it your way, Lois." He rolled away from him, essentially letting him know he was done playing with him. "I'll see you in the morning. If I'm not the one in cuffs, that is."

Asa closed his eyes, knowing he wouldn't get a wink of sleep with Zane free to roam the house. The bed shifted. Asa assumed it was Zane leaving, but then, there was the sound of metal on metal and the snick of not one, but two, cuffs sliding back into place.

Asa rolled back over to find the pillows had been pushed to the floor and Zane was now on his belly, both hands secured to the headboard. He faced away from him, like he just couldn't bear to see the smug look of satisfaction on Asa's face.

But there was nothing smug about Asa's reaction. He growled low, blanketing himself over Zane's prone body, burying his face against his neck. "The things I'm going to do to you."

Zane made a sound like a wounded animal, which only narrowed Asa's focus, until only his most primal instincts were left. He inhaled Zane's scent, raked his nails down his sides, rumbling when he arched his back with another helpless sound.

"Fuck, do that again," Asa snarled, biting down on Zane's shoulder.

Zane's surprised cry turned into a moan as Asa licked over the marks he left behind before moving lower, biting and soothing his way down Zane's body. Tomorrow, Zane's skin would be a roadmap of bite marks and bruises. Everybody would know he was Asa's. They'd know Asa had been inside him, had claimed him.

He growled at the thought, hauling Zane's hips up and shoving his sweatpants to his knees before burying his face where Zane's scent was strongest, fucking his tongue against his entrance, pulling off only to spread him open farther, push his tongue in deeper, anything to keep Zane making those sexy fucking sounds.

Asa wrapped a hand around Zane's cock, not so much jerking him off as milking him, squeezing from base to tip, giving him just the right amount of pressure, then taking it away. Asa wanted Zane to come, but only when he was done with him.

He raked his teeth over Zane's hole, then licked and sucked at it just as he had his other bite marks. "I can't go slow with you," he muttered. "I just can't."

He stretched himself across the bed to grab the lube, coming up onto his knees. Zane's breath punched from his lungs as Asa forced two coated fingers inside, working them in and out, stretching him.

"Does that hurt?"

"Yes," Zane hissed.

Asa chuckled, twisting his digits as he probed him. "Good."

Asa pulled free and poured the lube over his cock until it was slippery, lining up and thrusting past that first tight ring of muscle without warning, his cock throbbing at Zane's pained cry. Asa gripped his hips and drove all the way in, groaning as his cock was enveloped by the tight heat of Zane's body.

Asa didn't wait for Zane to adjust, didn't wait at all, just fucked into him, hands gripping his hips, holding him in place as he hammered into him hard enough to see each reverberation roll along his skin as they came together. The noises Zane made were barely human, which only further spurred on Asa's instinct to possess, control, breed. When Asa was done with Zane, there would be no doubt who he belonged to.

He put his full weight on Zane until he collapsed onto the bed, Asa following him down. He wrapped one hand around the slender column of his throat and fucked two fingers of his other hand into Zane's gaping mouth, another low growl erupting when he started sucking them greedily, desperately. Even in the low light, Asa could see Zane's cheeks were streaked with tears. He was so beautiful like this. He forced his fingers deeper, into the tight squeeze of Zane's throat, driving his cock into him faster.

Zane canted his hips back, like he wanted more, moaning like a whore as he nursed Asa's fingers. Asa licked the tears from Zane's cheek, bit at his jaw, his earlobe, his breathing ragged as he rasped, "That's it. Suck my fingers. So fucking needy. So desperate for it. Keep going. Show me how bad you want it."

Zane sobbed but his tongue worked between Asa's fingers in a way that was almost hotter than the tight squeeze of his ass. Almost. Asa was past the point of no return, his hips driving into Zane almost against his will as his orgasm chased its way along his body, punching from him with such force he bit down on the back of Zane's neck, snarling as he emptied himself inside him, hips working against him until there was nothing left.

He pulled free, flipping Zane onto his back, absently noting the way the cuff chain twisted, before he sank his mouth over Zane's painfully flushed cock. His whole body contracted as Asa sucked him off, working his fingers back into his hole, making a pleased rumble when he could feel how stuffed full Zane was.

Zane cried out as his release flooded Asa's mouth. He took a second to savor the bitter taste before pulling off, catching his weight on one hand as he loomed over Zane, gripping his jaw and forcing his mouth open, feeding him his own cum.

He wrapped his hand around his throat. "Swallow."

Zane did as he was told, his gaze hazy and disconnected.

"Good boy."

Asa kissed him again, gently this time, as he once more released the handcuffs. Zane's hands stayed where they fell, but he kissed Asa back.

Asa flopped onto his back, sucking in much needed breaths, before gathering a squirming Zane into his arms. "Stop. Moving."

Zane went rigid but then deflated against him, burying

his face in Asa's chest. He lifted his chin, forcing him to meet his gaze. He was a mess of tears and snot and saliva, but he'd never looked hotter. He looked defiled. Debauched. He looked like a goddamn crime scene, and Asa had never felt more warmed by a sight in his life.

Asa had done that. Asa had marked and claimed him and bred him, and it was the single most intense moment of his life, which was a lot when he held it up against the pile of bodies he'd left in his wake.

Asa grabbed Kleenex and gently wiped Zane's face, then kissed his forehead. "Go to sleep, Lois."

For once, Zane didn't argue, just rolled to face away from him. Asa sighed. Was their ceasefire over that quickly?

Zane reached behind him then and grabbed Asa's hand, pulling his arm around him before burrowing back against him. Asa curled his body around Zane, marveling at how perfectly they fit together.

When Zane started snoring softly, Asa buried his nose in his curls, finally letting sleep take him.

NINE

ZANE

Zane woke to the sound of Asa's voice. He pried his eyes open to find the sun blazing through the window and Asa sitting naked on the bottom corner of the bed, his phone pressed to his ear. He forced his gaze away from perfectly toned back muscles to give a stretch that sent his joints cracking. He was sore everywhere. He felt like a sneaker that had been tossed around in the dryer. Every part of his body ached, including his ass.

"—start local, then expand outward." Asa listened to whoever was on the other side of the line for a moment. "We already know about Henley. I want to see if August's and Lucas's school had a similar ring."

Zane forced himself to his feet. Asa turned at the movement, his heated gaze dragging over Zane like he had a right, a claim to his body. Zane pointed to Asa's bathroom, heading for the door before he said or did something they'd both regret. He left the door cracked as he emptied his painfully full bladder, all sense of shyness dissolved after the night they'd had together.

But, honestly, he just wanted to eavesdrop on Asa's conversation. If he was right, there was a story there. How much of a story, Zane wasn't sure, but enough to earn him a byline in a decent paper.

Wow. One good fuck and, suddenly, you're willing to give up your dreams of being a star journalist to beg for scraps over a story people will forget about in a day or two? Weak sauce, bro. Very weak.

Zane ignored his brother's snide tone. He didn't know what the fuck he would do about the Mulvaneys.

Liar.

He was lying. He was. This was why his mother thought he was a loser. As much as he wanted a big story, a byline, celebrity status, he craved something more. Attention. Attention he'd never get from his own family. Attention Asa lavished on him without a second thought.

He heard Asa ask, "So, they were happening in other schools? Fuck. Tell August and Lucas I need to meet with them at lunch. And let them know I won't be alone."

So, it was true? Those suicides weren't suicides at all but… accidents? That just seemed too convenient. Five deaths, five year increments—that seemed a strange coincidence. Except, it wasn't every five years if Gage had been involved. Because he'd died in a different year at a different school.

Zane stood at the door, listening. "Oh, and tell them not to tell Dad about my…friend." There was a brief pause. "Fucking Jericho. Yes, he's a friend. I've got it handled. Just please keep it to yourself." Another pause. "Thank you.

Hey, have you heard from Avi?"

Asa's voice was almost childlike, tinged with hope and something else. Zane got it. He couldn't really put a name on it, but it was probably the same catch in his heart that came when he thought about Gage. Zane would give anything to have a real conversation with him. The real Gage, not his imaginary version.

Zane probably shouldn't cut Asa slack simply because they both shared a similar attachment to their siblings. But Asa was awkwardly close to his brother, like Zane had been with Gage. Asa might be the only person who understood Zane's complicated relationship with his own brother. His dead brother. Who he still talked to like he was alive.

Zane turned away from the door, moving to the sink to splash some water on his face, but stopped short when he saw his reflection.

Yikes.

Zane rolled his eyes as said brother's voice rattled around in his head. *Shut up.*

If you didn't want me here, I wouldn't be, so blame yourself.

Zane ignored the logic. He had no interest in facing his own psychological demons today.

You called me a thrill seeker, but I think you've got me beat. You really chained yourself to a mass murderer's bed. That's like shackling yourself to a rabid dog. Honestly, you look like you were mauled by a rabid dog.

Gage wasn't wrong. His eyes were swollen and red ringed. There was an obvious bite mark on his shoulder, a dozen hickeys on his neck, and bruises in the shape of Asa's hands. They were everywhere. His hips, his upper arms, even his throat. He didn't even remember Asa's hands being in those places.

He probably cut off your oxygen supply. I hear that can cause memory loss.

Fuck all the way off. Seriously.

Zane turned, looking back at the mirror's reflection over his shoulder. The bite marks on his neck and shoulder were nothing compared to the numerous deep bite wounds on his back, his ass, and his thighs, or the nail marks along his sides. He racked his brain but couldn't recall any specific bite or bruise. They all blurred together. Once Zane had made the decision to put those cuffs back on, it had all gone hazy.

"The things I'm going to do to you."

That was what Asa had rasped in his ear a second before he'd turned Zane's whole world upside down. But he didn't remember pain or fear. He remembered a warmth pooling in his belly and spreading throughout his limbs. He remembered Asa's ragged, panting breaths in his ear, the way he growled and snarled and even purred as he took what he wanted, driving into Zane's body with a ravenous need that should have scared Zane but hadn't. It had made him feel wanted, desired…seen.

When he returned to the bedroom, Asa had pulled on a pair of gray joggers that clung to narrow hips, accentuating his perfect physique. Zane swallowed hard as he tried to tear his gaze from the deep vee visible above the waistband.

Asa closed the distance between them, spinning Zane

away from him, wrapping his arms around him from behind, burying his face where his neck and shoulder met and inhaling deeply, making Zane's nipples harden and his cock thicken in a way that was impossible to hide.

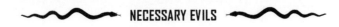

Asa made an appreciative sound as he held him tightly, sniffing at him and nipping at his skin.

"Morning…"

Zane had wanted to convey how weird this was, but what came out was a sort of breathless hitched sound that only seemed to spur Asa further, his broad hands sweeping from Zane's belly to sit low on his hips, creeping dangerously close to Zane's now very erect dick.

Asa tugged on the shell of Zane's ear with his teeth. "You look so fucking hot. I've never gotten to truly admire my work before. I always made sure my…dates…were gone before morning. But you… Fuck, you look amazing like this. Promise me, you'll let me take pictures. Just for me."

Once more, that almost childlike tone was back, like he was asking for another piece of candy instead of asking Zane if he could document the numerous ways he'd defiled him last night.

"You know people are going to see these, right?" Zane cautioned. "I can't run around in a turtleneck in the dead of summer."

"Good. I want people to see," Asa said, as if that were a perfectly normal response.

"You want people to see me looking like I was the victim of a violent crime?" Zane murmured, hating the way his hands closed around Asa's forearms—not to stop him but to anchor himself as Asa continued to explore him.

"I want people to know you're mine," Asa said against his ear.

Zane's heart skipped in his chest. "Some people might say that is presumptuous and a little insane considering we've barely known each other a day." Zane sucked in a breath. A day. Shit. It was morning. "What time is it?"

"Eight o'clock," Asa said, still leisurely exploring Zane's throat.

Blake. Zane slapped at Asa's hands. "I need my phone. Now."

Asa frowned at the sudden shift in the conversation. "What? Why?"

Zane gave him an exasperated look. "Because I really did tell my friend to send those coordinates to the cops if he didn't hear from me by morning."

Asa sighed, releasing Zane, and then turned back to where he'd abandoned his jeans the night before. Zane wanted to snap his fingers and tell him to pick up the pace. He really didn't seem to be giving the situation the gravity it deserved.

Asa fished Zane's phone from his pocket. "Are you saying you don't want me to get caught now?" he asked, a smirk forming over his full lips.

"I'm saying I want to see this through and figure out if something is truly going on with these deaths or if it's all just a bizarre coincidence."

"I don't believe in coincidence," Asa said.

"Me neither," Zane muttered, sliding his phone open and

punching Blake's picture with more force than necessary.

Blake answered on the third ring. "'lo?"

His voice was gruff with sleep. What the fuck? So much for Blake bringing the cavalry. Had Blake even bothered to respond to his text or just rolled his eyes and went to bed last night?

"Hey, it's me. Just wanted to let you know I'm fine," Zane said.

There was a long pause. "Why wouldn't you be fine?"

"Um, because I went to check out one of the Mulvaney properties last night. The one I sent you coordinates for?" Zane said hesitantly.

"Huh?" There was the sound of rustling on the other end and then, "Oh. I never saw this. I was chasing down Gizelle Sands and Naz King last night. Got some great shots of them cozied up in the back of some dive bar. Beach almost shit herself with excitement."

Zane scrunched his nose at Blake's assessment. "That's… graphic."

"Yeah, she tried to get a hold of you, but you were MIA, so she just published them straight to the site. So, what's up with the Mulvaney property? Find anything good?"

"Nothing. Dead end. But I got a lead on another, possibly bigger story. Can you let Beach know I need to take a few days off? Tell her my mom died or something."

"She knows you wouldn't take a day off to mourn that shrew. I'll tell her you got food poisoning from the press dinner. How'd that go, by the way? You and Thomas Mulvaney best friends forever now?"

Zane looked back at Asa, who looked too goddamn fine pulling a black Gemini hoodie over his head. "Not exactly," he muttered.

It really, truly shouldn't be legal for any man to look that good on no sleep, especially not when it looked like Zane had gone ten rounds with Muhammad Ali. When he caught Zane staring, he grinned, sliding his wallet into one pocket and his phone into the other. "Breakfast?" he asked, pointing to his watch.

"Who's that?" Blake asked.

"Nobody," Zane said, a little too quickly to be convincing, earning a smug smile from Asa and an infuriating chuckle from Blake.

"Did you get laid last night? Are you calling in sick to work because of a hookup? Did you fuck Thomas Mulvaney? That dude's, like...what? Twice your age?"

Zane shook his head. "No, I didn't hook up with Thomas Mulvaney." Though, Zane supposed it had never been truly off the table. Last night, he'd been willing to do almost anything for a story.

Almost? You're playing chew toy to a serial killer. Where the hell is this imaginary line of yours, bro?

"No, I'm not calling out sick for a hookup."

"But you did get laid last night," Blake said.

"I'm hanging up now," Zane warned.

Blake chuckled again. "Okay, man. I see you. Get som—"

Zane hung up on him before he could finish his sentence. When he looked back at Asa, he was watching him with an expression Zane couldn't quite place. Like he was...

studying him. "Don't you have work, too?" Zane asked, trying to fill the sudden silence.

Asa waved a hand. "I'm the boss. I make my own hours. I had my secretary clear my schedule. We're good." Asa fished a t-shirt out of his drawer. "Arms up."

Zane complied without thought, allowing Asa to pull the shirt over his head. "Don't you design skyscrapers worth millions of dollars?"

Asa grabbed a pair of black sweatpants and went to his knees before Zane. "Foot." Zane lifted his leg, sliding it through the hole, repeating the process on the other side, trying not to think about Asa's face now at eye level with his crotch.

Asa tugged the pants upwards. "No, I design *billion* dollar skyscrapers. And I do it so well, people are willing to tolerate my somewhat unprofessional behavior because I make buildings that stand out against the backdrop of our cities." Asa slid the fabric slowly over Zane's all too obvious erection.

Zane had thought that would be the end of it, but Asa didn't stand; he pushed Zane's borrowed shirt up, nosing along each inch of skin as it was revealed, making goosebumps erupt along Zane's skin as he licked a trail from the waistband to just beneath his belly button. These pants weren't loose enough for this.

Asa looked up at Zane from his knees. "Fuck. I wish we could just stay here all day. I like...playing with you."

Zane had meant to push Asa away, but his hands tangled in his hair instead. "I don't know if I can handle another session so soon."

"Your dick says you're more capable than you know," Asa teased, leaning forward to bury his face against said dick. Zane squirmed at Asa's hot breath on him through the thin material.

Asa rocketed to his feet. "Fuck. Okay. We've gotta get out of here. You look too good in my clothes."

Zane looked down at himself as he allowed Asa to snag his hand and pull him towards the staircase. He looked ridiculous, like a kid playing dress up in his older brother's closet. "Can we stop at my place so I can change into some real clothes? Please?" he tacked on at the end, almost like an afterthought.

Asa stopped at the top of the stairs, studying Zane with another enigmatic look. "Yeah, sure."

Once they were on the road again, speeding towards Zane's apartment, he said, "I just can't picture you as an architect? Like, why would somebody like you want to design skyscrapers? It seems a strange career for a person whose hobby is murder."

Asa glanced over at him. "It's not a hobby, it's more like a calling. As for the architecture, I was great at math and drawing. Avi was, too. He went into fashion design because he's good at it and loves the attention and celebrity of it. I went into architecture for somewhat similar reasons."

"Certainly not for the fame?" Were there famous architects other than Frank Lloyd Wright and I. M. Pei?

Asa gave him a look that sent a shiver down his spine. "Oh, no. I don't care about fame. My last name gives me more than enough notoriety for that."

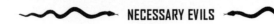

"So, why do it?" Zane asked.

"There's something about knowing that I hold thousands of lives in my hands every single day and I choose to let them live."

"What?" Zane said, heart contracting in his chest.

Asa shrugged. "Think about it. One misplaced beam, one bolt just slightly off, one sub par truss or anchor and… boom. It all comes down." At Zane's wide-eyed look, he said, "I've designed three skyscrapers in my career to date. That's roughly—what?—ten thousand people who go to work everyday and live, just because I allowed them to."

Zane blinked at him. "You sound like a—"

"Psychopath?" Asa countered with a wink.

"I was going to say megalomaniac," Zane managed. "You probably shouldn't tell people that you became an architect because you wanted to play God by turning skyscrapers into your own personal ant farm and that you're just one bad day away from shaking it like an Etch-A-Sketch."

Asa smiled. "I keep my thinking thoughts to myself."

"Your what?"

"Noah says, 'Those are thinking thoughts, not speaking thoughts.' But you asked why I do what I do, and I told you I wouldn't lie to you."

Asa looked so proud of himself for not lying about secretly being a nihilistic anarchist that Zane almost felt guilty for saying, "You're batshit crazy."

"Has anything you've learned about me in the last twelve hours led you to think I wasn't? But you like my crazy.

When I gave you the chance to leave last night, you locked your wrists in handcuffs and offered yourself up to me like some kind of virgin sacrifice. And I took it, took you, and would have done far more to you if you hadn't been so tired. But you consented. So, which one of us is crazier, Lois?"

"You kill people," Zane said, hating how pissy he sounded.

"And you fucked the guy who kills people, knowing I kill people, all for a story. I was born a psychopath. But you, you're an opportunist. I'm not complaining. I was mad about it last night, but today is a new day and in the cold light of day, I get it."

Then maybe he'd be kind enough to explain it to Zane. "Get what?"

"That this is a high for you. Not just the terrifying sex we've had—twice—but chasing a story, not knowing what comes next, being in the presence of a killer, knowing the effect you have on me. You're so high off the adrenaline I can practically smell it on you."

"That's not true."

"Sure, it is, Lois. But that's why this little partnership of ours works. I can be myself around you and you can be yourself around me. There's something kind of freeing about knowing each other's deepest, darkest secrets and not wanting to let them go."

Was that what was happening? Zane picked up his phone, covertly typing in: *How long before Stockholm syndrome sets in?* He grimaced when he noted the statistics weren't on his side. Less than five percent of hostages developed the phenomenon and not in just twelve hours. Which meant Asa was right. Zane was enjoying this, enjoying him, and though he wanted to be terrified, he wasn't.

"Would you kill me if you had to?" Zane asked casually. Some part of him hoped the answer would scare the common sense back into him.

Asa took his eyes off the road to look at him for a beat. "That seems like a loaded question, Lois. I feel like if I say no then the power dynamic of this little relationship is going to splinter."

"You said you'd be honest."

Asa sighed. "I did say that, true. But I meant in more of a you ask questions and I say yes or no kind of way."

Zane lips twitched in an aborted smile. "Would you kill me if you had to? Yes or no."

Asa stayed quiet for so long Zane started wondering if he'd survive the tuck and roll required to leap from the SUV if he brandished a weapon. "No, Lois. I don't think I could kill you. Luckily, we'll likely never know. Because my father would never kill an innocent man, and whether you believe it or not, neither would I."

That was the thing nagging at Zane. Was he really innocent? He was unscrupulous when it came to chasing a story. He hadn't reveled in the violent deaths of others, but he'd done his best to find a way to use those deaths to his benefit. He'd never wept over any of the victims of the cases on his crime blog. He'd never really cried over anybody. Not even his brother. The only time Zane had ever really cried was for himself, last night, when Asa was breeding him. Something Zane had consented to. With a stranger. For a story.

Maybe that made him a narcissist instead of an opportunist, but either way…he wasn't innocent. Which meant he wasn't truly safe from Thomas Mulvaney.

TEN

ASA

Asa was strangely relieved to see Zane eat—and keep down—a full breakfast at the small cafe they visited before heading to Zane's. But as he continued to nurse one cup of coffee for twenty minutes, Asa began to suspect Zane had ulterior motives for lagging behind at the restaurant. Was Zane trying to plot his escape? What was he suddenly so worried about? It was his idea to stop there so he could change.

When they pulled up outside a dilapidated building, Zane tried to convince Asa to wait in the car. Was he embarrassed of where he lived? Was that why he was so hesitant? Either way, staying behind wasn't possible for a million different reasons, most of which could be summed up in one small sentence. Asa didn't want to.

Seemingly resigned, Zane led him through the double doors with its Astro-turf colored carpet to a dingy white door, leading him up four flights of stairs to his apartment. Asa propped his arm on the door frame, leaning over Zane as he used the key to let himself inside.

Asa hadn't expected Zane to live in a house as grand as his, but he certainly wasn't prepared for what he saw. From the doorway, he could see the whole thing. The small kitchen, dining room, and family room combo could easily fit in one of Asa's bathrooms. One of his *smaller* bathrooms.

Jesus.

Despite its modest size, the apartment was clean, no dishes congealing in the sink, no dirt or dust, which was more than he could say for his and Avi's apartment in the city. His brother was hardly a neat freak. Luckily, they had a housekeeper who came daily.

But there was a large amount of clutter starting in what should have been the dining area but was actually Zane's version of a home office. There were two desks set up back to back, as if somebody other than just Zane worked there. Who else came and worked there with Zane? Who else knew of Asa's family? One wall held a dossier on his family that would have impressed the CIA, including a map of the city filled with pins Asa recognized as drop sights.

Beside one of the desks sat a pile of neatly stacked bound pages. Upon closer inspection, Asa saw they were manuscripts. Did Zane have secret aspirations beyond journalism? Did he want to write books? Fiction? True crime? Asa tucked that in his back pocket for later. It would be good to have leverage if Zane decided a byline was more important than Asa's attention.

While Asa moved around the apartment, he kept his ears trained on Zane and his movements around the space. He was currently in his room, rummaging through the drawers, likely looking for clothes. Or a weapon to brandish. He was giving Zane a lot of leeway. Avi would say too much leeway. That he was taking his life in his hands by not watching what Zane did in the other room. Maybe there was a landline. Maybe there was a gun. Neither of those thoughts swayed Asa away from his exploration.

There was a well-worn sofa in the small living room and a reasonably sized television. On the walls were a number of black and white photos, mostly landscapes, and a few of people on the street. They were all exceptional, but Asa had never heard of the photographer, Blake Marshall, though maybe, one day, he would.

On a shelf above the small TV were two family photos. One was of Zane and a similar looking man, standing beside two older people, presumably their parents. That must have been the brother. He had the same curly hair and honey eyes, but he was broader, sturdier, taller, perhaps more commercially attractive, but in a department store underwear model kind of way. Attractive but not runway worthy, not interesting in any way.

Not like Zane. Talent scouts would go crazy for Zane's insane bone structure and those crazy curls and that almost bashful smile he'd made when he'd so easily seduced Asa last night. Yeah, agents would line up to represent Zane.

Still, the man in the photo had kind eyes and a huge smile, and he hugged Zane close like he was the most important thing in his world. The same couldn't be said for the parents. Asa was no body language expert but it was clear the boys were attempting to distance themselves from the stern-looking people in the photograph.

Asa picked up the second picture, smiling at the insanely goofy grin on Zane's face as he sat perched on his brother's back like he'd snuck up on him just as the photo was taken. When was the last time Zane had smiled like that?

"That's Gage."

Asa turned to see Zane in a pair of black jeans and a hot pink t-shirt that shouldn't have worked on anybody but, somehow, looked killer on him. He'd thrown a gray beanie cap over his mop of curls and no longer wore his glasses. Asa did his best to tamp down his disappointment. Contacts were obviously more practical. Still, Zane looked so…innocent in those glasses.

Asa turned back to the picture, setting it down. "He looks…nice."

Zane wandered closer and picked the picture up, his shoulder's sagging as he looked down at their smiling faces. "He was. Most of the time. Sometimes, he could be a real dickhead."

Asa laughed. He could say the same of Avi.

Asa nodded towards the family photo. "Those are your parents?"

Zane grimaced, then nodded. "Bev and Irv Scott."

Asa knew everything he needed to know about them simply by the way Zane spoke their names. "They seem… intense."

"Bev is a lot. My father is just…whatever Bev wants him to be. Usually, that's silent."

Oof. "So, you don't get along?"

Zane cut his gaze to him, setting the picture back into place. "You really want me to get into my fucked up family dynamics?"

Asa shrugged, reaching out to snag one springy curl, pulling it straight just to watch it bounce into place. "I mean, you already know mine. How much worse can yours be?"

"I guess it depends on the yardstick you're using to measure it. I wasn't raised by a family of murderers, but I was raised to be invisible. Gage had the spotlight from the moment he was born. My mom had tried to get pregnant with him for five years. She was almost forty. He was her miracle."

"And you?" Asa asked, adjusting Zane's cap for no other reason than to have another excuse to touch him.

"I was the accident, the drunken mistake who destroyed my mom's body and almost killed her when she hemorrhaged at thirty weeks. I ruined her life. Just ask her."

There it was. The seven month age difference. "I can't imagine you being invisible in any way."

Zane gave a humorless laugh. "No? I can give you Bev's number. She has an alphabetized list of all the ways I've disappointed her. The number one reason being that I wasn't the one who died so Gage could live. Gage was going to be somebody, you see. I was just the screw up. Correction. I still am the screw up."

Asa could feel his teeth clenching as Zane spoke. He really believed that about himself. Asa's gaze cut back to the plump woman with her dyed blonde hair and sneer of a smile, contemplating giving Zane her eyes as a birthday present. If she couldn't see how perfect Zane was, maybe she didn't deserve to see at all.

"You can't kill my mother," Zane said, alarm creeping into his voice as he looked at Asa's mutinous expression. "She's the literal worst, but she makes her own misery. I promise. I don't care about her anymore."

It was a total lie and they both knew it. Asa didn't call him out on it, though. "I don't think anybody's ever shown her the real meaning of misery before," Asa said, unable to tear his gaze away from the woman who made Zane feel so badly about himself.

"She lost her son—the only one she cared about. That's enough pain for one person."

Asa shook his head. "You lost your brother. The only person who seemed to care about you. Who took care of you?"

Zane flushed, blinking rapidly. "I did. I'm fine. It's fine. I thought for sure you'd be more pissed off about my Mulvaney murder board than you are about my shitty parents."

Was that why Zane had been trying to keep him in the car? Over the stupid board? Asa huffed out a breath through his nose. "I don't know why you thought I would care? I already know you're investigating my family. I didn't know your parents were garbage."

A slow smile spread across Zane's face. "Garbage is a little strong."

"Do they know you live…here? Like this?"

Zane snickered. "Like what? Like a poor person? No. My family thinks I've just scored my first job as a big, fancy reporter, hence my rush to get as much dirt as I could on your family. If I don't come up with some kind of byline soon, my mom won't have anything to tell her fancy friends."

It gave Asa a strangely warm feeling in his chest that Zane was being so casually honest with him. It felt...intimate somehow. Asa reached out and gripped Zane's t-shirt in his fist, pulling him closer until he was near enough for Asa to dip his head, brushing their lips together in a soft kiss before letting him go again.

Zane's eyes were all pupil, his lips slightly parted. "What was that for?"

Asa shrugged, not really knowing why he'd done it. "I don't know. I just wanted to kiss you."

"You always do whatever you want, don't you?" Zane said, voice full of awe.

"Don't you?" Asa asked.

Zane's gaze strayed to the stack of manuscripts, his lips pulling down at the corners. "No, not really."

"Are those all books you've written?"

Zane made a noise of disgust. "Books I've started. I always talk myself out of finishing them." Asa marched across the room, picking up the first book on the stack. Zane scrambled to catch up, yanking the manuscript from his hand before he could open it. "What are you doing?"

Asa frowned. "What do you mean? I want to read it."

Zane looked scandalized, like Asa had asked to read his diary or look through his underwear drawer. Did Zane keep a diary? Was he wearing underwear? Asa's cock hardened, and he had to tamp down the thought of bending him over the desk and checking for himself.

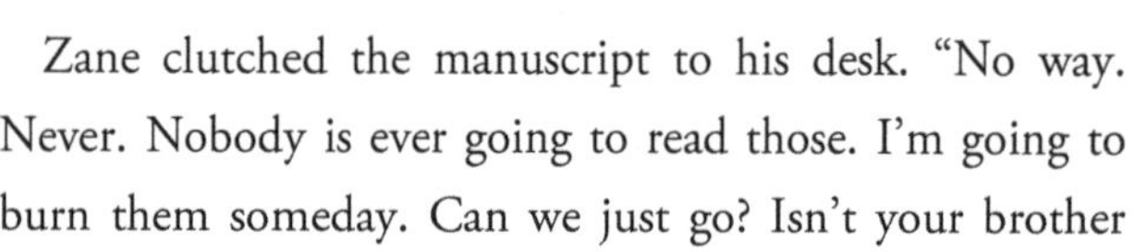

Zane clutched the manuscript to his desk. "No way. Never. Nobody is ever going to read those. I'm going to burn them someday. Can we just go? Isn't your brother expecting us?"

Asa glanced at his watch. "Yeah. But we're going to revisit this conversation again later. Let's go."

The look of relief that washed over Zane made Asa's stomach clench. Zane looked different standing in his apartment. The ballsy, confident badass he'd pretended to be was long gone. In its place was a boy with sad eyes and the weight of the world on his shoulders. Asa really did want to kill whoever made Zane feel like that.

"Who are you going to tell them I am?" Zane asked as the door closed behind them.

Asa grimaced. "I don't know. The way my family gossips, Jericho probably already told Atticus, who told August, who told Lucas, who told Noah, who told anybody who would listen."

Zane snickered. "Gossipy killers."

Asa threw his arm around Zane's narrow shoulders. "You have no idea."

Asa had expected Zane to push him away…but he didn't. His arm slid around Asa's waist, his head tucking in close to Asa's shoulder as they walked down the hall to the stairs. Once more, that warmth pooled inside him, lower this time.

Shit. It was already happening. Like some self-fulfilling prophecy. First Adam, then August, then Atticus, and now him… He was growing comfortable with the thought of having a person of his own. Someone other than Avi.

But this someone might still be out to destroy his family. Zane could just be luring Asa into some false sense of security with his sad family history. Was he just a good actor? Asa didn't think so, but some part of him whispered it was his dick who didn't think so and his brain that wasn't thinking at all.

Asa knew it didn't matter either way. He wasn't getting rid of Zane, and like Zane said, Asa always did whatever he wanted.

Asa breezed by Cricket's desk with a half-wave, dragging Zane along behind him, ignoring the look of confusion on August's assistant's face. Could they still call her that? She was one of a growing list of people who knew who they really were, and she was August's and Lucas's surrogate. Didn't that sort of make her family?

Asa shook the thought away as he pushed August's office door open to find his brother and Lucas sharing August's office chair. He shuttled Zane in ahead of him, closing the door behind them and pushing him deeper into the room. Zane stopped short at the two men, causing Asa to crash into him, his arm coming around his waist to keep him on his feet.

One look at August's frigid expression and Asa knew they knew who Zane really was. Which was going to make this a thousand times more confrontational. Fucking gossipy killers indeed. Before Asa could get a word out, Lucas's gaze narrowed in on the obvious bruises and marks on Zane's neck and forearms.

"Jesus, Asa. Did you do that to him?" he asked.

Asa crossed his arms over his chest. "What? He likes it. Tell them."

Zane flushed crimson, closing his eyes for a long moment before saying, "It's fine."

"Fine?" Asa echoed, tone testy. "That wasn't what you said last night."

"Oh, my God. It was consensual, okay?" Zane muttered.

Asa smirked, then said, "Zane, this is my brother, August, and his husband—"

"The psychic," Zane murmured, seemingly without thought.

"Most people just call me Lucas," he said, his amusement clear.

Zane dipped his head. "Sorry. Nice to meet you."

"Is it?" August asked. "I hear you're a reporter." His gaze flicked to Asa. "A reporter who knows our secret. What do you plan on doing with that knowledge?"

Asa sighed. He'd been expecting this. He leaned against the doorframe, crossing his arms over his chest. Time to see how Zane handled himself under pressure.

Asa's brows shot up as Zane sat in a seat across from the two other men, leaning forward until his elbows were on his knees. "I have no idea what I plan on doing with that knowledge. But your husband was an FBI agent when you met, no? Did he know your secret before you started seeing each other?"

Lucas grinned. "Yes. He broke into my house, told me he was Batman, and then stabbed himself."

Zane blinked at Lucas as he attempted to process August's bizarre courting rituals. "A reporter like me couldn't be more dangerous than an actual federal agent, right?"

August frowned like somebody had just beat him in a chess match, then turned to his husband, poking him in the ribs. "Why would you tell him that?"

Lucas batted his hand away. "A: because it's true. And B: because he's right. Just because he's a reporter doesn't mean he's out to screw the family." He then looked Zane directly in the eye. "I highly encourage you to not screw our family."

Asa's gaze slid to Zane, watching his cheeks flush as his posture straightened. *Feeling a little guilty, Lois?* "We need to ask you some questions."

"So Calliope said. About what, exactly?" August asked, his gaze still on Zane.

"Do you know anything about a string of suicides that occurred on campus? Would have been around four years ago?" Zane asked, then captured his bottom lip between his teeth, worrying it until Asa had to fight the urge to free it.

August shrugged. "I may have vaguely heard about that, but I'm not one for gossip."

Lucas snorted. "What he means is, he rarely knows what day it is, much less what the rest of the world is up to. Half the time, he forgets to eat."

"And you weren't here back then, right?" Zane asked Lucas.

"Afraid not."

"So, you haven't heard anything about a game some of the kids might have been playing on campus back then?"

"Game?" August echoed.

Before Zane could answer, the door burst open, and Cricket was standing there in her black polka-dot romper and cherry red heels. "I know this one," she shouted.

August sighed. "How many times have I told you not to eavesdrop on our private conversations?"

She gave him a look, waving a hand. "None. You told me to stop listening when you and Lucas were boning in your office. There's no boning happening here. Besides, don't you want to know what I know about those 'suicides'?" she air-quoted. Then looked hard at Zane's neck then gave Asa a knowing smirk. "Nice."

August sighed heavily, but Lucas said, "What do you know, Cricket?"

"It's part of some super secret game some of the students were invited to play on campus."

Zane's gaze snapped to Asa's, his eyes going wide. "Super secret game?"

"Have you ever heard of the Blue Whale challenge?" Cricket asked.

Asa frowned, relieved to see August and Lucas looking equally confused. "Blue Whale?"

"I know it," Zane said, looking pale. "It's an online game that originated in Russia. They claim almost two hundred kids have died worldwide playing this game."

"But what is it?" Asa asked. "What's the game…or

challenge? What do they have to do?"

Cricket jumped in before Zane could answer. "Fifty tasks over fifty days overseen by a 'curator,' who monitors to make sure the player is completing the tasks."

"How do you know all this?" Asa asked.

Cricket walked to the sofa, slipping off her shoes and sitting down, tucking her feet beneath her. "I didn't know anything about it until the deaths at Henley last month. Then the staff here started talking. It's become, like, a sort of urban legend that people in our city are playing and losing a game very much like the Blue Whale challenge."

"What kind of tasks?" August asked.

"It's hard to say. In the Blue Whale Challenge, the tasks are pre-set with the curator overseeing the player. Who knows if it's the same thing here," Cricket said with a gentle shoulder shrug.

"What kind of tasks are on the Blue Whale challenge?" Lucas asked Cricket. "If you know."

"I researched it on Reddit a couple of weeks ago," she said with a heavy sigh. "The first challenges are always easy. Watch a video the curator shows you. Draw a picture and show it to the curator. But the deeper into the game you get, the more insane the challenges. They say people are asked to carve letters into their skin, listen to certain music, meet other 'whales,' but it all leads to the same place. Jumping off a building."

"Jesus," Lucas muttered.

"Okay, but if the tasks are always the same and the last task is to jump off a building, then they're not playing the

Blue Whale Challenge here on campus, right?" Zane asked. "Because the suicides that occurred here and at Henley, the victims hanged themselves. So, if this is a game, it's not this Russian challenge. This is something else entirely."

Asa looked to August, who nodded, punching two buttons on his phone. The room filled with sounds of a phone ringing as August put it on speaker. "What's up, baby daddy? Or daddy of babies? How are the littles? Give them a squish for me."

August sighed. "Calliope, please stop calling me that."

"Don't," Lucas cut in. "Don't ever stop calling him that. The girls are good. I'll give them all the squishes. But we need your help first."

"What's up, Buttercup?" she chirped.

"Remember what I asked you about this morning? The string of suicides?" Asa asked. "We think it might be tied to a game, kind of like the Blue Whale challenge. Do you know how we could find out if any of those who died were playing the game?"

There was a long pause. When Calliope spoke again, all the joy had left her voice. "I would need to see the computers, check their browser history. And even then, I might not know for sure. These kinds of people are good at hiding their tracks."

"How do we get access to one of their computers?" Zane asked, looking back at Asa.

"I don't suppose you still have your brother's?" Asa asked.

"Your brother's?" Lucas echoed.

"My brother was a student here when the deaths happened

four years ago. My brother was one of them," Zane managed. "I'm sure my mother has my brother's laptop enshrined somewhere, but she'll never give me access. I'd have a better chance of stealing the Declaration of Independence."

Fuck. He'd suspected as much. "Calliope, can you patch in Jericho?"

Jericho wasn't going to like this favor, but at this point, he owed Asa for ratting him out.

There was a thirty second delay, and then Jericho's voice came over the speaker. "What's up?" Jericho said.

Before Asa could speak, Calliope said, "You're on speaker with August, Lucas, Cricket, Asa, and Zane." Quickly tacking on, "And me…obvi."

There was a moment of hesitation before he said, "Um, okay. What can I do for *all* of you?"

"I need a favor," Asa said.

"*Another* favor?" Jericho barked.

Asa huffed out a breath. "Yeah, one you'll actually follow through on and not rat me out over. Besides, that body didn't dismember itself."

Jericho scoffed. "Man, you said don't tell your dad. I didn't. You're welcome."

"Can you boys fight about this later?" Calliope asked.

"Yeah, whatever," Asa muttered. "Do you still have an in with the police? Like that ex-boyfriend of yours?"

Another snort of derision. "Gabe works at Best Buy now," Jericho reminded him. "And Gabe's former colleagues were all his buddies, so I don't think I can ask for their help either."

"Shit," Asa grumbled, looking at Lucas. "What about you? Still have any pull with your Fed friends?"

"No, pretty sure that ship sailed when I accused a fellow agent of being a mass murderer and then got locked up for thirty days."

"Um, I know someone," Cricket said, waving her hand with an irritated look on her face. "Why do none of you ever ask me?"

All eyes swung to Cricket as Jericho's voice popped up on the line. "There you go. I gotta get back to work." Then he was gone again.

"Who do you know, Cricket?" Lucas asked.

Cricket smoothed a hand over her black skirt with the white polka-dots. "My cousin, Jagger. He's a detective. Violent crimes."

"You have a cousin named Jagger?" Lucas asked.

Asa's gaze jerked to August. "You had a baby with a girl whose cousin is a homicide detective and you're giving me shit for dating a reporter?" he asked, exasperated.

"Dating?" Lucas said, a smirk forming. "Are you two *dating*? I thought he was just a hookup. That's what you told Jericho."

"Holy shit. Does Avi know you have a boyfriend?" Cricket asked, clapping her hands together like an excited child.

Zane was looking at Asa like he was insane. He hadn't meant to say dating. It had just slipped out. Asa could take it back, but he didn't want to. Dating seemed such an innocuous word for what they were doing. They weren't dating. Zane was his. He'd marked him. Claimed him. His obsessive need for Zane was so much more than a word as casual as that.

"Can you ask your cousin if any of the computers were confiscated in these most recent suicides?" Zane asked quietly. "They sometimes take them to look for a note."

"Yeah, I can ask. But what are we looking for, exactly?" Cricket asked.

Zane shrugged. "I don't know. Anything. Something out of the ordinary."

Cricket frowned. "But wouldn't the cops have noticed something?"

"Only if they knew what to look for," Calliope said. "I know what to look for. Cricket, if your cousin can get me access to one of the victims' computers, I can look for any hidden programs and websites he visited. In the meantime, I'm going to take a deep dive into the darknet abyss and see what I can find on a US version of the Blue Whale challenge."

"Cricket, can you also see what information you might be able to get from the staff? Any and all gossip might be helpful," Asa said.

Cricket stood and nodded. "Always happy to gossip for the Mulvaneys."

Once she was gone, Asa grabbed Zane by the arm, helping him to his feet. "Calliope, can you get me a list of names of all the victims and expand the search to look for more victims."

"Expand the search how far?" Calliope asked.

Asa grimaced, giving Zane's arm a squeeze. "Nationally.

Check the whole fucking country."

"Got it." Then Calliope was gone as well.

"You can't tell Dad about Zane," Asa said to August, pulling Zane closer.

"I'm not going to tell Dad about Zane," August said. Asa's shoulders sagged in relief. "You are."

"What?"

"You're going to tell Dad about your boyfriend. Today. There are no secrets in this family, remember?"

He stared down his brother for a full minute. August never wavered. "Fine. But only after we finish today's investigations."

August smirked. "Clock's ticking, Brother."

ELEVEN

ZANE

Zane waited for Asa to say something once they were back in the car, but he remained unnervingly silent. "You told your brother we were dating," he said finally.

"Mm," Asa responded, tone noncommittal.

When Asa didn't elaborate further, he asked, "Are you really going to introduce me to your father?"

Asa continued to stare straight ahead. "Yes."

Zane stared at the side of Asa's face, trying to gauge what was going on in his head. "What are you going to tell him?"

"The truth."

Zane's eyes went wide. "The truth? You're going to tell Thomas Mulvaney that I tricked you into taking me home with you where I then let you stalk and fuck me on the floor of your sex dungeon? After which, I followed you into the woods where I filmed you dismembering a body before you tased, kidnapped, and handcuffed me to a radiator, then blackmailed me into playing Dr. Watson to your Sherlock? Like…that's what you're going to tell your dad?"

Asa's lips twitched. "Maybe not with that level of detail, no. But I am going to tell him the situation."

Zane flopped back against the passenger seat. "He's going to kill me."

Asa sighed, turning to look at him. "How many times do I have to tell you? My father doesn't kill innocent people. He's going to kill *me* instead."

"And if he decides I'm not innocent?" Zane countered.

"Then I'll keep you safe," Asa promised, meeting Zane's gaze in a way that made his heart race but also made him nervous because he wasn't looking at the road ahead.

Asa was a complete and total mindfuck. In twenty-four hours, he'd turned Zane's whole life upside down.

What life?

Zane sighed. The last thing he needed was Gage's snarky voice rattling around in his already muddled brain. "Not now," he muttered.

Asa hooked a brow upwards, tone amused. "Pardon?"

"Nothing," Zane said, cheeks flushing.

"No, you definitely said something. Not now, what?"

Zane glowered at him. "If you know what I said, why did you say pardon?"

Asa laughed. "I know what you said. I just don't know why you said it."

"It doesn't matter. I wasn't talking to you," Zane huffed.

Asa was grinning now. "Well, I'm the only one here. Who were you talking to?"

My dead brother. "Myself."

Asa's gaze strayed from the road. "You said 'not now'

to yourself? What was it you wanted that you don't have time for?"

Zane could feel his face heating up. "Just let it go."

Asa jerked the wheel, pulling onto the side of the road and throwing it in park before turning to look at Zane, blue eyes bright. "Oh, now I'm definitely not letting it go."

Zane's heart slammed against his ribs, both from the terrible driving and Asa's now laser-like focus on him. "Are you fucking crazy?"

"We both know the answer to that. Now, answer the question."

"You're just going to think I'm crazy."

Asa reached out and pushed an errant curl off Zane's forehead. "Color me intrigued."

Go ahead. Tell him. I double dog dare you. Tell him all about me. Hey, he'll probably let you out of the car right now and you'll be free. Zane swallowed hard. That thought no longer gave him the thrill he thought it would. Somehow, he no longer really cared about being free of Asa.

"My dead brother talks to me," Zane blurted. "Or, I talk to him. We…talk."

Asa blinked at him. "What?"

Shit. "Like, not really. I know my dead brother isn't *actually* talking to me. But, like, you know that voice in your head that is constantly keeping a running monologue of all your thoughts and feelings like Jiminy Cricket? Mine sounds like my brother."

"Jiminy Cricket?"

Zane made a noise of exasperation. "Yeah, your conscience.

The voice that reminds you of the right thing to do."

Asa shook his head, a small smile playing at his lips. "Yeah, I don't have that."

Of course, he didn't. Who did? Just Zane. "Well, I do, and mine sounds like my dead brother."

Asa studied him for a long minute. "Yeah. Yeah, okay. That makes sense."

With that, he checked his mirror and eased back onto the road as if the matter was resolved. Zane continued to stare at the side of Asa's face as he drove another two blocks before not being able to stand it anymore. "What do you mean, 'that makes sense.' That makes no sense. Hearing the voice of my dead brother makes no sense."

Asa shrugged. "My brother and I have been…connected… our whole lives. I know what he's thinking, feeling, doing at any given time. If anything happened to Avi, hearing his voice in my head would be the only thing that kept me from setting the world on fire. Hearing the voice of your dead brother sounds like a coping mechanism. A pretty tame one considering how awful your parents seem."

Zane didn't know what to do with that. If he'd told his secret to any other living soul, including Blake, they would have insisted he make an appointment with a therapist immediately. Asa just took it at face value. Zane was living in some alternate universe where up was down and in was out. He'd fallen through the looking glass.

Asa's phone rang where it sat between them. He pushed a button on the steering wheel. "Dimitri, tell me you've got something."

Dimitri's voice came through the car's speaker. "I've got something," he said dutifully.

Zane perked up as Asa said, "What is it?"

"A name."

"Whose name?" Zane asked.

"The name of a person who may have played the game and lived."

Asa frowned. "May have?"

"Yeah, it's…complicated. People who play this game don't exactly advertise they're playing the game. It's kind of an underground thing. But his roommate seems pretty convinced that's why he dropped out four weeks ago."

Asa looked at Zane, who shrugged. It was a small lead, but it was a lead.

"Name?" Zane asked.

"Eric Sievers. He was a sophomore at Henley. Dropped out four weeks ago out of nowhere even though he was rocking a 4.0 GPA and was captain of the lacrosse team."

"Where can we find him?" Asa asked.

Dimitri made a hesitant noise. "Yeah, so that's the thing. Nobody can find him."

Asa shook his head. "What?"

"He's, like…on the run or something," Arlo's voice piped in. "Like, the game broke his brain or something."

"How do we know he's still alive?" Zane asked. "How are we supposed to question somebody we can't find?"

"You asked for information. This is all we could find. Our friend Jason had heard from his roommate David that Eric had played the game but got spooked when they asked him to do something horrible."

"Can we talk to this David kid?" Asa asked.

"Um, probably. Jason said he works at the Cantina on South Padre and Montrose. I don't think David knows that Jason told us what he told him about Eric, so maybe don't, like, kidnap him and torture him for information or something," Dimitri said. "He seems like a good guy and my mom will fucking flip."

Asa scoffed. "Would I do that?"

"Yes," Zane, Arlo, and Dimitri said at once.

Asa rolled his eyes. "Fine. I'll be nice. What's this David kid's last name? Do you know?"

"Robinson."

"Alright. Thanks, kid."

"We square?" Dimitri asked.

Asa grinned. "Yeah, we're good."

Asa disconnected and looked at Zane. "Let's go interrogate a teenager."

Zane sighed. "Question. Let's go question a teenager."

"Yeah, yeah. Whatever. Let's go find out what he knows."

David Robinson stared at them in confusion. He looked like every other college student Zane had ever encountered. He wore jeans and a black t-shirt with the Cantina logo emblazoned across the front and a backwards ball cap over his blond hair. "Who are you guys again? What happened to you? Are you okay?" he asked, looking at Zane's bruises with concern.

"I was mauled by a bear."

"I'm an otter at best," Asa murmured under his breath, earning a glare from Zane and a confused look from David.

Asa had asked to speak to the manager when they'd arrived and then offered him a ridiculous sum of money to speak to his employee. Zane had rolled his eyes but admitted it was amusing watching the manager's eyes bug out when Asa handed him the cash.

"We want to talk to you about your former roommate," Asa said, crossing his arms over his chest in a way that made David take a step back.

Zane sighed, stepping in front of Asa with a smile. "We're really sorry to bother you at work. My name is Zane Scott, and I'm a reporter working on a story about the recent string of suicides over at Henley."

David examined them both warily. "Who's he?" he asked, pointing at Asa.

"Security," Asa deadpanned.

"Asa Mulvaney. He's helping me with the story."

David snorted. "Asa Mulvaney designs athleisure for, like, soccer moms."

Zane didn't even have to look behind him to know Asa's expression had turned threatening; watching the color drain from David's face was enough. He leaned his weight against Asa, relieved when he felt his hands slide into his back pockets, holding him in place.

"That's his brother, Avi. Asa is an architect, but he's helping me out because...he's my boyfriend and this story might be dangerous," Zane said, improvising on the spot.

"A story about a bunch of suicides is dangerous?" David asked.

Zane nodded. "If it wasn't suicide…yeah."

David tilted his head. "Why would you say that?"

"Because there are rumors that these might not have been suicides. That it was part of a game," Zane said.

The color started to drain from David's face a bit more. "A game?"

"Yeah, a game your roommate was playing," Asa said.

"W-What?" David said.

"Eric. People say he was playing a game. People say they heard it from you," Zane said.

David's eyes started darting around, like he might bolt. Zane held both hands up. "Look, nobody will know you told us anything. We just want to talk to Eric."

David shook his head jerkily. "I can't help you. I have no idea where he is. His parents don't even know where he went. I don't even know if he's still alive."

"Can you at least tell us why you think he was playing this game? Like I said, nobody will know you spoke to us," Zane promised.

David seemed to vacillate on it for a moment before finally heaving out a sigh. "It started a few months ago."

Zane fought the urge to fist pump. "What did?"

"The rumors about the game," David said. "People were saying you couldn't apply, you were chosen. That it was some underground thing. They talked about it like getting chosen made you elite. Some said the game had already started, others said it hadn't. Some people said it was fake, others said it was like a mind game made to test, like, spies and secret agents. They said it was like…psychological warfare."

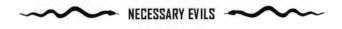

"Psychological warfare?" Zane echoed. "What does that mean?"

David waved a hand, then lifted his ball cap to run his hands through sweaty blond hair before replacing it once more. "It was all just rumors. Some of them were crazy. There was a million dollar payday. It was some supernatural thing, like out of a horror movie. Once you started to play, there was no way to stop it. Some said it was just some Japanese horror movie with a kitschy hook, like they did with the *Blair Witch Project*. It just took on this sort of urban legend-like quality for a few weeks. But then we all found something new to talk about…until the first death."

"Xander Hamilton," Zane said.

David gave a jerky half-nod. "People were shocked. Upset. Except Eric. He was weird about it. Said some people couldn't handle the pressure. It didn't make any sense. I didn't even think Eric knew Xander. But Eric was unraveling all on his own."

Zane frowned, leaning heavier against Asa's solid frame, something loosening when he felt Asa pull him back against him a little more. "How so?"

"Eric was solid. Nothing fazed him. He was literally the most level-headed, chill guy I knew. But just before Xander died, Eric started acting weird. Erratic. He stayed up all night, stopped showering. He looked sick. Pale. I think he started abusing his Adderall. It didn't matter what time of day or night it was, he was awake, watching weird ass shit on his laptop."

"What kind of weird shit?" Asa asked.

"Like people being tortured, people in foreign countries being beheaded. People torturing animals and kids. Sick fucking shit. I threatened to report him. That was when he said it was all part of the game. That he just had to make it through the thirty days."

Zane's stomach sloshed, goosebumps rising, as he pictured his brother participating in something that twisted. Would he agree to something like that? Would anybody? It sounded insane. "Why would anybody agree to something like that?"

"Money. I think he thought there was actually money involved. He was on scholarship. He was buying his grades. His parents were psychos. I think he thought if he had this money he could get out from under his parents' thumb."

Gage would do that. He hated the hold his parents had on him. He was on partial scholarship but they held other things over his head. Room. Board. He had to toe the line or the guilt trips would start.

"You okay, man?" David asked, snapping Zane out of his thoughts.

"Yeah. Sorry," Zane said. "Long day."

David's brow furrowed. It was only three o'clock in the afternoon. But Zane stood by his statement. It had been a long day. And it wasn't over. He still had to live through a meeting with Thomas Mulvaney.

"How do you know Eric ran away and something didn't

happen to him? Maybe he went off campus to end his life like the others," Asa said.

"I came home from class one day and his shit was gone. There was just a note that said, "I quit. Don't tell anyone."

"That could easily be a suicide note, no?" Zane asked.

David looked around again, like he was afraid there was a hidden camera crew. "I saw him a few days after that. He was waiting for me by my car at the end of my shift. He asked me if he could borrow some money. He looked rough. I…gave him what I'd made in tips, which was only, like, a hundred bucks. I never saw him again."

Zane frowned. "You gave him a hundred bucks with no expectation of getting it back?"

"Man, I work here for weed money. My parents are loaded, but they like to think having a job will keep me honest."

"Tell me about it," Asa muttered.

Zane snorted. "Do you have any idea where we could find Eric? Any idea at all?"

David shook his head. "Nah, man. I haven't seen him. I don't think he wants to be seen."

"Do you think people were really after him, or do you just think paranoia started to get the best of him?" Asa asked.

David shrugged. "I don't know, man. Five people are dead. I don't know how many were playing the game, but I'm pretty sure Eric was, and something spooked him bad enough to go off grid. Maybe there were others who quit the game and stuck around, but I just don't know. I don't know anything more than I've already told you. I gotta get back to work. Don't—" He shook his head. "Don't come back. Okay?"

David didn't wait for them to respond, just turned and went back inside, leaving Zane leaning against Asa, whose arms snaked around his waist. "Did we learn anything from that interaction?"

Zane shook his head. "I honestly can't tell. It definitely sounds like there was a game. But it also sounds like these deaths were all self-inflicted. What are we supposed to do with that?"

"I'd give you my opinion but you already think I'm a monster," Asa said, humor lacing his voice.

Zane shivered. "Tell me anyway."

"If there is a game and that game involves driving people to their breaking point, whoever controls that game is a murderer and should be treated as such."

Zane nodded. If his brother had played the game...if somebody pushed his happy-go-lucky brother to the point where he felt taking his own life was the only way out... fuck them. Asa could have them. He could tear them to pieces for all Zane cared.

Zane turned in Asa's arms, voice grim. "I think I'm ready to meet your father now."

TWELVE

ASA

Asa sighed, shifting in his seat once more, watching Zane from the corner of his eye. They sat in Asa's SUV just outside his father's house. Beside him, Zane sat with a death grip on the door handle, like he was worried somebody might wrench it open and drag him out. Asa found it both confusing and amusing.

This had been Zane's idea, yet he'd been stalling for at least fifteen minutes. All the bravado he'd had when he'd told Asa to bring him to Thomas appeared to have disappeared in the thirty minute drive across town. Asa understood his apprehension but didn't know if he should push the issue or wait. He had never had to worry about somebody's feelings before. It was…weird.

"So…did you want me to have my dad meet us out here or…" Asa teased.

"I just need a minute," Zane snapped.

"A minute to, what?" Asa asked around a laugh. "You get that my father isn't the one who kills people, right? That's me. You know, the one who's been inside you. Twice. The one whose bed you willingly handcuffed yourself to last night? I'm the one you should be afraid of." Zane gave him a pissy look, arching one brow, leaving Asa to roll his eyes. "You know what I mean. Listen, my dad isn't going to be mad at anybody but me."

"Yeah. Okay," Zane said. "Let's just do this."

Asa stifled a laugh at Zane's sudden fake gusto but exited the vehicle, going around the car to open the door for him. He laced their fingers together, walking directly up the walkway and up the stone steps to the wide glass double doors.

Inside, Asa called out, "Dad?"

The house was enormous but the acoustics were fantastic. Besides, at this time of day, his father was usually in his office. Except today. "Kitchen," Thomas called back.

Asa led Zane to the kitchen, stopping short with a grimace when he realized his father wasn't alone. His brother, Adam, and his fiancé, Noah, sat on the bar stools at the island.

Shit.

As soon as they caught sight of Zane, Noah and Adam began to smile, Noah's gaze instantly dropping to where their hands were joined. Asa resisted the urge to drop Zane's hand. They knew. They definitely knew. Fuck.

"Who's your friend?" Noah asked, voice full of mock innocence, a grin spreading across his face when he saw the hickeys on Zane's throat. "Jesus, Asa. You really are an animal."

Yeah, they knew. Jericho told Atticus, and Atticus had told the others.

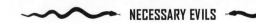

"What? What's going on?" Thomas asked, looking between the two.

"This is Zane. Zane, this is my father, Thomas, my brother, Adam, and his fiancé, Noah. They're about to be super invasive."

Zane blinked. "Oh. Okay."

Thomas studied each of his children carefully, Noah included, before saying, "Nice to meet you, Zane." His voice was hesitant, like he reserved the right to retract that statement later.

Adam narrowed his pale blue eyes in Zane's direction, a smirk forming as he leaned back. "So, Zane. What do you do?"

Thomas squinted at Adam's tone, gaze darting to Asa.

Zane opened his mouth to speak but Asa interrupted. "Dad. Can I talk to you…in private."

Thomas gave a huge sigh, already irritated with Asa without cause. "Sure. Let's go to my office."

Asa dropped Zane's hand, leaning in to whisper in his ear, "Show no fear. Adam feeds off of it. If you get into trouble, look to Noah for help. I'll be right back."

Asa left Zane gaping after him, following his father to his office. No sooner had the door closed, then Thomas turned on him. "What did you do? And why do your brothers know about it before I do?"

Shit. "Okay, it's a long story. Okay, well not a long story so much as a kind of convoluted story—"

"Asa." His name was a warning.

"Yeah, right. So…remember that awards dinner you made me go to?" Asa asked.

Thomas gave him an exasperated look. "Of course, I do, Asa. It was yesterday."

Oh yeah. Could he have really only met Zane yesterday? That seemed impossible. He shook off the feeling. "Yeah, so anyway. Um, I met Zane at the dinner—"

Thomas sighed. "Your hookup? The one you blew off my award for? Is that him?"

Asa leaned against his father's desk. "Yeah. I have to tell you something, and I need you to keep an open mind."

"Christ, Asa, whenever you say shit like that, my eye starts to twitch." He crossed the room to the mini-bar in the corner, opening the whiskey bottle and pouring himself two fingers full, throwing them back like a shot. His father's day drinking was a relatively new endeavor. "You and your brother have been apart twenty-four hours and already you've both lost your goddamn minds—"

Asa broke in. "What did Avi do?"

"This isn't about your brother. What did *you* do?"

"Zane is a reporter. Well, he wants to be a reporter. Right now, he's just a crime blogger."

Thomas closed his eyes, digging his thumb and forefinger into his sockets like he was trying to scratch his brain. "Okay…"

Asa tried to choose his words carefully. "After we… hooked up, he found his way to Jericho's and Atticus's murder cabin."

"Found his way?" Thomas asked through gritted teeth.

Asa did his best to keep his voice light. "Yeah, it's a long story. But he saw Jericho and me getting rid of that biker guy. You know…getting rid of?" He mimed bringing down an ax.

Thomas gave another long-suffering sigh, reaching for the bottle again. "Asa, please explain to me why you were holding hands in my kitchen with a reporter who saw you dissecting a biker."

"Because we've reached an understanding," Asa said, hoping this would ease his father's mind.

"An understanding? How much is this understanding going to cost me?" Thomas asked.

Asa shook his head. "No. Not like that. I fixed it. He's helping me figure out the suicide game situation, and, in exchange, I answer all his questions. At the end, he'll see that what we do is a public service, not a crime, and he'll get a better story out of it than ours."

"You're answering his questions?" Thomas repeated, voice low.

"Yes?" Asa asked, unsure whether his father was angry or not.

"What do you mean you're 'answering his questions'?"

"I needed his help with the case. I had to bring something more to the table than uncuffing him from the radiator."

"Uncuffing him from the *what*?" Thomas snapped.

Asa shook his head. "It's not like that. Okay, it was sort of like that," he said, correcting himself.

Thomas's voice was a low rumble as he asked, "Did you put those bruises on him before or after the radiator, Asa?"

"I mean, technically both? But he likes it. Like, it's a sex thing—"

"Jesus, Asa. I'm aware. I know what hickeys look like."

"But really, Dad. Zane likes me. Well, okay, I don't know that he *likes* me exactly, but we have this thing, this connection. We get each other. I think he might be my person."

"Your person?" Thomas echoed.

"Yeah, you know, like Noah, Lucas, and Jericho are for the others. I think Zane's supposed to be my person."

Thomas breathed heavily through his nose. "Is this you acting out because of your brother? Are you punishing me because I sent Avi to help Aiden?"

Asa rolled his eyes. "What? No. Well, at first, yeah, kidnapping Zane was probably acting out, but then we reached an understanding, and now, I think he actually really feels something for me."

"You've known him less than a day. Asa, you're smarter than this. You can't just abduct random strangers—especially reporters—and then decide that you're going to keep them like some kind of trophy." Thomas shook his head, gaze snapping back to Asa's. "Wait? What do you mean kidnapped? You kidnapped him?"

"Yeah, why else would I have had him cuffed to the radiator?"

"With you? God only knows," Thomas muttered.

"There are a million other things I could have chained him to for that. Trust me—"

"For the love of God, Asa."

Thomas wasn't being fair. He had to see that Asa did exactly the right thing. "What was I supposed to do? Let him go so he could share his little videotape with the world?" Asa asked, flinging his hands into the air. "I was thinking on my feet."

Thomas began to pace. "How much does he know, Asa? How much more have you told him?"

Asa shook his head. "Everything. He knows everything. It was the only way to explain to him what he saw. Jericho and I were dismembering a body, Dad. We were chatting about all kinds of very top-level clearance stuff. The best case scenario is him knowing the whole story. Better he think we're vigilantes than that we're psycho killers. What would you have had us do? Kill him?"

"Of course not," Thomas snapped. "He never should have been there in the first place."

Asa stood, moving closer to his dad. "Well, I don't have the ability to time travel, so we need to move past the shoulda, woulda, coulda portion of this lecture. Besides, I think this could work in our favor."

"How?" Thomas asked. "How will having a reporter know all of our secrets help us?"

"Good press?" Asa said.

"Good press? You want us to go public with this?" Thomas barked.

"What? No." Why was Thomas being so difficult about this? "Think about it. Talk of some superhero taking out the city's evil helps plant seeds, just in case things ever go badly. It might pay to have the public on our side. Besides, if they think it's one vigilante-like superhero, then they won't be looking for a whole family full of them. Right?"

Thomas closed his eyes. Asa could only sit there and wait for him to finally speak again. It didn't pay to push his father too far.

Finally, Thomas said, "Bring him to the war room."

Asa felt a sudden weight lift off his chest. "Yeah, okay. I can do that."

Thomas turned and left the room, not waiting to see if Asa followed.

In the kitchen, there was a strange stand-off happening between Zane and Adam. Zane leaned against the counter, arms crossed. Adam had his arms folded on the island. They were both locked in on each other.

"What's happening right now?" Asa asked Noah, the only person not participating in this weird staring contest.

Noah grinned, looking back and forth between the two of them. "I'm not really sure. I think this is like the eye equivalent of a dick measuring contest. Like…at some point one of them has to blink or they're going to lose an eyeball. Right?"

Asa was sure, whatever this was, Adam started it. He liked to torture all the newbies. They didn't have time for that today. "Zane. My dad wants us to meet him downstairs."

Zane's gaze snapped from Adam's to Asa's, but it was Noah who said, "No way. He's going to the war room already? When's the wedding?"

"Shut up," Asa muttered.

Noah laughed. "What? I'm just saying, once they make

it downstairs, you're sort of obligated to put a ring on it. Hope you're ready to change your last name, Zane."

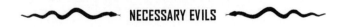

"Um, you and Adam aren't married," Asa pointed out.

Noah rolled his eyes. "That's because I want the wedding to be perfect. It's not perfect yet. Besides, legally Adam's shit all goes to me when he dies, so at this point, a wedding is just paperwork. We don't need paperwork."

Asa snorted. "Hopefully that holds up in probate court." To Zane, he said, "Come on."

Zane gave Adam one final long stare before turning and walking to Asa, who put an arm around his waist, leading him from the room and down the hallway. At the war room, Asa punched in the code that opened the heavy door.

Zane's head was on a swivel from the moment they entered, taking in the large conference table, the comfy office chairs, the speaker in the center, the murder board on the wall breaking down the targets Noah and Thomas were currently vetting. He looked a little overwhelmed.

"Go ahead, Calliope," Thomas said, aiming his words at the speaker in the center of the table. The wall lit up with hundreds of faces. Thomas looked to Zane. "Pick one. Any one."

"W-What?" Zane stuttered, looking from Asa to Thomas and back again.

"Pick a face," Thomas said, his tone letting Zane know this wasn't a request but an order.

Zane struggled, his eyes darting from picture to picture before finally settling on one. "Third from the top," he said, pointing out a fair-skinned man with a receding hairline and patchy facial hair.

Calliope's voice filled the room. "Gerald Mizner. Serial child rapist. Four proven victims, all under ten. Another eight suspected but never confirmed. Released from jail on a technicality. Killed by…Archer, 2017."

The muscle in Zane's cheek twitched at the rapid-fire information. A look of disgust pulled his lips into a grimace.

"Pick another," Thomas demanded.

Zane floated closer to the wall. "Him," he said, pointing to a blond man with jowls.

Thomas gave a nod. "Max Mason, Calliope."

"Maxwell Raymond Mason, human trafficker. Sold girls he smuggled in from Eastern Europe on the darknet, some as young as eleven. Killed by—"

"Me," Asa said, cutting off Calliope. "And Avi. Last year."

"Another," Thomas said.

On and on it went. Serial rapist. Serial killer. Child predator. Spree killer. Domestic abuser. Child pornography. Child abuse. Torture. Kidnapping. Child killer.

"Enough," Zane finally said. "I get it."

"Do you?" Thomas asked. "Because my son has inadvertently given you the power to destroy everything we've worked for. Do you think the world is better off with any of those people in it?"

Zane swallowed, falling into one of the plush office chairs around the table. "No. Of course not."

Thomas leaned his hip on the table, staring down at Zane. "I don't mean to sound like a bad movie, but you've only got two moves here. You're either with us or against us. I'm not a fan of threats, and I don't relish having to say things like this. But what we do here, this experiment of sorts, it's a pilot study for something much bigger than all of us. And there are very influential people who would kill to make sure this doesn't leave this room. So, I encourage you to make the right choice."

Asa dropped into the seat beside Zane. Was his father telling the truth? Were there others involved in this? Who were they? How were they involved? Was this some kind of fear tactic? Did the others know? Zane looked to Asa, then back to Thomas. "This is impressive and all, but I decided hours ago that I'd keep things to myself. Besides, it's like Asa said this morning. Who would even believe me? I have no proof. I'll just have to wait for my big break."

Asa felt a weird squeeze around his heart. It wasn't fair that Zane was having to sacrifice everything, even if he had used Asa. It wasn't like Asa hadn't used him right back. Several times. He looked to his father pleadingly.

"I can help with that," Thomas said. "I have connections everywhere. This could be of benefit to all of us."

Zane seemed to consider it, then shook his head. "No. I want to earn my place, not buy it. I'll have to find a different story for my big break."

Asa didn't like the hollowness of Zane's words or the disappointment on his face. It made him feel heavy somehow. He knew Zane was hurting but he couldn't do anything about it. It wasn't just a byline. This had to do with Zane's shitty parents and his dead brother. Asa was making Zane's life harder. He didn't want to do that to him.

"A story like a game that ends in mass suicide?" Asa asked. "That seems byline worthy to me."

"What have you found?" Thomas asked.

Asa nodded towards Zane, who said, "We interviewed a student who claims his roommate was playing, and he implied that at least one of the victims, Xander Hamilton, was also playing this game. This is all second-hand information, but it appears to have to do with completing a certain amount of tasks, each of them more unpleasant than the last, many of them having to do with watching or listening to disturbing material. This student's roommate skipped town four weeks ago, and he thinks the guy was running for his life."

"Are you able to track this roommate down?" Thomas asked.

"Not yet. Calliope, can you tell me what you can find on an Eric Sievers? He was a sophomore at Henley up until four weeks ago."

There was the sound of Calliope's nails clicking on keys. "Eric Sievers, date of birth September 25th, 2000. Son of Lisa and Grey Sievers. Mom is a real estate agent, dad is a professor. He is the youngest of…six siblings. Jeez. No wonder he needed that scholarship."

"Can you check to see if his phone has pinged off any towers or if his debit card has been used anywhere in the last few weeks?" Asa asked, earning a surprised look from Zane.

"Give me an hour and I can tell you what he had for breakfast this morning," Calliope said.

"In the meantime, can you send me the info you found

on the victims? Maybe we can work backwards and figure out how they pick their players," Zane reasoned.

"What good will that do?" Asa asked.

Zane shook his head. "Well, if we can figure out how they pick their players, maybe we can figure out who was playing this time and if they quit the game or are still playing?"

Thomas nodded, looking at Zane with a much different expression than just moments ago. "That's a good idea. Get Lucas to help you. Behavioral profiling is what he does. Maybe he can profile the students. Don't just look at the most recent five victims. You need a wider sampling. Calliope, look for any suicide clusters you can find throughout the whole country."

"I already have a bot running. I'll send that info over pronto."

With that, she disconnected, leaving the three men to stare at each other. After a minute, Thomas clapped Zane on the back. "Welcome to the family, son. I hope you know what you've just signed on for."

It wasn't quite the welcome Asa was hoping Zane would get, but it was far better than what he'd expected. When they were alone, Asa stood, looking to Zane. "What do we do now, detective?"

Zane let Asa pull him to his feet, his expression grim. "Now…" he trailed off, like he was gathering his strength. "Now, you meet my parents."

"What? Why?" Asa asked, hating the panic in his voice.

Asa was not ready to meet Zane's parents. Not now. Not ever. His mother was a vile creature, and his father seemed equally unpleasant. Zane and Asa were far too new for him to murder Zane's parents. Murdering his future in-laws might be one hurdle too many for their blossoming relationship. But he kept those thoughts to himself.

Zane shook his head. "Because there's a very good chance my brother was one of the victims of this game, and if anybody has my brother's computer lying around somewhere, it's my mother."

"You said your mother would never give it to you."

Zane shook his head. "She won't. But she'll give it to you."

Asa frowned. "She will? Why?"

"Because, more than anything else, my mother is about clout. Her reporter son will never trump her dead golden child, but his billionaire boyfriend will. She'll do anything to impress a celebrity. You're as close as she's likely to get. If she thinks there's a chance you're going to make an honest man out of me, she'll give you a fucking kidney."

Asa's lip curled in disgust. He had no interest in placating Zane's horrible mom. Not for any reason. "No fucking way."

Zane stepped closer, his hands falling on Asa's waist, his fingers dipping beneath his shirt and feeling their way along Asa's abs. "Please. You have to. I need to know if my brother was involved in this, and—God help us—my mother might be the key to that."

Asa was temporarily distracted by Zane's roaming hands and his pleading eyes and the way he caught his bottom lip between his teeth. Shit. "You're completely playing me right now."

"Is it working?"

Yes. "You shouldn't tease me like that, you know."

Zane's thumbs played over Asa's nipples, his gaze heated. "I'm not teasing. I'm…negotiating."

A slow smile crept across Asa's face. "I'm always open to negotiations. What's your offer?"

Zane's hands slid down to Asa's waistband. "You agree to take me to my parents and play nice and I'll be nice to you in return."

Asa hardened instantly. "How nice?"

Zane glanced around the room. "Are there cameras in here?"

Asa's breath punched from him. "No."

He hoped that was true. But even if it was a boldfaced lie and his father somehow ended up seeing whatever Asa was about to do to Zane in that room, he couldn't bring himself to stop. Especially not with Zane sinking to his knees, his hands already working open the button on Asa's jeans.

Shit.

THIRTEEN

ZANE

Asa was already hard, staring down at Zane with a smirk that he should have found humiliating but, instead, made his dick throb and his heart race. Asa pushed Zane's cap off his head, threading his fingers into his curls. He eagerly nuzzled the ridge of Asa's cock through the denim before his fingers scrambled to free him from his jeans, too turned on to be embarrassed by his forwardness.

It was hard to be embarrassed when Asa was looking at him with enough heat to make him spontaneously combust, like Zane was worthy and sexy and something Asa truly wanted.

"You look so fucking hot. I've been picturing you on your knees for me since the moment I laid eyes on you," Asa crooned, running his thumb over Zane's lower lip. "Go ahead, Lois. Be nice to me. I'll try not to be too mean to you."

Zane's pulse tripped at Asa's words. The old Zane might have been furious at being treated like some sex doll but *this* Zane couldn't get enough of it, couldn't get enough of Asa and the way he looked at him. It made Zane bold. It made him feel sexy and wanted. "I don't want you to be nice to me."

"You have no idea what you're saying," Asa warned with a chuckle, gripping Zane's curls tighter. "I have zero control around you as it is. If you let me off the leash, I can't promise I won't hurt you."

Warmth bloomed through Zane's core. He sat back on his heels, meeting Asa's gaze defiantly. "Then hurt me. It would hardly be the first time."

Zane let his mouth fall open, tongue out, making his intentions clear. He saw the exact moment Asa dropped his mask—that fake human exterior everybody wore to convince the rest of the world they were safe around them.

But nobody was safe around Asa. Except Zane. They'd barely known each other a day but Zane knew, deep down, that Asa would gut anybody who looked at him sideways, and that knowledge made Zane want to do very bad things for Asa. Made him willing to hurt for him, debase himself for him.

Asa ran his cock between Zane's lips, not forcing his way inside, just rubbing himself over his lips and cheeks, like he was marking him, letting him know he'd do what he liked, when he liked. He pushed Zane's face into the curls at the base of his cock, making him moan. Was it normal to crave a person's scent? Especially like this, his face buried in his thigh where the smell was strongest?

Zane didn't care. Didn't care if he looked needy or

desperate as he rubbed his face against Asa, unable to stop the groans that fell from his lips as he mouthed over Asa's balls.

"Come on, Lois, suck me." Asa pulled Zane's head back, forcing his cock between his lips. "Show me how good you can be."

Zane closed his mouth over his length, relishing the tang of his skin and the heavy weight on his tongue as Asa began to fuck his mouth, slowly at first, but then with more fervor.

Asa rumbled low as Zane moaned around him, the sound going straight to his dick until he was leaking through his underwear. Asa hadn't lied—he had no intention of being nice. Maybe he'd just been warming Zane up, easing him into what was to come. Asa's one hand stayed where it was, threaded in his curls, but the other closed around the back of his head. He took a step forward, forcing his cock to the back of Zane's throat in one swift motion.

He tried not to heave, but it was impossible. Asa was huge and Zane most definitely had a gag reflex. A reflex Asa seemed intent on testing as he forced his cock impossibly deep until Zane's muscles were convulsing around him.

The more he gagged and sputtered, the more brutal Asa grew until tears poured down Zane's cheeks, his nose running and both of them covered in his saliva as Asa kept his gaze locked on him. It was raw and brutal and felt a little bit like a felony, but despite the pain—or maybe because of it—Zane only grew harder, his cock leaking until he worried he might come in his pants like a teenager.

Zane liked being used by Asa. Craved it. There was something so intoxicating about being the only one who got to see Asa's truly dark side. Zane knew all of his secrets, knew every dark kink. Just Zane. Nothing had ever been just his. Nobody had ever cared just for him. Was this care? Had Zane been so abused that having a man wreck his throat was the equivalent of love in his mind? A therapist would have a field day with him.

"Touch yourself," Asa demanded, as if Zane had been waiting for his permission.

Had he? Either way, he jumped to comply with Asa's order, working his jeans open with one hand, groaning in relief when his palm closed around his overheated skin. He wasted no time, stroking himself in time with Asa's rough thrusts, pleasure sparking along his nerve endings until he couldn't stop the sounds he made.

Zane was already so close. Asa had been edging him since he'd gotten him dressed that morning. Asa would probably say the same about Zane. *Had* said it. Said he was a tease. But they both enjoyed this game, this thing between them. Whatever it was. This constant push and pull. The teasing. The taunts. The kidnapping. Zane felt like Asa saw all of it as foreplay. And, God help him, he did, too.

The more Asa used him, the faster Zane's hand moved, hurtling him closer to orgasm. The more brutal Asa was, the more intense Zane's pleasure until he wasn't even stroking himself anymore but squeezing off his release, afraid he'd come first. He didn't want that. He wanted to come with the taste of Asa on his tongue.

Asa was close. Zane could feel it in the way his hands gripped him tighter, the way his breath hitched. Asa wasn't exactly a talker, but that just meant Zane could hear how much he was unraveling, how much he turned Asa on.

"I'm gonna come," Asa grunted, forcing his cock into Zane's throat, holding him there. His hips pulsed against him until Zane worried he might actually suffocate on Asa's dick. It wasn't the worst way to go.

Just as Zane's vision grew fuzzy at the edges, a weird sense of euphoria overtaking him, Asa's release flooded his mouth, forcing him to swallow or choke. Zane chose to swallow, his hand finally working over his own aching cock once more. It only took three hard pulls and he was coming, his orgasm hitting him with the force of a tsunami.

Asa pulled free, but Zane stayed on his knees, trying to catch his breath, only slightly aware of Asa walking away. Then he was back, pulling Zane to his feet before picking him up and sitting him on the conference room table.

Zane's heart squeezed as Asa used a wet cloth to gently wipe his face. All the harsh intensity had melted from his features, leaving him looking at Zane in a way that made him catch his breath. Like he'd pleased him.

Asa gave him an amused look. "Are you alright?"

Zane nodded, swallowing hard, then wincing. "Nothing a little water and maybe some Tylenol won't fix."

Asa chuckled. When Zane was all cleaned up, Asa gripped his chin gently, dropping an almost chaste kiss on his lips. "That was hot, Lois."

Zane's eyes burned from tears and he still had the sniffles, but he felt hot, just because Asa had deemed it so. He looked around the room. "I really hope your father doesn't have cameras in here."

Asa's knuckles brushed against Zane's cheek in that way that made goosebumps erupt along his skin. "He doesn't, but I wish he did. That blowjob was worthy of being recorded for posterity."

"I don't think you should be showing that to any future generations," Zane said, a lopsided smile forming. "Though, I suppose it's nice you want something to remember me by." He hated how sulky he sounded.

Asa smirked, shaking his head. "You really don't get it, do you, Lois? You're never getting out of this. You and me? It's a done deal. We're kind of like the mob. Once you're in, you're in. I really hope you can learn to love me because this fucked up thing we have going…it's forever now. Hope you don't get sick of me."

This was all so surreal. Two days ago, he'd dreamed of taking down the Mulvaneys. Now, suddenly, he was going to be one. He had no idea what to do with that information. Falling in love with Asa wasn't going to be a hardship. But he couldn't shake the feeling it would forever be one-sided. "I think it's far more dangerous if you get sick of me."

"That's not going to happen, Lois. Relationships are what you make them. Our goals and values are very much aligned. We have an amazing sex life. You'll never want for any material possession you desire. If you need something from me emotionally, I'll learn. I'll figure it out. You don't have to be afraid of me. I decided you were it for me the moment you put those handcuffs back on."

Zane wasn't sure he was still breathing. As far as proposals went, it was a pretty good one. "Oh."

Asa grinned. "It's Avi you should be afraid of. He's very...possessive of me. He might see you as a threat."

"So, your psychopathic brother—who looks exactly like you—might want to murder me. Great. Excellent. I guess there's something to be said for me not seeing it coming."

"Don't worry, Lois. I won't let him kill you."

"How romantic."

Zane ran his fingers through his hair for the hundredth time as they landed on his mother's doorstep. He'd thrown his cap in the backseat, knowing she'd instantly hone in on it like a beacon. Beside him, Asa was taking in the small tidy white house with its neatly manicured lawn and beds along the white picket fence overflowing with only white flowers. His mother was dedicated to her aesthetic.

The houses on either side of his mother's house were larger and far more grand, but hers was meticulous. She told the neighbors she'd chosen the tiny house because she was downsizing since her children were gone, but the truth was, she'd rather have the smallest house in the nicest neighborhood than the largest house in a less desirable one.

Zane lifted his hand to knock, but he just couldn't bring himself to do it. Talking to his mother on the phone every week was hard enough, dealing with her scrutiny in person was torture. Listening to her discuss each of his flaws in detail in front of Asa would be pure, unadulterated hell.

He shouldn't have worn pink today. She hated when he did anything too effeminate. Just because he was gay didn't mean he had to 'look' gay.

Just turn and run, bro. She's never going to give you what you want. She guards that MacBook Pro like it's my death shroud.

Go away. I can't do this with your voice in my head and hers in my ears. Seriously, fuck off.

Okay, touchy. Damn.

It was then that he noticed Asa staring down at him with an amused expression.

"Do you prefer to take all parental meetings outdoors?" he teased. "Since I can't help but notice that we're once more just standing outside instead of, you know, not."

Zane rolled his eyes. "I'm…gearing up for it. You don't know what a nightmare my mother can be."

Asa reached up and rang the doorbell, earning a wide-eyed look of exasperation from Zane. "What? You said she'll find me charming. Let me charm her."

Before Zane could panic further, the door swung open. His mother stood there in her white linen pants and flowy magenta top, dripping with gold jewelry like she was afraid if she didn't wear it all at once, somebody might steal it. She blinked in surprise, her gaze darting back and forth between Zane and Asa.

"What are you doing here?" she said, her tone sharp enough to cut. She narrowed her eyes at Asa, taking in his full sleeve of ink and his casual attire with a sneer. "Who's this?"

Zane mentally took a deep breath. "Asa, this is my mom, Beverly. Mom, this is my boyfriend, Asa." She clearly didn't recognize him on sight so Zane said, "Asa Mulvaney."

The change was instantaneous, her expression serene but the look in her eye predatory. "Mulvaney?" she asked, feigning ignorance. "Why does that name sound so familiar?"

Asa gave her a dazzling smile. "You probably know my father. Thomas Mulvaney."

His mother's hand floated to her chest. "Oh, my. You are so handsome. Just like your father. And you're…with *my* son?"

God, she's a bitch. Zane had to agree with Gage on this one. It was no surprise to him that the only person who hadn't asked about the bruises all over him was his own mother. She either hadn't noticed or truly didn't care. Zane wasn't sure which option was worse.

Zane struggled not to react to his brother's musings. He was right, though. She was a bitch. No matter how much he steeled himself for her unwavering hatred of him, it never grew any less painful. The way she'd emphasized 'my' as if perhaps Asa had just grabbed the wrong boyfriend by mistake was just a twist of the knife she'd lodged in his heart at birth.

Asa stiffened beside him, but his smile never wavered. He wrapped his hand around Zane's, threading their fingers together and squeezing hard, though Zane didn't know if it was in solidarity or if even he wanted to punch Bev in the throat. Either way, something about that gesture eased some of the ache.

"You've raised an amazing man," Asa assured her. "I was never really one who believed in love at first sight, but one look at Zane and I was a goner."

Maybe it was just part of the act but Zane's heart skipped a beat, especially when Asa's thumb began to draw circles on the delicate skin of his inner wrist. His mother's look of confusion wasn't an act. She truly couldn't fathom a world that didn't find him as awful as she did. "Oh. Well, how nice. Has he met your father? I imagine he's used to you dating men who are far more…suitable."

What the fuck? Maybe you should let him kill her. At this point, it seems like a public service.

Zane fought not to crack a smile, but then Asa squeezed his fingers so tightly he worried they might break.

"Yes, just this morning. He loves Zane, too. Was excited to welcome him to the family."

Her hand fluttered. "To the family?" she gasped. She then seemed to remember her manners. "Oh, my. Come in. Come in. I apologize. My son rarely comes to visit, least of all during the week." She led them into the living room with its white carpet and white furniture, gesturing to the sofa. "Please, sit."

Zane dropped onto the nearest cushion. Asa followed, sitting close enough for them to touch from shoulder to calf, keeping their clasped hands on his thigh. "Thank you."

Bev let out a huge breath, her smile almost genuine. "Of course, my future son-in-law is always welcome here. Your family as well, though I can't imagine why they'd want to come to my humble little home."

"Your home is lovely," Asa said, sounding so sincere Zane couldn't help but gawk at him. Was this public Asa? Was this the Asa of interviews? The one who met with clients and dated supermodels? Zane would take the psycho killer Asa any day. “The truth is, we’re here because there’s something I was hoping—well, my father was hoping—you could help me with.”

Beverly’s well-manicured brows shot upwards. “How could I possibly help Thomas Mulvaney?”

Asa leaned in, still refusing to relinquish Zane’s hand. “This is a bit of a delicate subject and I apologize in advance for any distress it might cause you,” he said, giving her a sad smile.

His mother leaned in as well, always primed for gossip or a juicy story she could use to regale her bridge club. “I’m listening.”

“I suppose you’ve heard of the recent deaths at Henley?” Asa asked.

His mother’s face became a storm cloud. She crossed her legs and clasped her hands together, her lips forming a tight line. “Yes, of course. Such a tragedy.”

Asa nodded. “Yes. My father agrees. He’s creating an event. A memorial of sorts for all the students who’ve taken their own lives, not just at Henley but at your late son’s school as well.”

If his mother crossed any more limbs, she’d turn herself inside out. He could tell she was fighting with herself. If this had been anybody but a Mulvaney asking, she would have shooed them out of her house with a broom and told Zane to never come back.

“Oh, that’s nice, dear,” she said faintly. “But I don’t see how I can help.”

“We were hoping you still have Gage’s computer,” Zane

blurted.

His mother's eyes went wide, her face paling. "What? Why?"

Asa gave Zane a look that screamed *shut up* then turned back to Bev. "The other families have given us access to their loved ones' computers to look for any poems, art, essays. Anything that would allow us a glimpse into a side of them we might not otherwise see. We're going to turn it into an art installation of sorts. You know my father is a patron of the arts."

Zane fought not to roll his eyes as he watched his mother attempt to process Asa's logic. It was a good story. Better than what Zane had planned, which was just to beg or wait until his mother left, then ransack her closet.

"I don't think my son had anything so frivolous on his computer," Bev said. "He wasn't into that artsy stuff like Zane. He spent his time on important things like schoolwork and extracurriculars. He even did volunteer work with your father's foundation. You would have loved my Gage."

Asa squeezed Zane's hand harder, like he could feel the sting of her words and their effect on Zane's heart. "Our computer expert would just like an opportunity to see if she can find all the things Gage loved. If Gage's grades and extracurriculars were his primary focus, we'll make sure that is highlighted, front and center. But it would really mean a lot to us—to my father—if we could just borrow his laptop for a few hours. We can clone the hard drive and have it back almost immediately so it's not out of your sight for long. I promise it will come back to you in exactly the same way it left."

Once more, Asa laid that big smile on his mother. Zane could tell she was wavering. She loved Gage more than anything in the world, but Gage was dead and Thomas Mulvaney's attention would be social capital she could cash in on with her bridge club for months if not years, especially if Asa was telling the truth and they really were doing life together.

Finally, his mother sighed. "Okay, sure. Why not? But I want final say in what goes into his memorial. I wouldn't want people getting the wrong idea about my son."

"Absolutely," Asa assured her.

She gave a single nod, then stood and left the room. Zane sagged against the couch. Asa leaned down and nuzzled just behind his ear. "I could kill her for you."

"How would you do it?" Zane asked, breathless. The idea of Bev's death felt like a balm to his jagged heart.

Asa seemed to think about it. "Um, poison?"

Zane shook his head. "Too quick."

"Drowning?"

Zane made a face. "Not painful enough."

"Vat of acid?" Asa countered.

A startled laugh escaped. "Are you trying to kill my mom or take out all the toons in ToonTown, Judge Doom?"

"Did you just make a *Who Framed Roger Rabbit* reference?" Asa asked, looking at Zane in awe.

"I love that movie," Zane said, blushing for some reason.

"Me too," Asa murmured, leaning down to kiss his way

along the shell of Zane's ear.

"Tell me more ways you'd kill my mom," Zane said on a gasp.

"Aren't you afraid she'll catch us making out on her pristine sofa?" Asa purred, dropping Zane's hand to skim fingertips along his inner thigh.

"Please, you could fuck me on the dining room table and she'd just try to find a way to capitalize on the event."

Asa made an appreciative sound when he felt Zane starting to harden behind his zipper. "There's an idea."

"Fucking me in front of my mom? Um, no. Boundaries are a thing."

Asa shook his head. "Uh-uh. Fucking you bent over my dining room table. I miss being inside you."

Zane flushed. "You were inside me last night."

"I know, it's been hours. I'm going to die," Asa intoned dramatically.

Zane snorted. "I highly—"

"Here you are," Bev said, holding Gage's laptop in front of her as if it was an offering.

Zane jumped to his feet, not missing the look of amusement on Asa's face as he clasped his hands together in front of his crotch. What an asshole. Asa stood much more languidly, taking the laptop from her and leaning down to kiss his mother's paper-thin cheek. "Thanks, Bev. I'll have this back to you in no time."

His mother's cheeks turned pink and she fluttered her lashes. "Please, call me Mom."

Un-fucking-believable.

FOURTEEN

ASA

Zane was unusually quiet when they left his mother's house, staring out the passenger side window once more. Asa was quickly learning that when Zane was truly hurting, he turned his anger inward. Asa wished Zane would just yell or scream or make hostile accusations. Anything was better than the silence that Asa knew meant Zane was tearing himself to shreds.

Asa had seen his share of shitty parents. Hell, until Thomas, he'd had two very shitty fucking parents himself, but Bev was different. Her method of torture was insidious. Death by a thousand cuts and her weapon was her sharp tongue. She wanted every barb to pierce just deep enough to wound but never enough to kill.

To people like Asa and Avi, there was no way to psychologically torture them. They lacked the capacity to be wounded emotionally. But not Zane. He tried to hide his soft heart behind biting words and dark humor, but there was no masking the pain in his eyes and that was what made Asa fear for Bev's safety. Zane was his. He belonged to him. *With* him. Forever. That meant protecting him with extreme prejudice, even if the attacker was Zane's own mother. Maybe especially so.

But Thomas would never approve of Asa taking matters into his own hands with Beverly Scott, and he didn't think 'it was a wedding present' would be a valid excuse for unaliving the woman, no matter how odious she was. But she was definitely not invited to the wedding. He'd have her dragged out of there in cuffs if he had to.

"Where are we going now?" Zane finally asked, bursting the bubble of tense silence.

"My brother, Atticus, has his research facility nearby. I can clone the hard drive from there and then we can have a courier return the laptop to your mother."

Zane nodded. "What do you think Calliope will find on Gage's computer?" he asked, voice dull.

Asa knew what he was asking. Would they find out his brother was murdered or that he took his own life? But Asa knew the truth. It didn't matter. There was no answer that would bring Zane any real comfort. His brother was still dead either way.

"What do *you* think she'll find?" Asa countered, hoping the question would let Zane vent some of the feelings he seemed to be bottling inside.

"Part of me hopes nothing. It would almost be better to never know why he's gone. There was a suicide note, but my mother never let me see it. Maybe Calliope will find that. But knowing that there was a game being played invalidates the authenticity of the note, no? Like, it could be fake, right? So, that doesn't matter, right?" Zane asked, voice cracking.

"I wish I knew the right thing to say in this situation," Asa said sincerely. "I can tell you that, if my brother died, there would never be a reason good enough to satisfy me. There would never be a way to stop the bleeding in here." He tapped his aching chest. "There would be no punishment harsh enough, no retaliation barbaric enough for the person who took him from me."

"But what if you found out the person who took him from you was him?" Zane asked, voice thick.

"I would probably go crazy," Asa answered honestly. "You're much stronger than me."

They pulled into a parking space outside of Atticus's fancy office, but before Asa could open the door, his phone pinged with a text message from Avi: **What's wrong?**

Of course, Avi had felt Asa's pain and panic over the idea of losing him. **I'm okay, just comforting a friend.**

Avi's response was immediate. **Comforting somebody? You? A friend? You mean your little reporter? That friend? I hear congrats are in order.**

Shit. The Mulvaney's gossip hotline never closed. **It's not like that.**

Avi: So, you didn't decide to wife up a reporter less than forty-eight hours after I left the state?

Okay, maybe it was a little like that. What could he say? Yes, he'd moved at lightning speed with Zane. Yes, he was planning on keeping him forever. Asa loved his brother more than anything in the whole world. He was the only person Asa had imagined ever being capable of loving. But what he had with Zane was more than that. So much more.

He looked at Zane and there was this gut punch of need, this primitive, animalistic knowledge that Zane belonged to him, was made for him, was meant to be loved and fucked and protected by him. He wanted to hurt him so he could heal him. He wanted to know that he was the only one Zane trusted to bend him without breaking him.

Avi: I'd ask if Dad's making you do this but I can feel how much you want him. I feel it so much it's distracting.

"Are you good?" Zane asked, frowning hard enough to cause tiny lines to form between his brows.

Asa gave him what he hoped was a reassuring smile. "Yeah, brother stuff. Two seconds."

Asa typed out his response and hit send, hoping Avi would be reasonable about this. **Listen, I need you to like him.**

He received three rage face emojis and then: **Not going to happen.**

Asa made a disgusted noise, earning another anxious glance from Zane. Asa didn't know why Avi was being so difficult about this, so he called his bluff. **Why do you even care? Do you think I don't know who's distracting you across the country? It's not Aiden.**

Three dots bounced for an inordinate amount of time considering the short response. **I brought him along so we can work.**

Asa snorted. **Work on what? His gag reflex? Don't forget, I feel what you feel, too, you know. You've wanted Felix since the moment you laid eyes on him. You can**

pretend all you want, but this is a two-way street. Be nice to my reporter and I'll be nice to your…intern.

This time, the dots started and stopped four times before his response arrived. **There's nothing going on between Felix and me. You're imagining things. I just like playing with him. He's so easy to rile up. Just because you've decided to tie us to a stranger doesn't mean I'm going to give up my bachelor status.**

Asa rolled his eyes. **Who even says bachelor anymore? Gotta go. Very busy.**

He didn't wait for his brother to text a response, just exited the car and slid his phone into his back pocket before coming around to extract Zane from the passenger seat.

The inside of the research facility was as sterile and boring as Atticus himself. It was all wood and chrome and linen-colored walls. It was like he'd put some kind of filter over the entire office that made even his employees look faded and drab.

The girl behind the desk raised her head, eyes widening when she saw Asa. "Um, hi. Are you looking for Atticus? I mean, Dr. Mulvaney? You're his brother, right? One of the twins?"

Asa hit her with a grin. "Yes, can you let him know I'm here? I just need to borrow his office for ten minutes."

The girl's perfectly manicured fingers fumbled over the phone keys and then she spoke into her little headset. When she glanced back up at him, she gave a smile, revealing a slightly crooked bottom tooth. "You can go straight back. His office is past this door on the left."

Asa nodded, taking Zane's hand and practically dragging him down the hall. Despite this being Atticus's office, he was still surprised to find Atticus in it. Asa stopped in the doorway so abruptly Zane ran into him. Atticus was usually in the lab. But he wasn't wearing his lab coat.

"What are you doing here?" Asa asked.

Atticus arched one imperious brow. "This is my office. What are you doing here?"

Asa tugged Zane inside and closed the door, handing over the slightly clunky laptop. "I need to clone this hard drive so I can get it to Calliope."

Atticus nodded, taking the computer and plugging it into the necessary equipment before opening the top and stopping short. "Password?"

Asa turned to Zane. "Do you know his password?"

Zane gave a humorless laugh. "His password was the same for everything: Borden1221."

"Borden?"

Zane nodded. "As in Lizzie. Axed her parents to death? Gage used to joke it was aspirational. He had a very dark sense of humor. He would have liked you."

Atticus typed in the password then gave a grunt of satisfaction that let Asa know it had worked.

After a few keystrokes, Atticus sat back. "This is going to take at least forty-five minutes. Have a seat."

"Don't you have to get back to the lab?"

Atticus looked Zane up and down. "It's my lunch hour."

Asa snorted. "Don't you usually spend that sexting your husband?"

"He's busy. Rush job," Atticus said, his gaze dropping to where Asa held Zane's hand. "This is him, huh?"

Asa sighed. "Zane, meet my brother, Atticus. Atticus, meet Zane."

There was a long moment of silence while Asa waited for Atticus to start ranting about responsibility and protecting the family, but he just sighed, then said, "Nice to meet you, Zane. Welcome to the circus. Hope you know how to walk a tightrope."

"I'm figuring it out as I go," Zane said.

"Just a word of advice. You should probably invest in a good foundation to hide my brother's…enthusiasm for you, before rumors start circulating that my brother here is an abusive partner. Also, if you betray us, they'll never find your body. My father has some powerful friends. Friends who would kill a reporter and make it look like an accident."

There it was. "Don't threaten him," Asa warned.

Atticus flicked his gaze to his brother then back to Zane. "He won't be able to help you. These people…they're looking at the big picture. The bigger plan for my father's research. They won't allow one person to ruin it. My father has a code, but they don't. It would be in your best interest to show them, sooner rather than later, that you're on our side."

"What do you mean?" Zane asked. "How?"

"You're a reporter, right?"

Zane shook his head. "I'm just a crime blogger."

"What crimes have you been blogging about?"

Zane's face paled, and his gaze darted to Asa, who asked, "Zane…what crimes have you been blogging about?"

"Crimes that seemed unrelated but might actually have a connection. Your father's crimes," Zane managed. "I never implied it was your father, just sort of tested the waters to see if others saw the pattern I did."

"Shit," Asa muttered.

"No. No, this is good," Atticus said, earning a surprised look from Asa. "I think you're right. About seeding the idea of a single crime-fighting vigilante."

"A what?" Zane said.

"Dad told you about that?" Asa asked.

"Told him about what?" Zane pressed, his confusion obvious.

"I told my father that having a reporter on our side—one who might be able to shape the public and their opinion about certain cases—could be beneficial to our cause."

"You want me to lie," Zane realized, voice dull.

"No. Exactly the opposite. We want you to tell the truth. Just not the whole truth," Atticus said.

"What does that even mean?" Zane asked.

Asa looked at Atticus, who gestured for him to go ahead. Asa turned to Zane. "It means the victims in these murders you're discussing are all very bad men. Some of the men we killed, the police knew were monsters. Like Noah's father, Wayne Holt. They knew he was a child rapist and predator, but they could never prove it in a court of law. We aren't bound by bureaucracy. Imagine if you just happened upon information about some of the unsolved murders in this town that showed the world who these men really were? Monsters."

Asa could see Zane's wheels starting to turn. "So, you want me to use my crime blog to out your victims and their crimes? Won't that bring more attention to your family?"

Atticus shook his head. "We're well insulated. We've got ourselves covered a dozen different ways. But we can't afford somebody asking questions about our father. Nobody can ever even whisper about Thomas Mulvaney being anything but the bleeding heart philanthropic billionaire the world loves. If you're covering these stories, if you're the authority on these possibly related crimes, if we're the ones controlling the narrative, it only helps. Thomas Mulvaney's journalist son-in-law would never delve into crimes that his own family committed. That would be crazy."

"So, you just want me to…expose their crimes?" Zane asked.

Atticus steepled his fingers together like some supervillain. "We want you to do what you do. Research the victims. Report your findings. Muse out loud about the possibility of a single vigilante killer. When your blog blows up—which it will the moment you become a Mulvaney—you can gently steer your audience in any direction you like. As long as that direction is away from us. Your new family."

"You should start a YouTube channel," Asa said with a grin. "Way more visibility." He pushed an errant curl from Zane's forehead. "People will love this nerdy, adorkable persona you have. Especially when you wear your glasses."

Zane flushed. "I don't really have a face for video."

Asa scoffed. "You're beautiful. Besides, I don't think you understand the amount of time you're about to spend in the public eye. We constantly have cameras on us. You will always have to be aware of your surroundings. We don't care if people track our day to day movements. They'll always try to catch Noah and Adam out at lunch or making out in their car. We live for that kind of press. As long as you're living our public life, you can look annoyed about the cameras being there but you need to tolerate them. Make sense?"

Zane gave a hesitant nod.

"When you're engaging in some non-public activities, you'll learn evasive measures," Atticus said. "Hopefully better than Asa did with you."

Asa gave him the finger.

"This is…a lot," Zane managed.

"This is being a Mulvaney," Atticus retorted. "Being the son-in-law of a rich billionaire is better than being dead. Even if you're married to *him*."

Asa gave Atticus another finger. "Can you get the cloned drive to the drop-off location and have a courier send the laptop back to Zane's mother?"

Atticus frowned. "Zane's mother?"

"Yeah, we think Zane's brother might have been involved in this case Dad's having me look into."

Atticus's brows hooked upward. "The game?"

Zane nodded, swallowing hard. "He was part of a suicide cluster at a different school, during a different year."

"Sorry to hear that," Atticus said, sounding sincere. "Write down the address and I'll have my receptionist get it back where it belongs. I'll drop the cloned drive on my way out when I leave for the garage."

"The garage," Zane gasped, as if suddenly remembering something. "I can finally ask about the garage. What's going on there? What's with all the kids going in and out all hours of the night? Your husband's obviously not running drugs, so what gives?"

Atticus glanced at Asa, who shrugged. "He's going to know it all soon enough."

Atticus looked at Zane, his tone rigid. "My husband takes in troubled kids who need a safe space. Those boys have created a…neighborhood watch. Bad people take advantage of good people who have limited options, whether that be residential status or finances, often both. My husband…discourages those people from preying on the vulnerable in his neighborhood."

Zane blinked. "Discourages them…"

"Yes."

"So, Jericho does what you all do," Zane said faintly. "He kills bad guys."

"It's what you do, too," Asa said gently. "You don't have to pick up a gun or a knife, but you're part of this family now, and you'll be expected to protect it, protect *us*, just as fiercely as we'll protect you."

Zane nodded, still looking a little dazed.

"And when Avi gets back, you're going to need protection," Atticus said. "Feel free to hide at our place."

Zane's startled gaze flicked back to Asa. "How long am I going to have to worry about your twin wanting me dead?"

Asa sighed. "Maybe a week? Maybe a day? With Avi, who knows. With any luck, there's a lethal twink fashionista keeping him distracted from any murderous impulses."

"That lethal twink fashionista is my brother-in-law," Atticus muttered.

"The heart wants what the heart wants," Asa intoned, earning an eye roll from his older brother. "Okay, we're leaving. I'll text Calliope that you'll drop off the hard drive at the pick up spot."

"Pick up spot?" Zane asked.

Asa nodded. "Yeah, it's where we drop stuff for Calliope to retrieve."

Zane frowned. "Why not just have her come get it? Or take it to her?"

"We've never met Calliope face to face," Asa said.

"But you've met her son?" Zane countered. "Right? Dimitri is her son?"

Asa looked to Atticus. "Yeah…he is. Does this mean we can meet Calliope now? Like, do we want that? I don't know how I feel about seeing the woman behind the curtain."

Atticus rolled his eyes. "That's a crisis for another day. Let's just figure out the game and keep your fiancé alive long enough for you to make an honest man of him."

Zane looked at Asa, his expression pleading. "I need a nap."

Asa flung an arm around Zane's shoulders, pulling him in to drop a kiss on his curls. "I got you, Lois. I got you."

FIFTEEN

ZANE

Zane blinked himself awake, stretching for longer than necessary before flopping onto his back and staring up at the ceiling above. Asa's bed was much more luxurious when Zane wasn't cuffed to the headboard. He wasn't sure how long he'd slept, but the moonlight shining through the window bisected the otherwise darkened room.

He dragged himself into a sitting position and frowned at the pile of clothes folded neatly on the edge of the bed. They were his clothes. From his apartment. Had Asa gone and retrieved Zane's clothes while he was sleeping? His heart did that funny thing it did whenever Asa did something thoughtful. Which was surprisingly often for a psychopath who liked hunting his bedmates instead of seducing them.

Had Thomas taught them to be this attentive? Was it all part of the…curriculum? Maybe every man should be forced to take Thomas Mulvaney's *How to Be a Human* class. He should send his future father-in-law a fruit basket.

The man brought you clothes, not a kidney. Is the bar really that low, Zaney?

Zane rolled his eyes. "Yeah, well, you can blame Mom for that, too. Now, if you'll excuse me, I'm gonna go into his apartment-size bathroom and make use of his fancy ass shower. You're not invited," he said out loud to the empty room.

Once under the water, Zane realized Asa had also brought his soap and shampoo. Zane must have been tired. He'd slept through Asa's movements throughout the bedroom. He ignored his own soap, instead lathering up with Asa's expensive spicy body wash. There was just something about wrapping himself in Asa's scent that made this whole situation feel more real and less like some kind of fever dream.

He leaned his forehead against the cold tiles, letting the jets beat against his skin. If this was a dream, Zane had no interest in waking up. He'd never been impulsive, not until Asa. Now, he was just allowing himself to be swept along with the tide of the Mulvaney family's chaotic existence, and he had never been more at peace.

Asa had said he should start a YouTube channel to really start dissecting the murders. The murders his own family committed. Now, Zane's family, too. There was an evil sort of genius behind the plan. It wasn't like Zane would be lying. He wasn't making up the crimes the victims had committed. The people they'd killed had deserved it.

The truth was, the Mulvaneys weren't killers, they were karma. And Zane could be part of the problem or part of the solution. Being part of the solution meant having the career he'd always dreamed of, a man he couldn't fathom ever having had a shot with, and a life out of a fucking fairy tale. And he was on the right side of history. There was no downside.

The idea of being in front of a camera was a little intimidating—he definitely had a face for radio—but it wasn't like Zane wasn't used to criticism. His mother had made sure of that. He snorted at the thought as he turned off the water and stepped from the shower to towel off before throwing on a t-shirt and joggers.

Zane wandered from the room, listening for sounds of Asa as he jogged down the stairs. Living in these houses was a constant game of Marco Polo. He tilted his head, his pulse tripping as he caught the sound of Asa's voice and followed it.

He was in his office. It sounded like he was talking actual business this time, something about budgets and time restraints. It was weird to hear Asa talking about mundane things like construction costs, like he was just another guy and not…well, a Mulvaney.

When Zane stuck his head around the corner, his dick instantly stirred. Asa was reclined in his big, black leather chair, his hair askew like he'd been raking his hands through it. He was also dressed casually in a vee neck t-shirt that showed off just the barest hint of his ink. He was so goddamn sexy, it took Zane's breath away.

Asa caught him looking and gave him a slow smirk that shot through Zane like lightning, then crooked his finger, beckoning him closer. Zane followed without thought.

Once he was in reach, Asa's hand snagged him, dragging him down into his lap. He continued his conversation without skipping a beat.

"Listen, Gil. It's too late. The plans are already nailed down. You and the board approved them. Budgets have been set, people have been contracted. The foundations poured. You're beating a dead horse, buddy," Asa said, his voice rich and smooth, his tone unbothered.

Zane couldn't say the same about the other man. He couldn't make out his words, but he definitely did not appreciate Asa's candor. Zane let his head fall back against Asa's shoulder, content to just feel the warmth of his body heat seeping through the thin layers of fabric separating them.

Asa was not content with that, it seemed. Zane sucked in a sharp breath as his free hand snaked beneath the waistband of his pants, making an appreciative sound when he realized Zane wasn't wearing any underwear. He bit off a moan as his fist closed around his soft cock, teasing him until he hardened in his hand.

"If you didn't like the design, the time to bring that up would have been a year ago. You know, when the board voted on the design," Asa said, rubbing his thumb over Zane's slit, gathering the precum there and smearing it over the head in a motion that had pulses of light flashing behind his lids and a moan rising in his throat.

He couldn't help but press himself back against Asa's now obvious erection as the man continued to shout on the other end of the phone. Asa clamped his teeth down on Zane's ear, forcing him to bite his lower lip to keep from crying out. How was he so fucking composed all the time? Why was it so hot?

Asa squeezed the phone between his cheek and his shoulder, nudging Zane to lift up, then hooking his thumbs in Zane's pants and tugging them down before doing the same to his own like it was the most normal thing in the world. When they were both exposed, he pulled Zane back against him, slowly rocking his hips so that his cock worked into the furrow between Zane's cheeks. Oh, fuck. He was going to have his own teeth marks permanently imbedded in his lower lip if Asa didn't stop torturing him.

"That's between you and Jensen, Gil. You approved the building and material costs. You can't decide you want to change the design once the project is under way just to save a few bucks. This isn't your personal residence, it's a fucking high-rise."

Zane nodded as if agreeing with him as he continued to grind himself against Asa, the catch of skin on skin making him crazy and desperate.

Asa spun his chair just enough to reach his top drawer and pulled what looked like hand cream from inside, pumping some into his hand before working it between their bodies. Zane shifted, feeling Asa slicking up his cock and then working the rest into his crease. Was he really doing this?

Asa cut the other man off mid-rant. "Gil, hang on for one second. I just have to deal with an urgent matter."

Zane watched as Asa hit mute on his cell phone and set it on the desk. "Lift up. You know what I want." Zane's insides shivered at his low rumble, an entirely different Asa than just seconds ago. "You're going to fuck yourself on my cock while you get yourself off. And you're going to do it without making a single sound or being handcuffed to the radiator will feel like a vacation. Understand?"

"Yes," Zane managed, breathless.

Asa took his mouth in a dirty kiss. "Good boy."

Before Zane could even process his words, Asa forced his way into Zane's body, robbing him of breath, his mouth falling open in a silent cry as his insides rearranged themselves to accommodate him. He was so fucking huge. Tears slid down his cheeks at the searing burn, but his cock was flushed and aching, and he shifted, trying to get Asa even deeper.

Asa arranged Zane so he had leverage to do as Asa requested, then picked up his phone, giving Zane a firm stare that made goosebumps erupt along his skin. "What are you waiting for?" he asked. "Oh, and you better make sure we both come before this phone call ends or else…"

Or else what?

There was no time to ask. Asa picked up his phone and unmuted the call. "Sorry about that. Where were we? Right, you hate the design." He led Zane's hand back to his cock as if reminding him what was expected of him.

Zane shifted, biting off a groan as Asa's cock shifted inside him. He had to forget about the phone call, about Asa's casual tone and his dismissive demeanor, and focus on the scent of him and the way the words he spoke puffed against his skin and the burn of his thighs as he worked Asa's cock.

Asa never broke. His voice never cracked, his breathing never increased. His affect remained bored as he discussed figures and design details, but his other hand roamed, sliding up under Zane's shirt to play with his nipples then down over his belly, his fingers teasing over his inner thighs, tugging at his balls until Zane's whole being felt like a live wire, every touch sending shocks of pleasure along his body.

When Asa shifted in his seat, forcing himself impossibly deeper, Zane couldn't help the desperate low groan that escaped. Asa smirked, slapping his hand over Zane's mouth. "What was that, Gil? No, that was just one of the housekeepers. She's emptying my trash can." Asa knocked Zane's hand out of the way, and Zane practically wept with relief as he began to jerk him off with a singular purpose until he was fucking up into Asa's hand and then back down onto his cock. He was so fucking close, but he had no idea if Asa was into this or not. He was giving him literally nothing to go on.

"I don't compromise. Ever. You hired me for my experience, my expertise, and my style. If you wanted to design your own building, you should have found a different architect."

Zane's gaze snagged on a black glass orb in the corner of the ceiling. A camera. Asa had said there were cameras everywhere in the house. Somewhere, there was a digital file recording them together. What did they look like together? Maybe Asa would show him the film?

Zane whimpered as Asa's hand worked him faster. Did he have any idea how close Zane was to falling over that edge? Too close. In another second, it would be out of his hands.

"That's just how it is, Gil. No need to get yourself all

worked up about it. This isn't emotional, it's business."

Asa's mouth found Zane's throat, licking and sucking a trail up to his jaw as he held his phone away so Gil wouldn't catch on to their game. Asa bit down hard on Zane's already bruised shoulder, right through his t-shirt, maybe even abusing the same marks. That was it; Zane was coming, his release spilling over Asa's hand. He didn't stop stroking him, though, even when he was squirming with discomfort and fighting to keep quiet.

"I am saying it. You're being irrational. Emotional. You've been screaming this entire conversation."

The man began to really let loose, his voice an almost guttural roar. That was when Asa released Zane's cock, his arm locking around his waist like an iron bar, his hips grinding up against him. Then Zane could feel his cock throbbing as he spilled within him. He dropped two delicate kisses onto the teeth marks he'd left, then on his neck.

This was so Asa. Two people. Two personalities. One for the public and one just for Zane. Nobody else got to see Asa as he truly was. Nobody. Except him. That alone was worth any discomfort, any risk, any…anything.

"Gil, why don't you take some time to get yourself together and then we'll talk about it on Monday before the board? See you then."

He didn't give Gil a chance to answer, instead just hitting the end button and dropping his phone on the desk to wrap both arms around Zane. "Mm, that was hot, as always. Is this what marriage is going to be like?"

"I fucking hope so," Zane said, deflating against him. Asa

pulled Zane's t-shirt away from his shoulder to lick and suck at the mark he'd left.

"Did you have a good nap?" Asa asked against his skin.

"Yeah, the best. But now, I'm hungry. You need to feed me."

"Your wish is my command. Do you want me to cook?" Asa said with a flourish of his hand.

"You can cook?" Zane asked, genuinely shocked.

Asa grinned. "I'm exceptional with knives."

"Yeah, but that doesn't mean you can cook," Zane said around a laugh. "Thanks for going to get my clothes."

"You're welcome. But now, for the bad news."

Zane's heart sank. "Bad news? What bad news?"

Asa kissed his ear again. "In about ten seconds, you're going to have to stand up and things are going to be real messy."

Zane rolled his eyes. "Oh, my God. Shut up."

Zane's leg bounced nervously the entire way to Thomas's house. This was what they'd been waiting for. A lead. Finally. Calliope had called that morning and had laid the good news/bad news situation on them. The bad news was that she had spoken to Jagger, who had let her know that any computers collected from the victims had been returned to their parents, and that she couldn't find anymore obvious suicide clusters, either at school or in other large social groups. At least, none that didn't have to do with cults or politics. The good news, she said, was that she had something but had refused to say what without a field trip to the mansion. She said it was easier to show them what she found on the big screen in the war room, but Asa said not to be surprised to find they were being lured into an ambush.

The last forty-eight hours had flown by with very little to show for it with the exception of some new bruises for Zane. During the day, they'd spent hours researching everything they could about games like this, where they originated, how they were played, who played them, who built them, who was responsible. But there was nothing.

Profiling the players was proving much harder than he imagined as well. All he could say was they were all popular, all at the top of their game, all killing it when it came to their college years. It wasn't hard to imagine somebody having a grudge against those kinds of people.

Their nights were much more interesting. Asa liked playing games, too. Games of the role playing kind. House. Doctor. Captor versus captive. Predator versus prey. He was very inventive and he really didn't have a line he wouldn't cross if Zane let him. And Zane found he had little interest in refusing Asa anything.

The hardest part of their relationship was enduring the strange looks he received whenever he left the house covered in Asa's bruises. Those looks varied from pity to disgust to even lascivious from those in the know. Zane had finally made Asa stop at the drug store so he could buy makeup to conceal the evidence of his enthusiasm, but Asa had pouted about it for a solid hour. He was very proud of those marks. Zane was, too, but Atticus was right. At some point, rumors would start that wouldn't paint Asa or the Mulvaneys in a good light. He didn't want that.

When they entered the war room, Zane stopped short. Asa had been right. It was an ambush. The entire family waited inside. Nobody looked particularly threatening, but this many Mulvaneys in one room felt a lot like they were about to tie him to the conference room table and offer him up as some kind of sacrifice.

Atticus and Jericho were there, August and Lucas, Adam and Noah. Even the gambling brother, Archer. It was Archer who caught and held Zane's attention. He sat slumped in his seat, clothing rumpled, wearing sunglasses in the dim lighting of the room. He had at least two days of beard growth on his chin and his wavy hair was pulled back off his face in a bun that sat askew on the top of his head.

"Is he okay?" Zane asked.

"We're not entirely sure he's even alive," August said drolly. "It's possible he's just been well-preserved by all the alcohol in his system."

Adam snickered. "Yeah, sometimes, I think Dad just pulls a *Weekend at Bernie's* and stages him in different positions so the public doesn't realize he's dead. Bad for optics."

Archer didn't speak but did raise his middle finger in the general direction of his brothers. Before anyone else could retaliate, Thomas swept in wearing a pair of perfectly tailored gray pants and a black sweater that hugged his form and made those not related to him stare just a smidge too long.

Zane tried not to be obvious, but when Asa pinched his side, he forced himself to drag his gaze away. It wasn't his fault Thomas Mulvaney was a snack. Asa led him to the two chairs at the end of the table, even holding his out for him. The rest of the family took notice.

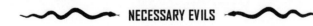

"We're all here, Calliope. What have you got?" Thomas asked. "And be quick, please. I have a meeting in an hour at the club."

"No, 'hi Calliope.' 'How are you, Calliope?' Just chop-chop," Calliope muttered.

"Hello, Calliope, how are you?" Thomas said, his voice dripping with impatience.

"Don't humor me," she said primly before her voice became all business. "Okay, I found something. Well, I think I've found something. Maybe."

"Which is...?" Asa asked, irritation creeping into his tone. Zane gave him a look. They didn't need to get on Calliope's bad side.

"Okay, so I've been scouring Gage's computer for two days for anything out of place and there was literally nothing. So then I started thinking about how that could be. I mean, obviously, there could have never been anything there, but I had to start thinking like a person who knew something had once been there."

"Are you following any of this?" Zane asked under his breath.

"No, but she'll get to the point eventually," Asa said.

"So then I thought about self-destructing emails which, before you ask, are exactly what they sound like, emails that delete themselves after a set amount of time."

"But if they self-destruct, how do you find them?" Noah asked.

"In the hands of lesser people, you don't, but *moi*, supreme goddess of the interwebs, has a program that allows me to at least find the dates that these emails were received, even if there's no way to know what was in said email. When I ran the program on your brother's system, I found a series of destructed emails. I then cross-referenced those dates with any downloads—"

"Good luck making that meeting, Dad," Adam muttered.

"You want to do this yourself?" Calliope asked. "I work pro-bono, pal. I'm only here because I want to be. If you think somebody else can do a better job—"

"I'm sorry, jeez," Adam said, sounding much younger than Zane knew him to be.

"Stop making people hate you," Noah murmured. "Please go on, Calliope."

"I found this." A picture of Gage popped up on the screen. A selfie taken from a webcam. Zane's pulse quickened, though he couldn't say why. There was nothing overtly ominous about the photo. "That's my brother. It looks like a selfie. Why is that weird?"

"Well, one, because somebody sent that photo to him in one of those embedded emails."

"How do you know that?" August asked.

"Because there was a file embedded in it that I don't think he would have had access to."

Lucas shifted, leaning forward to prop his elbows on the

desk. “What kind of file?”

“This.”

A screen appeared. It was a low budget graphic like something out of an old school nineties video game. There was a man with a large gaping mouth repeatedly making an evil laugh. Above the screen, it said **DO YOU WANT TO PLAY?** with a yes or no button flashing in green and red boxes.

That uneasy feeling was turning into a bugs crawling beneath his skin feeling. He couldn’t tear his eyes away from the man and the mechanical laughter leaving his mouth. There was something not right about all of this. Did nobody else see it?

“Is this some kind of retro thing? This is the second bad guy website where it looks like some kind of Atari throwback,” Adam said.

“The dark net is fond of old school,” Calliope quipped.

“Did you click the button when you first saw this?” Atticus asked. “Do you know what happens next?”

“No,” Calliope said. “I wasn’t sure I’d get another opportunity once I did. Should I?”

There was a long pause as the group exchanged worried glances before all looking to Thomas.

“Do it,” Thomas said.

Calliope’s mouse moved to the button, then clicked **yes**.

The screen exploded into a thousand bricks and then the words **GAME OVER** formed in the rubble. Then the screen went black.

“Well, that was anticlimactic,” Jericho said, leaning back and scrubbing his hands over his face before asking,

"Anybody want to go get lunch? I'm starving."

Atticus rolled his eyes. "You're always starving."

"We have to get back to the girls," August said. "They'll be waking from their nap soon."

Suddenly, three words appeared.

WHO ARE YOU?

But nobody seemed to notice. "Uh, guys?" Zane said.

When they looked at him, he pointed at the words on the screen, his heartbeat pounding in his ears.

A text box now blinked on the screen.

"Um, what do I do?" Calliope asked.

Zane shifted in his seat, swallowing audibly, before saying, "Tell them you're my brother."

He pulled one of the water bottles from the bar and twisted off the cap as Calliope typed in Gage's name and hit enter. The response was instantaneous.

LIE. PLAYER SELF-TERMINATED. WHO ARE YOU?

Self-terminated. What the fuck? This was obviously not an if/then prompt from a computer program. They were speaking to a real person hiding on the other side of the screen.

"We need to keep him talking," Calliope muttered, nails clacking as her fingers flew over the keys. "He's masking his IP address, bouncing it off a million different routers, but if you can keep him talking, I might be able to trace it back. Give me questions."

Zane's leg began to bounce beneath the conference room table as he rubbed his sweaty palms on his jeans.

"Oh," Noah said excitedly, hand waving. "Tell them you want to play the game."

Calliope did as suggested.

YOU DON'T VOLUNTEER FOR THE GAME. THE GAME FINDS YOU.

"Jesus, dramatic much?" Adam said.

Calliope gasped, then snapped, "Oh, hell no."

"What? What's wrong?"

YOU'LL NEVER FIND ME. BUT I CAN FIND YOU.

Zane knew he wasn't talking directly to him but it felt like it. "What's happening?"

"The fucker is trying to back-hack me. Keep asking questions."

Zane's heart was in a vise grip. "Ask why the game found my brother."

Asa snagged his hand beneath the table as the question appeared in the box.

THE HANDLER CHOOSES HIS PLAYERS. NOT THE GAME MASTER.

Calliope didn't wait for input before typing: **You're the game master?**

I AM.

No hesitation. No fear. Almost cocky. Who was this person? What the fuck was a game master? Like the Hunger Games? Was that somehow the point of the game? Players cannibalizing themselves? None of this made any fucking sense.

"Why is this person so willing to answer your questions?" Zane asked the room.

"Because he knows she'll never find him," Lucas said somberly.

"That's what he thinks," Calliope muttered under her breath.

Lucas's response was an icy shock, like being doused in cold water. Somehow, no matter how grim, some part of Zane always imagined there would eventually be an answer. But maybe not. Maybe there truly never would be any closure. Maybe Zane was doomed to forever wonder why his brother did what he did. Why did he play the game? What was the final straw? Why did he leave him behind?

"What does the game master do?" Noah asked, watching as the question appeared in the box.

I ENSURE PLAYERS ADHERE TO THE RULES.

"Nothing fucking ominous about that," Archer rasped, startling Zane, who sat beside him.

It really was like having the dead speak directly in his ear.

"Ask what happens when players don't adhere to the rules, Calliope," Thomas said.

PLAYERS ARE TERMINATED.

"And if they win?" August asked.

PLAYERS ARE TERMINATED.

Zane felt sick. "So, there's no winning the game? This is all some sick fucking way to get off on forcing people to self-harm?"

Calliope ignored Zane's outburst, typing only: **So, you can't win the game?**

PLAYERS ARE PAWNS. HANDLERS ARE PLAYERS. I'M THE GAME MASTER. YOUR TIME IS UP.

Zane stared at the blinking cursor on the now black screen. "What the fuck?"

"Tell me you got a location, Calliope?"

Calliope huffed out a breath. "I got nothing. But, on the

bright side, I don't think he did either."

"So, we're back at square one?" Zane managed.

August shook his head. "Not exactly. We know there's a game. We know the players are picked ahead of time. We know the players are dead the minute they start playing the game. We know the handlers are the real players, which means the handlers are just as culpable as the game master. They're breadcrumbs, but we've found more with less."

"There's something else," Lucas said. "And I think August and I can help."

"What's that?"

Lucas looked to August, then to Zane. "The game master said the handler picks the players. We know that every five or so years, players from our school and Henley are picked and that they all have similar backgrounds. We can work backwards. If we profile the players, we can profile the handler. If we can profile the handler, we can find him. Find him, we flip him and get the game master."

"Thomas suggested profiling the victims a few days ago, but there's so little to go on?"

"I also suggested you contact Lucas," Thomas pointed out, looking at Zane like a disappointed father.

Oh, yeah. The truth was, he and Asa had spent far too much time wrapped up in each other and not enough wrapped up in the case, but in Zane's defense, playing kinky games with Asa was far more fun than learning his brother might have been taken from him for such a stupid reason.

"That's what we do," August said, gesturing between him and Lucas. "He's a profiler. I'm an expert in statistics

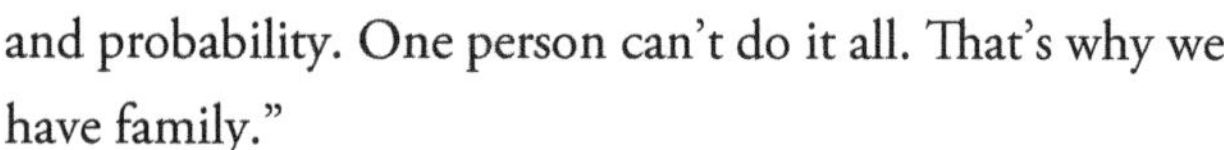

and probability. One person can't do it all. That's why we have family."

"So, what do *we* do?" Zane said.

"Track down the player who lived," Calliope said. "I might have a lead on him. It's tiny, but it can't hurt."

"Send me what you've got, Calliope," Asa said. "Zane and I will check it out."

It wasn't much to go on, but it gave Zane something to cling to. And right then, he really needed something—anything. Fuck.

SIXTEEN

ASA

Calliope's lead wasn't so much a lead as a hunch. Eric Sievers' mother was a real estate agent. Properties bought and sold quickly in the current real estate market, yet two properties had sat vacant for far longer than they should have. Maybe David had been wrong? Maybe his parents knew exactly where he was. Who wouldn't help their son hide from a murderer?

It was possible there was something unmarketable about the homes, but when Calliope had called Sievers' mother and posed as a potential buyer, she'd agreed to show the house on Maple but said the one on Bliss was under renovations. Now, sitting across the street from the craftsman-style home, it was clear no external renovations were under way.

There was no indication of any interior design changes either. No workers, no supplies stacked outside the house. Maybe the workers were off that day, but Asa wasn't buying it. The two-story home with its white paint, black shutters, and red door was meticulous. There wasn't so much as a blade of grass out of place.

The house was most of middle-class America's wet dream. There was no way it would have stayed empty on the market like this for as long as it had, not even for renovations. Through the binoculars Asa held, all was still on the inside—not that he could see much through the obscured windows.

"I think Calliope's right," Asa said. "I think this is where we'll find him."

"Why do you say that?" Zane asked, glancing back at him with interest.

"There are only curtains on the downstairs windows and no blinds. Who leaves curtains behind when they move?"

"People in a hurry?" Zane said with a shrug. "I don't think that's quite the clue you think it is."

Asa handed Zane the binoculars. "Look closer. The house is for sale but there's no 'for sale' sign. There's no lock box on the door. Why would a realtor not want a sign? Why would they not want other realtors to show the house? Because her kid is hiding in there."

"Yeah, maybe."

Asa shrugged. "Maybe not, but I think we should go check it out."

There was no reason to wait. It wasn't like this Eric kid was a fugitive. He was just a scared college kid hiding out from ghosts.

"Go check it out…" Zane echoed.

Asa nodded. "Yeah. Let's go around back and see if we

can look in the windows."

"What if there are cameras?"

Asa rolled his eyes. "There aren't. We'd see them."

Zane's hand flailed. "What if he sees us around the back and tries to bolt out the front?"

Okay, that was a fair point. "Right. You go around back and I'll stay at the front door just in case."

Zane gave him a hard look, pushing his glasses up the bridge of his nose. "What if he has a gun?"

Asa chuckled at the tiny frown lines between Zane's brows. "Do you want me to go around back and you go to the front door?"

Zane appeared to mull it over, then sighed. "No. I'll go around back. But if you hear a gunshot, tell my mother I died a hero."

Asa smirked. "You're surprisingly dramatic."

Zane tilted his head, giving Asa a pissy look. "You made me pretend to be an inmate trading sex for favors from a guard last night. I'm not the dramatic one."

Asa's grin was feral. "*Made* you, huh? I don't know, those sounds you made while you were riding me last night were pretty dramatic."

Zane flushed to the tips of his ears. God, he was fun to play with. He was so sexy, so open, so responsive. So willing to dive headfirst into whatever insane scenario Asa could make up. He'd yet to get him in his dungeon, but only because he was having far too much fun living out his fantasies with a person he actually enjoyed spending time with, even with their clothes on.

The pain that felt like fish hooks catching in his skin whenever Avi wasn't around was just a dull ache when he was with Zane, more irritating than excruciating. Was that because Avi was also distracted with whatever kill they were working? Or was Avi distracted with something else entirely? With *someone* else. Someone like Felix. Why didn't that bother Asa more?

"Should we wait until dark?" Zane asked.

"People pay more attention when it's dark outside. This Eric kid will be on high alert once the sun goes down. If you just look like you belong, nobody questions you."

Asa hopped from the car before Zane could find another reason why they shouldn't do what they were doing. He walked around, opened the passenger door, and helped Zane up from his seat. Asa wasn't too worried about being recognized, but he wore a ball cap anyway. Just in case.

Once they walked up the steps, Asa nudged Zane to walk around the side of the house, listening to the faint squeak of hinges as Zane opened a gate to the backyard. Asa was a little disappointed when no shadow moved behind the curtains until he heard Zane let out a sort of cut-off yelp.

Asa forced himself to walk until he was out of sight of the passing cars, then bolted through the gate only to run directly into Zane's back. He appeared to have found Eric enjoying the sunny weather by the pool. He was shirtless, wearing only a black and red bathing suit. He was also brandishing a barbeque fork.

"—here to hurt you," Zane was saying, hands up where Eric can see them.

"Who the fuck sent you?" Eric asked in a stage whisper, poking the air with his makeshift weapon.

"Nobody sent us. We need your help," Zane said, keeping his voice calm.

Asa didn't intervene, but he did keep himself plastered against Zane's back, ready to step in if he had to. But he wanted to see how Zane fared under pressure. Though, he'd had Jericho's gun to his head and had been cold as a cucumber. Maybe it was an act, or maybe this was. Zane was a complicated guy.

"My help?" Eric asked. "Who are you?"

Zane glanced back at Asa, who nodded for him to keep going. Zane gave a stilted nod in return. "My name is Zane Scott. My brother played the game."

There was no missing the shock of recognition in the boy's there-and-gone wide-eyed response. It was quickly replaced with wariness. "What game?" he asked, clearly knowing the answer.

"*The* game. The game that ended his life," Zane said.

Eric's hand trembled at Zane's words. "Why should I believe you?"

"Why would we lie? Do you think we'd just wander into your backyard in broad daylight if we were? My brother's name was Gage. He wasn't suicidal. He died anyway. I'm just looking for answers."

Eric's gaze darted back and forth between the two of them. Asa didn't blame him for being nervous. The game master was enough to creep out anybody who had the ability to be uneasy. Asa just wasn't one of those people. To him, this game master guy sounded desperate, like he was trying too hard to be the villain. But then, Asa never had to work hard to be the bad guy. He was born that way.

"You can keep the meat fork if it makes you feel safer," Asa reasoned. "But nobody followed us. We won't tell anybody where you are. If you help us, we can find the game master and you can get your life back," Asa offered.

Eric's face paled beneath his golden tan. "You can't end the game. The game ends when you die."

"How do you know that?" Zane asked, gesturing towards the chairs under the awning of the patio before pulling one out and carefully sitting down so as not to spook their host. Eric hesitantly did the same, white-knuckling the meat fork as he sat. Asa opted to stand, leaning against the post so he had eyes on both the boys and the back gate. Just in case.

"How do you know the end of the game is your death?" Zane asked again.

"Other than my fellow students dropping like flies?" Eric asked bitterly.

Zane winced. "Yeah, other than that."

"It started with my marketing class," Eric said, as if that made perfect sense. "And this."

He turned his forearm over to reveal faint lines from what were obviously healing cuts. Someone had carved *I'm already dead* into his skin. "I only vaguely remember doing it."

"You did that to yourself?"

"Yeah, with a piece of glass. I puke at the sight of blood. I would have never done this to myself voluntarily."

"You're saying somebody made you do this to yourself?"

Zane asked. "Like you were drugged? Or like hypnosis?"

Eric gripped the meat fork's handle with both hands, like he needed something concrete to hold on to. "That's what I thought at first, too. Drugs. Hypnosis. But then I remembered my marketing class. Lesson one: Advertising. Chapter one: Subliminal messaging."

"Like splicing porn into kid's movies in *Fight Club*?" Asa asked, earning an exasperated look from Zane.

Eric nodded solemnly. "Theoretically, yeah. The videos my handler had me watch didn't start out disturbing, but by the fourth one, I would get sick watching things that appeared perfectly innocent. I was depressed, distracted, paranoid. In-between the videos were activities, some ridiculous, like drawing a purple cat on a piece of paper or drawing a red X on the back of your hand. But that was when I realized they were driving home that they could always see us. That they were always watching."

"They had access to your camera?" Zane clarified.

"My webcam, my phone cam, but it went further than that. The seventh task was to go to a specific train track at a specific time and lie down on the tracks. We had to set a stopwatch and stay there until the alarm went off, even if the train was coming. I'd decided to blow it off and go to a party instead. That was when the messages started coming."

Zane leaned in, expression equal parts fascinated and horrified. "What did they say?"

"First, it was just my handler letting me know they could see me and that they knew I wasn't completing the task as required. When I ignored them, the pictures started.

Pictures of my mom, my dad, my sisters. Pictures from mall cameras and from their phones, their security feeds, businesses, traffic cams. I got the point. I hauled ass to the tracks and I did what they wanted."

"What happened?" Asa asked.

"I almost got run over by a fucking train," Eric said, breathless, like he was reliving the moment. "When I got back, there was another video and a warning to never ignore my handler or I would be punished. It was after that video when I woke up to the cuts on my arm."

"You think the message was in the video?" Asa said.

Eric nodded. "I know it was. I couldn't go back and check the past videos because they self-destruct after viewing. So, I screen-recorded the next one they sent on my cell phone and took the file to my friend, who helped me go frame by frame, and what we found was dark shit. 'Kill yourself. Do it. You're a burden to your family. Do it. Now. End it. End it all. Slit your wrists. Hang yourself.' It was relentless. And that was just one video."

Zane looked like he was going to be sick. "Jesus."

Eric grimaced. "Yeah. That was when I realized the only end is death. Having this carved into my arm would make any cop not even question my suicide. Clearly, I was self-harming. I had suicidal tendencies. Then other tasks began to make sense. Writing letters to my family, writing my eulogy, writing down my deepest fears. When you add that up, it looks like I took my own life."

"And that was when you ran?" Asa asked.

Eric shook his head. "No. That was when the handler

tried to kill me himself."

"You've seen him? This handler?" Asa asked, walking closer, dropping his hands onto Zane's shoulders. Zane leaned back like he just needed to be closer to Asa. Maybe he did. This must be a lot. Somebody had psychologically tortured his brother to death.

"Not enough to pick him out of a line-up. He tried to run me over with his car. Or with *a* car. I doubt it was his."

"What can you tell us?" Zane asked.

"He was in an old Buick. Like the big ones that old people drive. It was, like, a gold color. He was fat. Like, his face was super round and he wore those serial killer glasses."

Zane looked over his shoulder at Asa, then back at Eric. "Serial killer glasses?"

Eric looked at them like they were stupid. "Yeah, you know, like those seventies black-frame glasses. Thick. Ugly."

"Can you remember what kind of hair he had?"

Eric shook his head. "He was wearing a hat. Not like yours." He pointed to Asa's cap. "Like one of those edgelord neckbeard types."

Asa frowned. "What?"

Zane laughed. "Um, the kind of guys who sit around posting on Reddit about how women don't date nice guys while calling them bitches and other not-very-nice names."

"Incels," Asa said, understanding dawning. "Got it."

"How did you end up here?" Zane asked.

"I couldn't go home. So, I called my dad's burner phone."

Asa dropped down into the chair between Eric and Zane. "Your dad is a professor. Why does he have a burner phone?"

"My dad teaches math at a community college, and my mom sells real estate. They have six kids. My dad has a… side business."

"Your college professor dad is a drug dealer?" Zane clarified.

Eric's shoulders went up, his expression guarded. "Just weed and shrooms mostly. Sometimes, some E. It's just so he can take care of us. He's not, like, selling to little kids and shit."

"We're not judging," Zane promised. "How did you explain this to your father?"

"Carefully. He talked to my mom away from the house and any technology since we had no idea how far their reach extended. My parents can be relentless assholes, but they don't want me to die. It took me a whole day to get to this house and feel like there was nobody following me."

"You know you can't hide out forever," Zane said.

Eric's chin thrust forward. "Well, the alternative is they kill me. They know I recorded the video. I violated the rules. I'm as good as dead if they find me."

"Did your father, by any chance, give you a burner phone to keep here?" Asa asked.

Eric hesitated, then nodded.

Asa handed over his own burner phone. "Put your information in there. I'll let you know when this is over."

When Eric just stared at the phone, Zane said, "You can trust us. I promise. We're going to get you out of this."

Eric's weary gaze looked back and forth between the two of them, then he finally grabbed the phone and put in the number, looking like he was going to vomit into the gardenia bush beside the porch.

Zane stood, and Asa gave Eric one final nod, before they left the way they came. They were a block away from the house when Zane lost it, punching Asa's dashboard with such force that he hit the button to disconnect the airbag, causing it to deploy directly into his face.

Asa let him yell and scream and punch the dashboard until his knuckles were bleeding and his voice was raw. "This is a game," he said, voice cracking. "My brother's life was a game to them. Do you know what living with my parents was like? Not just for me but for him? I was invisible and it sucked, but their love for him was so conditional. Get an A, get affection. Get a B- and Mom gives you the silent treatment for a week. To think that while he was watching those videos, somebody was driving home his worst fears about himself, brainwashing him… making him think nobody wanted him…" Tears flowed down Zane's cheeks but he brushed them away angrily. "I want these fuckers dead. All of them."

"It's as good as done," Asa said. "I promise."

Zane turned his furious gaze to Asa. "You know what you did to that biker guy in the cabin?"

"Yeah?"

"I want you to do it to them…*before* you kill them," Zane said, voice trembling.

"Anything for you," Asa promised, reaching out to cup Zane's cheek. "I'll even let you pick the weapon."

"Good," Zane said, seething. "Good," he repeated under

his breath.

There were a few more working hours in the day, but it was clear that Zane was in no shape to handle anything else. "I think I need to take you home, Lois. You don't look so good. It might be a night for junk food and emotional support vodka."

Zane blinked red-rimmed eyes. "For what?"

"I'll explain everything once we're home. For now, why don't you just close your eyes and get some rest. We'll go to my apartment in the city. It's closer."

Zane nodded. Asa turned the radio to something soothing as Zane let his head rest against the glass, his eyes falling shut.

Asa was imagining all the ways he could exact revenge for Zane's brother when he reached out and snagged Asa's hand, threading their fingers together. Asa stared at their joined hands for a long minute, unable to explain the mixture of emotions flooding his system.

On the one hand, Asa was enraged that somebody would dare to harm something that belonged to him. On the other, there was the anticipation of violence, of exacting his revenge in Zane's name. He'd hang them all up on rusty hooks and take them apart piece by piece if that was what Zane needed. It would be Asa's fucking pleasure to do so.

Was that love?

SEVENTEEN

ZANE

Zane was drunk. No, Zane was very drunk. Room tilting, head spinning, why-is-the-bed-moving drunk. It was all Asa's fault. He gave him the vodka. The emotional support vodka. That was what it was called. Somebody had even written it on the label with Sharpie. *Noah's Emotional Support Vodka. Do Not Touch.* But he had touched it. So much of it.

Sorry, Noah.

But it did bring up questions. Did Noah come to the twins' apartment often enough to keep an emergency booze stash? Did Noah keep vodka in all locations? Was Noah an alcoholic or just easily overwrought?

Zane wasn't exactly one to be pointing fingers, even if that was what he was currently doing. Pointing a finger at Asa who watched him, clearly amused and boringly sober. "Why do you like chasing me down before you fuck me?" Zane asked, noting the way his mouth struggled to form words. "Is it, like, a serial killer thing?"

"Has anybody ever told you that you're chatty when

you're drunk?" Asa asked.

"Has anybody ever told you you're invading—nope—evading the question?" he countered.

Asa smirked up at him from where he lay on the couch, Zane straddling his hips. "I'm not *invading* the question, your honor. I just don't know how to explain it. It's the closest I can get to killing without actually doing it. There's an adrenaline rush. The same kind of high I get when I hold somebody's life in my hands. When I make them suffer."

"Is that why you like chasing me down?" Zane asked, not sure why he needed more from Asa's answer. "You want to make me suffer?"

Asa pushed an errant curl off Zane's forehead, then pushed his glasses up the bridge of his nose, smiling when they slid right back down because of Zane's tilted head. "No, I like chasing you down because you're mine, and there's an animalistic need inside me to stalk and claim what belongs to me. I like knowing you can't outpace me, that you're physically weaker than me. That you need me. That we're so connected that, no matter how far or fast you run, I'll always find you and remind you who you belong to."

Zane's whole body flushed with warmth, his dick hardening at the promise in Asa's words. "That's sweet," Zane said, trying to boop Asa's nose but poking him in the cheek. Asa snickered, but Zane frowned, trying and missing again. "Don't laugh at me. That's not sweet. Be sweet."

"You're a very cute drunk," Asa said, reaching up to cup Zane's face. "A very cute drunk who has zero ability to gauge what's sweet and what's borderline abusive behavior."

Asa was the cute one. No, not cute. That was such a weak word. Asa was…hot. There was no other word for it. He was supermodel, thirst-trap, next level A-list celebrity hot. And he wanted Zane. He wanted everybody to know Zane belonged to him. It just didn't make sense. Zane's own family hadn't wanted him. How could Asa Mulvaney?

Maybe this would be some kind of marriage of convenience. Maybe Asa was taking one for the team because Zane knew their secret and Daddy wanted to keep him close. Marrying him was far more palatable to Thomas than killing him was cold comfort. He did his best to stuff all his insecurities deep down where he couldn't think too much about them, but the vodka laid them bare.

"Am I out of your league?" Zane asked suddenly, unable to stop the words from bubbling up. "Or are you out of my league? Whatever. Like, are you too good for me? Am I not good enough for you?"

Asa barked out a surprised laugh that made Zane feel small somehow and had him choking back tears. "What?"

Zane swayed backwards slightly as the room tilted on its axis. Asa gripped his shirt and pulled him back until he hovered over him once more. But Zane couldn't let the thought go. The vodka had dissolved what little filter he had. "Like, are you just with me because I know your secret? To keep me quiet or whatever? 'Cause I would never tell on you guys. You can be honest. I mean, I probably wouldn't even say no to marriage anyway. It's not like men were beating down my door before you got bored and took me home."

Asa tugged him forward until Zane had no choice but to

lie down on top of him, tucking his bare legs between Asa's pajama-clad thighs. He rested his folded hands on Asa's chest, then dropped his chin on them, feeling like he was screwing everything up.

Asa wasn't smiling anymore. He studied Zane for a long moment. "You think that's why I took you home? I was bored?"

Zane shrugged, looking away to stare at the coffee table with its untouched copies of *Architectural Digest*. "I don't know."

Asa sighed. "You definitely weren't my usual type."

Zane's face burned, his insides curdling, at Asa's bold statement. He started to squirm away, but Asa's arm came around him, holding him still until he stopped moving.

"*Because* I usually went for cheap hookups with himbo types. All muscle, no substance, wanted the same shallow quickie that I wanted." Asa stroked Zane's cheek with his knuckles in that way that made his insides shiver with pleasure. "But you were…pretty. That was the first thing I thought. Rockstar pretty. That you had amazing hair and gorgeous eyes, and that I wanted to see those perfect lips wrapped around my dick."

Zane couldn't fight the smile that crept across his face, so he buried it against Asa's chest.

"I thought you were beautiful. I also thought you were playing me. That you were trying to seduce me into a story."

Zane blinked up at him. "I was…"

Asa laughed. "Yeah, I know."

Zane was so in love with this man. The thought hit him

like a school bus, stealing his breath and making his heart pound until he was sure Asa must be able to hear it. He loved him. Even if it was only one-sided. Zane had never loved anybody before. Still, he forced the thought out of his alcohol-pickled brain. "Why'd you take me home if you thought I was playing you?"

Asa shrugged. "Because I had to. You called my bluff. And once I thought about chasing you down and breeding you, there was no way I was going to say no. I had to know what it felt like to have you underneath me, to bury myself inside you. And you were so fucking perfect. You played the game so well. You made me work for it and it made my reward even sweeter."

Zane could feel himself flushing even more, if such a thing were possible, his cock throbbing almost painfully at the heat in Asa's gaze. "You should chase me and fuck me right now."

Asa grinned, running his thumb along Zane's bottom lip. "I think that's probably a bad idea."

Zane frowned. "Why? You don't want to fuck me?" He closed his lips around Asa's thumb, sucking it suggestively, his tongue tasting the tang of salt on his skin.

Asa tugged his thumb free, pinching Zane's chin and forcing his gaze upward. "Just so we're clear, there will never be a time when the answer to any question will be because 'I don't want you.' But at the moment, you're very drunk."

Zane batted Asa's hand from his face, then propped his chin up on his hand, his elbow wobbling with each breath Asa took. "I promise I'm fully consenting."

Asa shook his head. "I'm more concerned about your coordination than I am your consent, Lois."

Zane began to rock himself against Asa in what he hoped was suggestive and not sloppy. "Do you think I'll fall off your dick or something? You can be on top. You know I like you on top of me, especially when you tie me up. I like when you take what you want."

"Jesus, Lois," Asa rumbled before taking a deep breath and letting it out. He was hard—Zane could feel it pressing against his hip—but Asa seemed content to play with the curl spiraling over Zane's forehead. "And I love being on top of you and inside you any way I can get you, but I think we'll save that for when you're not quite so glassy-eyed. I would be very sad if you died."

Zane's eyes went wide. "You would?"

After a moment of heavy contemplation, Asa nodded. "Yeah, Lois. I think I'd be really fucking sad if you died. Inconsolable even."

Zane felt like his heart would explode from happiness. "That's really…nice."

Asa chuckled, his fingers pushing through Zane's curls in a way that made him want to purr. "I'm glad you think so."

"Do you think you could ever love me?" Zane blurted.

Asa frowned. "I don't really know what love is. I want to say yes, but I don't know what it feels like, so I don't know if I can do it."

Zane couldn't stop the words from tumbling past his loose lips. "It feels like your heart skips when the person walks in a room. It feels like you're sad when they leave, like you think about them when they're not around, and you care about their day and what happened to them. That you don't want them to be unhappy. That you'd be unhappy if it saved them being sad."

Asa studied Zane's face, a little breathless when he asked, "Is that how you feel about me, Lois?"

Zane screwed his face into an expression of mock seriousness, doing his best to imitate Asa's sexy-talk voice. "I feel like if I tell you that, it might change the power dynamic of this relationship."

The way Asa kept looking at him was making Zane feel goosebumpy. "I think we're long past that."

Zane hated how vulnerable he suddenly felt, but he nodded anyway, "Yeah, it's how I feel about you. But you better not hold this against me tomorrow. This shit is going to be super embarrassing in the morning."

"You being in love with me is embarrassing?" Asa asked.

Zane snorted. "It is if I'm the only one, yeah."

"I can assure you, lots of people are in love with me," Asa teased.

Zane slapped his shoulder. "I'm serious. You can't make fun of me for this."

Asa's hands came up under Zane's arms, dragging him high enough to reach his lips in a slow, almost lazy kiss that made Zane's toes curl. "If I can love anybody, Lois, it will be you. No question. I don't know if I will feel all of those things you mentioned. We haven't been apart since we met. But I don't ever want you to be sad. I want to kill people who hurt you. I spend half my day thinking of how

I can't wait to be inside you again, to fill you up, leave my marks all over you. I knew days ago that, even if my family didn't accept you, I wouldn't let you go."

"Even Avi?" Zane asked, voice barely a whisper.

Asa gave a slow nod. "Even Avi. But I think he'd come around."

Zane didn't want to be the reason Asa and Avi didn't spend time together. "I hope so."

Asa narrowed his eyes. "This seems like a good time to mention this. You know we're probably all going to live together. My brother and I just like to be…near each other. I know that seems weird to people. Believe me, I've seen the rumors, read the headlines. But it's not like that."

"Like what?" Zane asked, trying to follow the conversation.

"We're not *that* close."

Asa made an obscene gesture that had Zane's eyes going wide. "Oh. Do people think that you have sex with people, like, together?"

"Oh, we've definitely had sex with people, like, together, just not…crossing swords. I don't want to fuck my brother, but that doesn't mean we don't like to share."

"Are you going to want to…share me?" Zane asked, far too drunk to give this conversation the attention it deserved. His dick had one hundred percent taken over all of the thinking, and the idea of having not one Asa but two was something Zane's smaller head was very much on board with.

"Is that something you want?" Asa asked, not sounding as jealous as Zane had imagined he would.

"It's not fair to ask me this question when I'm drunk and

horny," Zane said honestly. "Would you do that? Want me to have sex with other men?"

"Other men? Hell no. But Avi isn't 'other men.' Avi's like the other half of me. It's not a deal breaker."

"Doesn't he have a boyfriend? Jericho's brother?"

Asa snorted. "Not according to him. But yeah, probably. You'd like Felix, though. He's kind of like one of those super small and pretty but highly venomous fish you see in the ocean. I think if my brother ever admits they're perfect for each other, the four of us could be happy together. In whatever way works for us. For all of us. Is that going to be a problem for you?"

Zane wasn't exactly sure what Asa was asking. Was he okay with fucking his brother? Was he okay with fucking Felix? Was he okay with Felix fucking Asa? There were too many bisecting lines in this conversation. But like Asa said, none of those things were exactly a deal breaker. Except one. "Only if Avi hates me. I don't know if I can handle living with somebody who looks like you but who can't stand me."

"I think my brother will find it very hard to not like you, Lois."

Zane looked around. "So, there will be four of us living here or at the house?"

Asa nodded. "Yeah, maybe. Does that bother you?"

Zane let his head drop to Asa's chest, listening to the solid thud of his heart beneath his ear. "No. It would be nice to have a family who actually likes me and wants me around."

Zane felt a little like he was going to cry when Asa said, "I want you."

Fingers began to thread through Zane's hair once more and he found his lids growing heavy. "My father likes you. Noah, Lucas, and Jericho will be allies. They remember what it was like to be the new guy. My brothers don't really like people so much as tolerate them, so that's as good as you'll get with that. And Avi… Avi will come around."

Zane rubbed his face against Asa's t-shirt, the warmth of his body lulling him to sleep. "I hope so."

"Let me worry about that."

Zane nodded. "Okay… I'm going to be really hungover tomorrow, aren't I?"

Asa chuckled, pulling the blanket from the back of the couch onto the both of them. "Oh, yeah. But I've got you, Lois. I promise."

EIGHTEEN

ASA

Asa had woken with Avi on his mind and a skull-splitting headache. They'd been apart too long. Was he feeling it, too? Maybe it was all the talk of Avi between Asa and Zane last night. Maybe the distraction of Zane was no longer the buffer it had been. His near constant presence made Avi's absence feel even bigger.

Asa buried his face against Zane's neck, smiling when his head tilted to give him better access. "Time to get up, Lois."

"I'm totally awake," he grumbled, voice sleep-soaked.

"That's what you said when I scraped you off the bathroom floor at five a.m.—"

"A gentleman wouldn't bring that up," Zane rasped.

"A gentleman wouldn't bring up that you weigh a lot more when my dick isn't buried inside you."

Zane crushed his face deeper into the pillow. "That's scientifically inaccurate."

"Whatever you say, Lois, but it's a good thing I don't skip leg day."

"Shh," Zane said, holding up a finger. "I'm awake. I mean it."

"And that's what you said when I woke you up at six-thirty to drink water. And again, at seven, when I made you take ibuprofen."

Zane squirmed away from him to do one of those big joint-popping stretches he did every time he woke up, then rolled back into Asa's arms, facing him. "Maybe I'd be more well-rested if you'd stop waking me up."

Asa bit the tip of Zane's nose. "Maybe I wouldn't have had to wake you up so many times if you hadn't drank a liquor store," Asa countered.

Zane buried his face against Asa's bare chest, wiggling his knee between his thighs, clearly intent on going back to sleep. "This is nice," he murmured with a contented sigh.

"Uh-uh. No time for that, sleepyhead. We have to go to my dad's."

Zane leaned back, cracking open painfully bloodshot eyes. He had drool dried on his face, his hair was a wreck, and he smelled like vomit and stale vodka, but if given the opportunity, Asa would have gathered him back into his arms and let him sleep off his hangover.

"Did somebody call?"

"Yeah, Lucas and August worked up victimology, and they want us to meet at Dad's house so we can help narrow it down."

"How am I supposed to leave the house like this?" Zane asked pitifully.

"Buck up, little camper. We could finally be close to

solving this thing, and that means we can finally get with the killing. That's the fun part."

Zane stared at him for so long, Asa thought, for a minute, he'd broken him somehow. Then, finally, he said, "Did you ask me to fuck your brother last night?"

Asa blinked at him, dumbfounded. "Well, that was a hell of a non sequitur, Lois. No, I absolutely did *not* ask you to fuck my brother. Which, by the way, is a sentence I never expected to utter out loud."

"Did I imagine that?" Zane said. "God, that's embarrassing."

"No, what I said was that my brother and I have shared… bedmates…in the past, and then you asked if I expected you to have sex with my brother."

Zane frowned until creases formed between his brows in that way that he did when he was concentrating really hard. "What did you say?"

"I countered and asked if you wanted to fuck my brother."

"Then what did I say?" Zane asked, dread leaching into his tone.

Asa grinned. "I believe you said it wasn't a deal breaker."

"Oh, my God," Zane said around a groan. "That's so embarrassing."

"That you'd consider fucking my brother and Felix?"

"And Felix?" Zane shouted, then winced. "I've never even seen Felix. Why was I so horny?"

"I don't know, but you definitely wanted to get down last night. Were rather insistent, even. I feared for my virtue," Asa teased.

"I am willing to bet you don't even know what that word

means. For the record, I don't want to bone your brother. I don't even know him. Is he going to think that I'm, like... available to him if I live here?"

"No. I can say this with one hundred percent certainty. My brother will never look at you sexually unless you give very clear indicators that you're open to it. He's so wrapped up in Felix at the moment, he can't see past him."

Zane chewed on his bottom lip for a long moment, studying Asa. "Do you want me to be...open to the idea of, like, sleeping with him and/or Felix?"

"I was never trying to get you to have a four-way with my brother and his maybe boyfriend. But four men living together in a house can either make us really close or it could start a war. I just want us to all be comfortable together."

"How comfortable?"

Asa sighed. Zane was definitely searching for something. "I don't want anybody inside you but me. I don't want you loving anybody but me. I don't want you needing anybody but me. But that doesn't mean I don't want you to go without something you need, something maybe I can't give you, physically or emotionally."

If possible, Zane frowned even harder. "Like what?"

"Sympathy. Understanding. Empathy. My brother can't give you that either, no matter how much we've been taught to fake it. Others in the family can. Noah, Lucas, hell, even Jericho and my father. But Felix will likely be in our house on a daily basis, not them. I would understand if you became...close."

"'Close,'" Zane air-quoted.

"Yes, close. In whatever way works for the two of you. Though, like I said, I don't want anybody else inside you. That's just for me. But I can't be…soft for you. I can try, but it might not be what you need. I don't want you to feel like I'm not giving you everything you need. We're going to be together for a long time."

Zane threw his arms around Asa, causing Zane to tip over on top of him. "You're so dumb. What we have is raw and painful and soul-snatchingly real. I like what you do for me. What you give me, physically and emotionally. In all the ways. Nobody has ever treated me as good as you."

"That's a really low bar, Lois," Asa teased. "You have more bruises on you than a prize fighter. Just know, if I'm not giving you something that somebody else can, we can talk about it. But that person will only be inner circle. And that circle is very small."

"Like a circle of four small?" Zane asked, a touch of humor returning to his voice.

"Yeah, that."

"You really think Avi is in love with Felix?"

Asa thought about it, pushing Zane's wild hair back from his forehead. "Not exactly. Well, maybe as much as he can be. Have you ever met two people who fight as foreplay? That's Avi and Felix. They taunt each other so hard that it's almost too intimate to watch. I think when they finally admit that there's something underneath the fighting, that's when it will all turn around and my brother will be shocked to find that he's the one with a leash around his neck, not Felix."

"There's nothing wrong with a leash around the neck," Zane said, sniffing delicately, pretending to be offended.

Asa attacked Zane's neck, dragging his teeth over his skin. "Oh, I definitely like you leashed. And collared." Asa forced Zane's thighs open with his legs, rocking against him in a way that had Zane whimpering in seconds. He bit the shell of his ear. "I like the way you respond to pain. I like the way you look when you cry, when you beg." He bit along his jaw. "When you're so far gone, you don't even hear the sick shit you beg for. But my brother, he's the complete opposite. He wants to be hurt. Loves a good fight. Will never back down. The problem with him is that he thinks he'll always win."

"But he won't?" Zane gasped, already hard beneath Asa.

Asa chuckled. "Not against Felix, no. And Avi will never see it coming."

"Keep doing that. It feels so good," Zane begged.

"Uh-uh. You need to get in the shower. But, if you're a good boy, I'll suck you off while you get clean."

"I never thought I'd let somebody call me a good boy without punching them in the face," Zane mused.

"You can punch me in the face if you want, Lois. But I might retaliate by holding you down and reminding you who you belong to."

"I don't think that's the deterrent you think it is," Zane teased, pumping his hips up against Asa in a maneuver that in no way should have been sexy but was most definitely getting the job done.

"Nope, shower blowjobs is all you're getting. Now, get

your ass up."

Asa rolled them before sitting up, depositing Zane on his feet. "Oh, God. I'm going to puke again."

Then he was off in the bathroom. Asa sighed as the sound of retching reached him. Well, at least he was up. Asa stood, stretching his arms over his head. "Hang on, Lois. I'll come and hold your hair back. That's what married people do, right?"

When it came to looking disheveled, Zane was giving Archer a run for his money. Some might say Archer actually looked more alert than Zane, who currently laid with his head on the conference room table, drooling like a high school student sleeping through math class. He wore a black beanie cap, one of Asa's Gemini hoodies, and a pair of jeans that molded to his ass and thighs in a way that almost made Asa forget about the meeting.

"What happened to him?" Noah asked, keeping his voice down, as if he was afraid to wake him.

"I'm no expert, but I'm going to guess alcohol," Archer mused.

"Oh, you're definitely selling yourself short," Adam chided. "If there was a gold medal for alcoholism, you'd definitely be an Olympic champion."

Archer tipped his fake cap at Adam as if he'd fed him a compliment. Maybe that was a compliment to Archer. Someday, scientists were going to study Archer's liver under a jar and marvel about how it had survived years of abuse. He honestly couldn't remember a time before the drinking started.

Lucas and August entered together, both in casual attire. Lucas was in jeans and a henley and August was in dress pants and a zip-front cardigan, which was the equivalent of jeans shorts when it came to August's level of casual wear. Jericho was there as well, clothes clean but hands stained, and there was grease under his nails.

"Where's Dad?" Adam asked August.

August shrugged, dropping into a chair while Lucas grabbed himself a diet soda from the fridge. "I thought he'd be in here."

"What happened there?" Lucas asked with a smirk, pointing at Zane's barely conscious form.

"Maybe he succumbed to his injuries," Jericho mused. "Asa finally succeeded in fucking somebody to death."

"Bold of you to assume I've never fucked a man to death," Asa said before dropping his hand to rub Zane's back. "Lois just needed some emotional support," he added, using his pinky and thumb to mime drinking.

"Oof. Been there," Noah said, looking at Zane sympathetically, before turning to Asa. "You know, I'm gonna need you to—"

Asa cut him off with an eye roll. "Yeah, yeah, replace your bottle. I'm aware. Seriously, where's Dad? He's never this late."

Lucas shrugged. "We haven't seen him. We left Cricket and the girls in the nursery and came straight down here."

"Wait, the snot faucets are here?" Asa asked.

"I don't think anybody whose boyfriend is actually drooling a puddle on the table gets to call our precious daughters snot faucets," Lucas said.

Asa rolled his eyes but gently shook Zane. "Wakey, wakey, Lois. You can sleep later."

Zane groaned but sat up, surreptitiously attempting to wipe the drool from his chin and the table.

"It's too late. We've all seen your shame," Asa said, handing him a bottle of water. "Drink this. All of it."

"If the girls are here, you know where Dad is," Archer said. "Hey, Calliope?"

Calliope's voice echoed around them like the voice of God. "Yes, Captain Sparrow?"

Zane snickered, then quickly stopped when Archer raised one brow in his direction.

"Can you show us the nursery?"

"Any excuse to see those sweet, adorable angel babies," Calliope crooned.

"See, that is the level of respect my children deserve," Lucas said, looking at each of them in turn.

The screen came to life. Calliope panned around the sprawling nursery with its carousel-themed wallpaper and custom-built cribs, stopping when she found Thomas. He sat in the overstuffed rocker, his ankle crossed over his other knee, two tiny bundles nestled in his lap.

When Thomas had requested a nursery be built in his home for the girls, Asa had thought it strange. He was the grandfather, not the dad. Wasn't spending thirty grand on a designer nursery a parent thing? But now, he got it. Or, at least, he got why his dad had wanted it.

The proof was there in 4k resolution. Even with no sound on, it was easy to see his father was in love. Whatever he was saying or doing had the two girls smiling and cooing and blowing spit bubbles. Maybe this was what his father needed. It probably hadn't been easy raising six kids who could never love him and a teenager Asa was starting to suspect maybe loved him a little too much.

"Should we get him?" Noah asked hesitantly.

"I can fill him in afterwards," August said. "Let's just get started. Calliope, did you get the information I asked for last night?"

"Yep. Got it right here."

Lucas opened the folder he'd had in his hand when he entered, putting on a pair of reading glasses. "Okay, August and I spent all night going over victimology and building a profile of the handler. Here's what we suspect. We're looking for a white man between the ages of thirty to forty-five, likely still living at home. Someone with a massive chip on his shoulder who thinks the world owes him something."

"Well, that's sixty percent of the population," Adam muttered under his breath.

August gave him a sharp look, and he dropped his head. "He has a knack for technology and believes he's smarter than most people. He's not. People will always think he's slightly off. He has a God complex. And any perceived slight will become a vendetta with him whether the other party knows it or not."

"Perceived slight? Like what?" Zane asked.

Lucas waved a hand. "It could be literally anything. Bumped him in line at Starbucks? Took his parking space? Didn't smile back when he smiled at you? He will consider you an enemy for life."

Asa leaned back in his seat, his fingers playing with the hair that curled over the nape of Zane's neck. "How does that help us get closer to finding the handler?"

Lucas looked to the speaker in the center of the table. "We had Calliope pull up a list of people who had been rejected from both of the targeted schools.

"Spoiler alert, there's a lot of them," Calliope said.

"Okay, well, you can eliminate any women," Archer said, then looked at Lucas for confirmation. "Right?"

Lucas nodded. "Yeah."

Rapid-fire typing filled the room. "That only gets rid of about twenty names."

"Eric said the guy who tried to run him over was very overweight and wore dark-framed glasses," Asa said. "I don't suppose there are photographs attached to any of those applications."

"No, but I did pull DMV photos of the men," Calliope said. "Unfortunately, there's no law that demands people update their photos, so some of them could be decades old."

A series of faces began to fill the screen. She was right. There were a lot of them and some of the pictures did, indeed, look decades old. People could change a lot in that time.

"Of this list, only fifteen are listed as needing corrective lenses. Four or so might classify as 'very overweight' but there's a huge margin of error. The handler might have put on weight since any of these photos."

Lucas tapped his pen on the file. "Okay, run deep background checks on the fifteen who need corrective lenses. We can probably use their employment and criminal history to at least eliminate them from the suspect pool."

Calliope made a noise in the affirmative. "I can do that, but it will take me some time."

"Hey, Calliope?" Zane asked.

"Yes, Zane?" she asked, her voice full of sweetness. She never talked to the Mulvaneys like that. Only the spouses.

"Can you cross reference those fifteen names and see if any of them own an old Buick?"

"An old Buick?" Jericho repeated, perking up.

Zane nodded. "Yeah, Eric said the guy who tried to run him down was driving a really old Buick."

"Do you think he'd be stupid enough to use his own vehicle?" Archer asked.

"Have you seen those vintage Buicks? It would be like being hit by a Sherman tank. Those cars were built to last," Jericho said, sounding fond. "What else do you know about it?"

"Just that it's gold."

Jericho nodded. "Okay, Calliope, look for anybody who has a registered Buick Riviera or Skylark. They were very popular back in the day and, up until the mid-seventies, came in a color called Cortez Gold."

"Who knew having a mechanic in the family would come in handy?" Adam said, earning a middle finger from Jericho.

"Okay, there's nobody on the list who has ever owned that kind of car."

"Shit," Zane muttered.

Asa knew Zane was stressed and hungover. He was a wire stretched to its breaking point. He needed this settled once and for all.

"Let me try searching for something else," Calliope said.

They all sat staring at each other as they listened to Calliope typing away for an obscenely long time. "Jackpot! Holy shit. Jericho, I think you just earned a cookie."

"You found him?" Jericho asked.

"Not exactly. I found a 1971 Buick Skylark in Cortez Gold registered to a Henry Devlin. Oh, damn. He's eighty-seven years old."

Zane suddenly came to life, leaning forward. "Does he have a son or grandson, Calliope?"

More frantic typing ensued. "Um, two sons. Maxwell and Jerome. One is sixty-seven and the other is sixty-four. Jerome has a son and a daughter. The son is thirty-eight. Jerome Jr. Maxwell…never had kids."

"Jerome Jr. could be our guy. Can you cross reference him with the list of rejections?" Zane asked.

Calliope made a disappointed sound. "He's not in the list we narrowed down. But," she said, dragging the word out. "Let me check the ones we eliminated."

Asa could feel Zane practically vibrating beside him as they waited for Calliope to do all her complicated computer shit. When she cackled like a witch in a horror movie, Asa knew they had a winner. "Yep, Jerome Jr. was rejected by both schools."

"What's his background?" Noah asked.

"Our creepy friend got his GED—"

"And he applied to our school?" August asked. "He does have delusions of grandeur. We barely allow anybody who wasn't in the International Baccalaureate program with over a 5.0 GPA."

"You sound like a snob," Noah said.

August leveled a flat stare at Noah. "I am a snob. But facts are facts. He's in no way qualified to apply to an Ivy League school, yet he did. That speaks to the profile."

"Um, he works as a Geek at a tech store. That tracks," she said, almost under her breath. "Never married. Was arrested three times. Once for stalking, once for sexual battery, and…one for peeking into ladies windows—never a good sign. Um, his LinkedIn profile says he's a member of MENSA."

August scoffed. "There's a database for members, Calliope. You should be able to access it from my phone. I bet you a thousand dollars, he's lying."

"Calliope has access to August's phone?" Zane whispered.

"She has access to every single aspect of our lives. She will be all up in your phone and everywhere else you live digitally. It's how she fakes GPS locations, tags, and a shit ton of other things I don't understand. It's part of the Mulvaney Murder, Inc. membership, so if you have any weird fetish porn on your phone, you might want to get rid of it sooner rather than later."

"Glad I didn't take that bet," Calliope said, "because you are correct. Definitely *not* a MENSA candidate."

"You think this is him? You think this is our guy?" Adam asked the group.

"I think it's worth delving into," August said.

"Same," Adam and Jericho agreed at the same time.

"Yes," Zane added fiercely. "When can we start cutting off appendages?"

"I like him," Archer said, pointing in Zane's direction. "You can keep him."

Asa rolled his eyes. "Thanks ever so much for your approval." To Zane, he said, "We need a little more proof before we start hacking off appendages." Zane puffed up like he was going to protest, but Asa said, "I know, it's annoying and tedious. But my father insists."

"We just need more proof," Jericho said.

"Like what?" Zane asked, slamming his fist on the table. "That guy mind-fucked my brother into killing himself, and I want to watch him fucking bleed."

Even Asa's eyes went wide at the venom in Zane's tone. He had a lot of fight in him. That was good. Willing to fight meant not giving up. He needed Zane to keep fighting. "Easy, Lois. If he's the guy, I'll make him suffer. I promise. But let's do a tiny bit of recon. Calliope, you know where he lives?"

She typed for a few more minutes. "He appears to dwell in his father's and stepmother's basement."

"Shocker," Lucas muttered.

"Well, that's going to make this slightly more difficult. Can you shoot me the address and maybe track down his work schedule, Calliope?" Asa asked.

"Sure, buttercup."

"Meeting adjourned?" Asa asked August, already standing up.

August nodded. "I hate to pry the girls away from my father, but I think we'll reconvene after your recon session."

Zane was already halfway to the door. "I want to go check this guy out right now."

"Lois, you're sick and hungover. It's broad daylight, and this is not the kind of guy who won't notice people snooping. I guarantee you he's got security cameras. Good ones. I know you're out for blood, but you need to trust me on this," Asa said, tone firm.

"Fine. But I want him dead. I want them all dead."

"How quickly you've corrupted him," Archer said as he passed.

Asa wrapped his arms around Zane. "Let's go get food and then we'll swing by his house—just drive by—and scope out what we can. Just once. And only if you eat all your lunch."

Zane made a noise of disgust. "I don't want to eat."

"That's my final offer."

"I could just go by myself."

"Lois, believe me when I say this. It will be a cold day in hell before I ever let you do anything murdery without me." There was no missing the way Zane's pupils dilated, his tongue darting out to lick over his lower lip. Asa pressed his lips to his ear. "That turned you on, didn't it? You're such a freak, I love it. Let's go eat, Lois. I'll even let you give me a handjob on the way."

"Wow, what a treat," Zane quipped.

Asa grinned. "I'm a giver."

NINETEEN

ZANE

The drive past Jerry Jr.'s house had turned into a stakeout of sorts. Not because Zane had managed to change Asa's mind about the timing, but because the aforementioned handjob turned into a blowjob and—for once—Zane seemed to have driven Asa to the point of distraction. Enough so that he pulled over, anyway.

Road head was a little painful. The center console jammed into his ribs, and he felt a bit like a contortionist with his ass all but in the air as he sucked Asa off. But when Asa had looked at him in that way he did that made Zane feel flushed and shivery, he knew it would never matter how painful Asa's request might be. He'd always do it.

Which was how he'd ended up with Asa's hands clenched in his hair, holding him in place so he could fuck up into his mouth, crooning exceedingly dirty things to Zane, telling him about all the people who could see him—could see them—right there in broad daylight while Zane choked on his cock like the perfect little whore.

His perfect whore. Zane had never enjoyed name calling or humiliation, but when Asa said it, there was nothing humiliating about it. It was the highest praise. Zane was a whore for Asa. Just Asa. He knew the talk was just as much for Asa's excitement as Zane's, just like he knew it was impossible for anybody to see past Asa's illegal limo-tinted windows, but that didn't make the thought any less hot.

By the time Zane swallowed Asa's cum, his throat hurt and his eyes were watering, but he didn't care. Seeing that look on Asa's face—that gobsmacked, shocky look that Asa got when he was cum-drunk, the way he looked at Zane like he was lucky to have him…that he was a gift and not a curse—only added to the heady experience that was sex with Asa. It made Zane feel both powerful and powerless somehow.

Though the first trip to Jerry's hadn't accomplished much, they had confirmed he lived there with his parents, and, with Calliope's help, they'd learned there was a security system and cameras. Why that alone wasn't proof enough that this guy was guilty, Zane didn't know. Asa had laughed at his reasoning, but Zane didn't think it was funny. This Jerry guy was shady.

Still, they were back to do their due diligence and bring the Mulvaney Council some kind of hard and fast proof that torturing this guy was the right thing to do. It was dark out. Jerry's shift was due to end in another hour, so they had to move quickly. Luckily, the night was on their side.

The new moon brought an almost inky darkness with it, the cloud cover obscuring the stars in the sky. There was no light but for the single yellow street lamp three houses down. It seemed as though Jerry's parents lived in the upstairs part of the house. Asa seemed confident that they'd discover Jerry was a basement dweller. Zane didn't question how he'd come to that conclusion.

"I really hope you know what you're doing," Zane muttered. "I really don't want to get popped for robbery. I won't do well in prison."

Asa gave him a long, lingering kiss, his voice low and sexy in a way that was entirely inappropriate given what they were about to do. "I don't know. You did a great job pretending to be an inmate the other night." His lips dragged from his jaw to his earlobe, biting down hard enough for Zane to flinch. "But if you tried to trade favors with the guards in real life, I'd have to kill them. All of them. I don't think you want that kind of blood on your hands. Right, Lois?"

Zane shivered, his pulse tripping and his cock hardening. "Are you saying you'd kill anybody who touched me?"

Asa's raspy chuckle was knife sharp. "Killing would be the kindest thing I could do to somebody who touched you without my permission. And I know that turns you on, you bloodthirsty little thing."

Zane scoffed. "It does not."

Asa's breath panted against Zane's ear as he whispered a single word. "Liar."

Zane grinned. "I plead the fifth. Now, can we go break into this guy's house?"

Asa grinned. "Okay, Lois. Just follow my lead. And stay close."

With the signal jammer, a few other toys, and balaclavas over their faces, they ran in a crouch across the side yard, stopping at a small basement window at the back, lying on the ground to peer inside.

"Gross," Zane muttered, face twisting in disgust.

No matter what Lucas's profile had told them about their possible suspect, nothing could have prepared Zane for the filth within. Even through the grimy window, there was no missing it. The only light was from the glow of five computer monitors, each with separate dizzying screensavers, set up slapdash on a desk that took up almost an entire wall.

There was a bed—well, a mattress—pressed against one wall, but Jerry hadn't bothered to put sheets on it, leaving every questionable stain front and center for all the world to see. There was no comforter. Instead, there was a grungy sleeping bag and some kind of fur blanket with a naked woman on it.

"If this isn't a red flag, I don't know what is," Zane said with a shudder.

"Red flags don't always mean murderer," Asa murmured. "Sometimes, people are just dirty."

Zane gave him a stunned look. "That's not dirty. That's… vile. The carpet looks black. There's definitely roaches. I don't even want to know what's in those jars on the floor by his computer."

"You are the guy who wanted to be an investigative journalist, no?" Asa teased.

Zane leveled a glare at him. "I didn't know that meant entering places like this without a hazmat suit," Zane said, wrinkling his nose.

"Do you want to just play lookout and I'll go in alone?" Asa asked. "I wouldn't want to upset your delicate sensibilities."

"You don't have to be condescending," Zane said, his tone pouty.

Asa shook his head. "I'm not being condescending, Lois. I'm trying to be accommodating. If you don't want to do the dirty stuff, I'll do it for you. I like getting dirty for you. It would be my honor to crawl through this window and wade through…all that…so I can get what we need to torture this guy. For you."

Zane narrowed his eyes at Asa. It was always hard to tell whether he was being sweet or sarcastic. "No. Let's just do this. But if a roach crawls on me, I cannot be held responsible for what I do."

"Noted."

Asa turned on the jammer, waited a moment, then tested the window. When it didn't give, he pulled out a strange flat metal rod that looked a lot like what locksmiths used to open locked cars from the inside. He slid it beneath the window, using it to pull up the gold latch from the interior of the lock. The window still took a bit of maneuvering but then finally slid up, making a shuddering sound Zane hoped sounded louder than it truly was. Asa slid in feet first, looking around, before gesturing for Zane to follow.

Zane temporarily forgot the grime as Asa helped him inside, letting him slide down his body before his feet found the floor. But before he could contemplate anything fun, he covered his nose and mouth. If he'd thought the place looked bad, the stench was so much worse, almost incomprehensible. It smelled like mold, sweat, stale beer, and weed. The air felt…damp, like Zane could feel the spores settling into his lungs.

"What exactly are we looking for?" Zane whispered.

Asa leaned in. "Anything that could prove this piece of shit is the handler we're looking for. These creeps like to keep trophies."

"Do you?" Zane asked.

Asa frowned. "Do I what?"

"Keep trophies?"

Asa gave Zane a grin that made him feel both hot and cold. "Remind me when we have time, Lois, and I'll explain to you what my tattoos really mean."

He turned away before Zane could question him further. Zane was grateful he had gloves and that had nothing to do with leaving behind fingerprints. It was impossible to move one thing without dislodging a thousand other things. Moving a magazine sent a stack careening onto the floor. Moving a box caused another small avalanche of computer equipment.

Asa gave him an exasperated look.

"What? It's not like I made the mess," Zane hissed.

When Zane got to Jerry's computers, he grimaced. Underneath the desk, behind the mystery jars of liquid, was a shoebox. He gave a low whine as he pulled it towards himself. He'd rather find a half-eaten human heart than a single roach. He was relieved when he didn't find either. It was a box of newspaper clippings.

He unfolded the first one and stopped short. "Asa," he said, unable to stop the raw rasp in his voice.

Asa stopped what he was doing and wandered closer. Zane handed him a couple of the slips of paper. "It's him."

The clippings were newspaper articles about the suicides, not just at those two schools but at others. High schools. Jesus. Had they even thought about high schools? Had he gone after younger kids, too? Zane couldn't think about it. There was clearly no end to his depravity. It wasn't just newspaper clippings of the stories. There were obituaries. Funeral programs. The fucker had attended their funerals.

Asa kissed the top of his head. "Good find. Photograph as many as you can with the camera phone I gave you, then put them back exactly as you found them. He strikes me as being the kind of person who likes to go back and revisit his crimes."

Asa continued to rummage around softly behind him until the silence was broken by another rockslide of items making a small clatter. This time, CDs in clear holders. They were unlabeled. Zane watched as Asa opened his bag and placed them inside. "What are you doing? I thought we were supposed to look, not touch."

"Nobody hides a bunch of unlabeled DVDs unless there's something he doesn't want people looking too closely at. I'm taking a calculated risk."

"Does that mean we can—"

There was the creaking of hinges, and then a sharp feminine voice said, "Jerry? Did you come home from work without even saying hello?"

Zane's heart rate skyrocketed, but Asa just held a finger to his lips and shook his head, cool and calm as always.

"You're hearing things," a gruff voice called from deeper within the house. "I'm telling you, you're getting senile."

"Oh, hush. I definitely heard something," she said.

"Probably a rat," the gruff man shot back.

A rat? Zane shot a panicked look at Asa, eyes wide. Did they have rats down there? Zane hated rats more than roaches. Shit. Finally, the door at the top of the stairs slammed shut. Asa nodded towards the window, and Zane eagerly complied, letting Asa boost him up so he could wiggle out. Asa followed, needing no help from Zane whatsoever.

Zane didn't start breathing again until they were back in the truck and out of Jerry's neighborhood. He peeled the mask off his face. "I… Yeah, I hated that. I do *not* want to be a field reporter. Give me the highlight reels and let me piece it all together. Ugh. No. Just no. I need a shower. Like, now."

Asa snickered. "That can be arranged. But let's drop the DVDs for Calliope to catalog and digitize. She can make us a highlight reel if there's anything on there worth looking at."

Zane nodded. "Okay. Then you can feed me. I'm starving."

Asa gave him a funny look. "I remember when I had to force-feed you. Now, you're hungry all the time. Like a baby bird. 'Feed me. Feed me. Feed me.'"

"Are you complaining?" Zane asked, narrowing his eyes.

Asa grinned. "Nope. Believe me, you'll need the energy."

Zane studied Asa's face. "What's that supposed to mean?"

Asa gave him an innocent look. "Nothing. Nothing at all, Lois."

Zane was pleasantly full and finally squeaky clean. That basement had been nightmare fuel, the scent lingering in his nose until Asa had taken him to get food. He turned the knob to turn off the scalding water, using one of Asa's fluffy white towels to dry himself off, running it over his damp curls before wrapping it around his waist.

He didn't make it two steps outside the bathroom before he found himself shoved against the wall, his face pressed against the cold surface. Asa yanked his arms behind him, two soft leather cuffs going around his wrists.

"What are you doing?" Zane asked, breathless.

Asa bit down on Zane's shoulder, his teeth fitting into the bite marks he'd left just hours before. "Taking what I want."

Zane couldn't stop the whimper that slipped free.

"You going to be good for me, Lois?"

Zane couldn't even form words, just gave a stilted nod as Asa led him up the stairs, keeping a hand around Zane's bicep to keep him from stumbling. They were going to the sex dungeon. Or attic. The sex attic. They hadn't played up there yet. Asa seemed to prefer making Zane run or spinning exceedingly dirty role play scenarios that always landed Zane as the submissive and Asa the aggressor.

Maybe he'd just been working Zane up to the sex attic.

Maybe he thought Zane hadn't been ready for what was about to happen. He might be right. Zane was never truly ready for the things Asa threw at him, but no matter how extreme their play, Zane was addicted. He couldn't get enough of Asa.

"You have a safe word, Lois?" Asa crooned in his ear.

"Do I need one?" Zane asked, swallowing audibly.

Asa pushed the door open and flipped on a light, illuminating a rather impressive collection of devices that ranged from mundane, like paddles and floggers, to truly baffling things that looked almost like medical instruments.

"My safe word is superman," Zane said quickly, making it up on the fly.

Asa gently kissed his throat, unknotting the towel at his waist, his hands roaming where they pleased. "Don't worry, Lois. I'll keep the training wheels on. I just want you helpless. Totally at my mercy. Completely immobile."

Zane couldn't stop the whimper that escaped. He leaned his weight back on Asa, unable to do anything but let him touch him, tease him, play with him.

"You love being helpless for me, don't you, Lois?"

"Yes."

"You love being a whore for me, don't you?"

Zane's whole body burned. "Yes."

Asa's hand came up to close around Zane's throat. "Just for me," he rasped in his ear.

"Yes," Zane managed around a soft cry.

"Good boy."

Asa walked him towards a darkened corner of the room

to a strange black leather…table? It was just above waist-high, but there were four padded platforms at each corner that sat lower than the table.

"Knees here," Asa said, patting the two lower padded risers.

Understanding dawned, and a shiver ran through him. He wasn't kidding. He wanted Zane completely immobile. Once he kneeled, Asa unlocked the cuffs that held his arms behind his back. Zane shook his arms out.

Asa's lips pressed against his ear. "Assume the position, Lois."

Zane hesitated for only a moment, realizing that the bench was slanted so his head was down, his arms and legs falling naturally into place. The cuffs that closed over each wrist and ankle were lined with something soft. It wasn't uncomfortable so much as nerve-wracking. Zane was trapped. Immobile. Completely at Asa's mercy.

Asa trailed fingers along the knobs of Zane's spine. "Do you know what this bench is called?"

"No," Zane managed.

"It's got a lot of names, really. Punishment bench." He raked blunt nails over Zane's skin. "Spanking bench." Asa's hand came down hard on Zane's ass cheek, fire trailing in its wake. He couldn't fight the low moan that escaped."But my favorite name for it, Lois…" Zane's legs suddenly splayed wide, leaving him completely exposed. Asa spread Zane open. "...is breeding bench."

Zane's breath punched from him as Asa's two fingers, somehow now slick with lube, pushed into him roughly. "Fuck."

"Oh, I will," Asa said, his fingers working inside Zane in a way that made him dizzy, especially when he added a third. "You like this? You like being completely helpless? Completely at my mercy? I could do literally anything to you right now. Anything at all."

That was Asa's real kink. Not the pain—or maybe not *just* the pain—he inflicted, nor the almost animalistic need to mark Zane, but the power. Asa needed to play God. He needed Zane fully dependent on him. Needed to know that Zane's life hung in the balance and only Asa could give him what he needed.

Zane moaned. "Yes."

It mirrored Zane's kink nicely. He wanted Asa to want him, to care for him, comfort him, pick him, choose him. He wanted to be everything to Asa, just like Asa was becoming to him. Underneath all of the pain was just need. Zane needed Asa to love him. Protect him. Keep him. Needed him to hurt him and then soothe him.

Asa's fingers disappeared abruptly. He came to stand in front of Zane and that was when he realized why the bench tilted downward at the top. It put Zane's mouth exactly where Asa wanted it. "Open up, Lois."

Zane didn't have a choice. Asa was pushing his cock between his lips, holding his head in place so he could fuck roughly into his throat. "Relax for me. That's it. Fuck. Your mouth is so hot. Swallow around my cock. Good boy." The muscles of Zane's throat burned. He tried to breathe slowly, tried not to trigger his gag reflex, but Asa wasn't making it easy. He liked the noises Zane made when his life was in peril. He gagged, coughed, sputtered, but Asa was relentless, pulling back only when Zane's head began to swim.

Then he was pulling free, hunkering down in front of him to wipe the saliva and tears from his face. "What should I do with you tonight? Hmm? Other than fill you with my cum?" he mused. "How many loads do you think you could take before you were begging me to stop? Three? Four? Can you imagine how full you'd feel?"

"Asa…" Zane moaned, trying to wiggle to give himself at least some friction, something to ease the ache, but there was nothing. The table was made to deny pleasure to the one strapped to it.

"What's wrong, Lois?" he asked, his voice dripping with sympathy.

"Touch me," he said, voice barely a whisper. "I need it. It hurts."

Asa stroked Zane's cheek. "I am touching you." At Zane's frustrated noise, Asa gave him a soft kiss, tongue sliding inside briefly. "Is that not what you meant, Lois?"

"I hate you," he muttered.

Asa's chuckle was maddening. "No, you don't. You love me. Love this. I bet I can make you come untouched. But once I do, I'm going to fuck you so hard, so deep, you'll feel me every time you sit down for a week."

Zane couldn't even answer. He could only whimper against Asa's lips. He kissed his slack mouth and then stood and walked out of Zane's line of sight. He sucked in a breath as a finger pushed back inside him, probing until pleasure spasmed through his whole body.

Asa did it again. Zane's nipples were painfully hard, goosebumps erupting along his skin. "Oh, does that feel good, Lois? Did I hit the spot?"

Asa's finger pressed and released again, and Zane tried to speak but couldn't. His blood felt hot, his nerves on high alert. Asa played Zane like some kind of exotic instrument, pressing and rolling and teasing until tears leaked from his eyes and pleas fell from his lips.

Asa always made sure Zane came, knew just how to touch him to make it happen, but it was subtle or, sometimes, abrupt. It had never been a deliberate attack on his senses. He'd never played with Zane like this. Asa was right. He could make him come untouched. But he wouldn't. Each time Zane felt that tell-tale tingle at the base of his spine, Asa's fingers disappeared, like he had some kind of sixth sense.

Zane was no longer fully aware of his surroundings. He felt like one giant live wire. Whenever Asa pulled his fingers free, he'd wrap a slick hand around his cock, and it would feel like an entirely different type of orgasm building until Zane was frantic. "Huh-Oh-Oh, fuck. Please. Please. Please. It's too much."

Asa's hand continued to stroke Zane, and his fingers returned, starting up a new rhythm, this *circle, tap, grind* that had Zane crying out. And then just crying. His pleas became barely-there babbling as he lost his train of thought again and again as Asa tormented him.

"Please, Asa," Zane begged, voice low and raw. "I'll do anything."

Asa chuckled, biting his ass cheek. "You're tied up, Lois. You'll do whatever I want anyway." Zane wailed as Asa twisted his fingers in a way that made him feel euphoric, like he was high.

When Asa's hand disappeared again, Zane literally sobbed. Asa's fingers were back, sending shocks of bliss through his blood with each stroke. "Oh, feel that? Look at all that fluid oozing from your cock. You're so hard, so flushed. You're so close. Can you feel it, Lois? I can make you come with just the slightest flick of my wrist. Is that what you want?"

This time, Asa didn't remove his fingers but wrapped his other hand around his cock, using the fluid to work it around his shaft. "Tell me."

"Yes, it's what I want."

"Tell me how much you like being my whore. I need the words."

"I love it. I love it."

"Say it," Asa growled, his fingers tightening over Zane's shaft.

Tears rolled unchecked down Zane's cheeks. This pleasure pain loop was making him crazy. He just needed to come. So badly. "Please."

Asa twisted his fingers, his knuckle pressing on his prostate in a way that robbed Zane of all reason. "Say it," he demanded. "Tell me. Tell me and I'll make you come so hard, you black out."

"I'm your whore," Zane sobbed. "Just yours. Please, Asa."

"Shh," Asa said, stroking Zane's painfully hard cock. "I

got you, Lois."

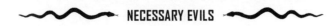

Zane couldn't think anymore. His whole body was just one tightly coiled spring, and every touch was almost too much pleasure. He couldn't stop begging, couldn't stop pleading with Asa to make it stop or make it better. He didn't know what he wanted except relief.

"Oh, you're leaking so much. You're so close. Come on, Lois. Come for me." Asa twisted his fingers and he felt this wave of pleasure crash into him, but when Asa jerked Zane just one time, Zane made a sound he wasn't even sure was human. He could feel himself coming but it was like his whole body was just one pleasure center, his orgasm going on and on until his world went black.

When he came to, Asa was inside him, using him hard, his hands gripping his hips hard enough to know he'd have bruises tomorrow. Asa was chasing his own pleasure, bending over him, biting whatever flesh he could reach, his hand clenching in Zane's hair to drive into him even deeper. Then he was coming, the sound he made somewhere between a growl and a shout, before collapsing on top of Zane and the bench.

He had no idea how long they laid there, but as the haze of pleasure wore away, Zane ached everywhere. With the scene ended, Asa was dropping soft kisses on Zane's back, his shoulders, his hair. "You did so good, Lois. So fucking good. Are you okay?"

"No. I think you broke me," Zane murmured, wiggling his ass beneath Asa, muscles contracting around his cock. Yeah, he ached literally everywhere.

Asa stood, slipping free of Zane before spreading him open, running fingers around his rim and then inside in a way that felt almost clinical. "You're good, Lois. I didn't break anything. You'll just feel like I did for a few days."

He undid Zane's wrists and ankles and then helped him off the bench, catching him when his knees gave out then swinging him into his arms. "I think we should take a bath together. What do you say?"

Zane rested his cheek against Asa's chest. "I can't lift my…anything."

"That's alright. I'll take care of you."

"You better," Zane said, voice barely above a whisper.

Asa stopped and looked down at him. "You can trust me, Lois. I promise."

Zane swallowed the sudden lump in his throat. "Yeah. I know."

TWENTY

ASA

The war room was crowded, with everybody in attendance except Avi, who was still out of town, and Archer, who'd left town for another poker tournament. Asa stared at his brother's empty seat—the one closest to the bar. Was he really at another tournament, or did Thomas send Archer out on secret gigs the others weren't aware of? Maybe it was a combination of both. Archer was an enigma.

August and Lucas had left their squishy angelic-faced distractions with their mother, ensuring the handler would have Thomas's undivided attention. Well, as much attention as he could manage, anyway. He was often present but never truly all there, as if his thoughts were split. He sat in his chair at the head of the table, his silver hair perfect and a drink dangling from his manicured fingers.

Asa shook his head. He was far too introspective today. He made a point of ignoring the others in the room before he started musing about their lives when he truly didn't give a shit why they did what they did. The only person whose private life mattered to Asa was Zane, and he was right there beside him, gripping his thigh hard enough for Asa to have bruises in the morning.

"We're all here, Calliope. What did you find on those DVDs?" Thomas asked.

Calliope let out a shaky breath but said nothing for a long moment. Asa's gaze darted to Thomas. Calliope rarely hesitated, no matter how bad the details.

"Calliope? Did you find anything?" Asa asked.

"Enough to keep me in therapy for another three years," she muttered.

"Let's hear it," Atticus said, his hand threaded with his husband's.

"This is more of an audio-visual thing," Calliope said reluctantly.

"What does that mean?" Zane asked, voice sharp.

"Maybe… Maybe I should just tell you what I found?" Calliope said.

Asa looked at his brothers. They also seemed confused. The others—those with the ability to feel human emotions—looked concerned and a little apprehensive. They'd seen a lot of horrific shit in this room. Stuff most normal people could never cope with.

Noah had confronted photos of the men who had traded him for sex as a child. Lucas had learned just how depraved a fellow agent was when they learned he wasn't only a murderer but that he tortured women for the entertainment of others. Jericho had learned how much his sister had suffered before she died. Calliope had never attempted to shield them from any of it. Or maybe she had and Asa never noticed.

"I'm fine. I'll be fine," Zane amended when he realized the others were staring at him.

Asa knew that wasn't true. Zane's sweaty palm now rested on his, his leg bouncing double-time beneath the table, and Asa could practically hear his teeth grinding. But that was nobody else's business.

"Okay. But, honestly, everybody should prepare themselves. This shit is… It's fucking awful."

The color blanched from Zane's cheeks, but he said nothing.

A video appeared on the screen. A man—presumably Jerry—sat at the desk they'd seen at his house. A different image appeared on each of the monitors before him, but they were all similar. People clearly in the throes of death. When Calliope hit play, it soon became clear why she'd been so nervous.

"Is he—" Noah started.

"Yeah," Adam said, cutting him off, as if he couldn't bear to hear him say it out loud.

Noah's nose crinkled. "Gross. What the fuck?"

The sounds the man made as he watched those on the screen dying were familiar to anybody who'd ever watched porn. Though the view obscured his movements, it was clear he was jerking off to them. He was jerking off to a group of people killing themselves. A group of people he'd *convinced* to kill themselves.

Yeah, this guy needed to die.

The screen went black, and then a dozen videos appeared. These clips couldn't have been more different. It was clearly footage from webcams. The people on them looked healthy and happy, though they were watching something on the screen intently.

"This is them when the game first starts," Calliope said.

The videos morphed into a different day, different time. There were only five videos now. It took Asa a moment to realize that the people on the screen were the same people. They looked sickly. Eyes bloodshot, hair a mess. Some looked as if they'd been crying, and all of them looked on the verge of a breakdown.

"This is the halfway mark," Calliope muttered.

"Halfway mark?" Zane asked, voice thick.

"Why are there only five videos now?" August asked.

"Because he fails the ones he can't manipulate. They 'lose' the game. These are his finalists," Calliope explained.

"What does that mean?" Lucas asked.

"I don't know," she said. "That's how they're listed in his collection. The finalists."

"Sick fuck," Jericho muttered.

"What did you mean by the halfway point?" Zane asked.

Calliope sighed. "This is where the game changes. He switches tactics."

"How so?" Thomas asked.

"Let me guess. He starts to befriend them?" Lucas asked.

"How did you know?" Calliope asked.

Lucas's expression was grim. "It's an interrogation technique. Break them down, then try to make them think you're their friend."

"Befriend them how?" Atticus asked Calliope.

"From what I can see in the chat, he starts to create this sort of intimate bond with them. Convinces them that he's not like the other handlers. He seems encouraging at first. Tells them that they can do it, they can beat the game, that he has faith in them. That the money they'll win will change their lives. But once he gets them talking to him, confiding in him, that's when it all changes."

"Changes how?" Thomas pressed.

Calliope cleared her throat, still hesitant. "He starts questioning reality. The videos he forces them to watch are the worst kind of conspiracy theory propaganda. Like flat-earther, 911 was an inside job, the country is being run by lizard people conspiracy theory stuff. The kind of things nobody in their right mind would watch if they hadn't already been broken down psychologically."

"But why?" Zane asked. "Like, what's the point of that?"

"He's systematically stripping down their defenses, making them more susceptible to his ideology," Lucas said.

"Ideology?" Zane echoed.

"Keep going, Calliope," Lucas said, without supplying any more detail.

The videos advanced again. "This is where he starts to convince them that none of this is real."

"None of what?" Zane asked, frustrated.

"Life," Calliope said softly. "He's unraveling their reality, convincing them that they're Neo and he's Morpheus and they're all caught in a Matrix-like creation.

One they can unplug from if they just complete the final challenge. And die."

"No fucking way," Zane snapped. "My brother wouldn't fall for this bullshit. Gage was the smartest person I knew. There's no way he'd fall for this. No way."

"I have the video, Zane," Calliope said gently. "But you don't want to watch it."

"Show me," Zane said, seething.

"Zane—" Calliope started.

"Show me!" he shouted.

The other videos disappeared and Gage appeared on the screen. Zane sucked in a sharp breath at the sight of his brother. His hand, which had rested on Asa's, now curled around Asa's wrist, his blunt nails digging into his skin.

"Day one," Calliope said.

It was clear the footage was coming from Gage's webcam, though whether he knew it or not was unclear. He looked much like he did in the picture in Zane's apartment. Good-looking, clear-eyed, dressed in a sweatshirt and a backwards ball cap. Behind him, somebody—possibly his roommate—moved around behind him completely unaware that Zane's brother was embarking on a game that would take his life.

"Day ten," Calliope said.

Zane made a sound like a wounded animal at the sight of his brother on the screen. He looked strung out, unkempt. His eyes were red, swollen, bloodshot. There was no sound, but he was speaking animatedly, either to somebody on the other side of his computer or possibly recording himself. He looked terrible, like someone days from succumbing to a serious illness. Asa supposed he was, whether he knew it or not.

"That can't be ten days," Noah said. "He looks ten years older."

"That's what psychological torture can do to you," August said. "There's an entire industry dedicated to learning the best way to systematically break down the human psyche. Even the strongest people have little hope of making it through unscathed."

"Eric did," Zane said, voice raw.

"Eric figured it out early. He said it himself. If he hadn't taken that advertising class that talked about subliminal messaging, he never would have put it together," Asa reminded him.

"Is that why he tried to kill Eric? He disqualified the others. Clearly, he wanted the number down to five. Why not disqualify Eric?" Zane asked.

"My guess is he worried Eric would spill about the game, the tactics," Asa said.

That did little to nullify Zane. He was unnaturally pale, his body trembling. "Show me the final clip."

"No," Calliope said, tone equally strong.

"You have to," Zane said, voice suddenly thick with tears. "I need to see it, need to see *him*. I need to see it with my own two eyes."

"Please, Zane…" Calliope said. "Don't watch this."

Zane swallowed the lump in his throat. "Show me."

Asa put an arm around him. "Maybe you shouldn't. You can't unsee this."

"I've seen plenty of dead bodies and even murders," Zane managed, his whole body stiff beneath Asa's touch.

"But those people weren't your family," Asa said, looking to the others for help.

"Asa's right," Adam said. "Noah still has nightmares about what he saw in his videos."

Asa hadn't expected Adam to be the one to come to the rescue. Of all the brothers, Adam was the one who appeared to feel the least. His only real solid emotion was envy—or maybe jealousy. Whatever it was that compelled him to protect Noah at all costs while disregarding the feelings of all others.

"Lucas, tell him," Calliope said.

"Witnessing a suicide, especially that of a loved one—" Lucas started.

"Makes me more likely to take my own life," Zane finished. "I know the studies. I've read them all. When somebody in your family decides to kill themselves, you become an expert."

Asa leaned into his space. "I can't lose you."

Zane looked at him, startled. "You won't. I'm not going to unalive myself just because I see my brother—" His voice caught in a sob, but he quickly stuffed it down. "Just show me."

"Do it, Calliope," Thomas said, studying Zane as if he could look inside and know he was making the best decision.

The film was clear, but because it was a webcam, there was only so much that could be seen. Gage sitting at his desk, nodding to the camera. He was pale, gaunt, dressed in the same clothes they'd seen him in days before. He didn't seem distressed so much as exhausted. When he stood, Asa could see he wore pajama pants. Gage walked to the closet just outside of the frame, but the belt that appeared in his hand was visible.

They all watched in taut silence as he stepped up onto his bed. Asa was glad they could now only view Gage from the thigh down. Zane's nails were drawing blood on Asa's wrist but he said nothing. He would have let Zane tear him to shreds if it could somehow prevent the inevitable breakdown.

Then it happened. Gage stepped off the bed. It wasn't a quick death. He didn't jump from enough of a height or with enough force to break his neck. He died slowly, over three minutes. They watched the whole thing. Nobody moving. Maybe not even breathing.

Zane stared at the screen, unblinking, until his brother's legs stopped twitching, and then he bolted from the room so fast it took Asa a moment to even realize he was on the move. He followed, catching sight of Zane rounding the corner, quickly overtaking him. He gripped him by the shoulders, leading him to the closest bathroom where he dropped to his knees and promptly threw up.

It was clear Zane had a weak stomach. He was going to end up with a bleeding ulcer. He had a delicate constitution, which was definitely not suitable for the Mulvaney lifestyle. Asa needed to start taking better care of him.

"I'm fine," Zane managed between heaves. "Just go."

Asa sat on the floor behind him, rubbing his back. "I'm not going anywhere, Lois. So, save your breath."

When Zane's stomach finally seemed too empty for him to vomit, Asa wet a washcloth and forced Zane to hold still while he wiped his face. "Why did you insist on watching that?"

"Don't lecture me," Zane said. "I needed to see it. I just… I needed to know."

"I'm not lecturing you, Lois. I just think you should let me handle the wet work and you stick with the brainiac paperwork stuff."

Zane snorted, letting Asa pull him back against him on the floor. "You act as if I don't know how smart you are. You build skyscrapers for a living. You're the smart one and the hot one."

"Now, see, the hot is subjective, Lois. Because I definitely think you're the hot one in our relationship. You like to keep it under wraps, but it's there. Nobody knows better than me just how fucking sexy you are, especially when you're naked and begging. Covered in my bruises. Nobody else will ever come close to that. And, as for smarts, I'm math smart. You're cop smart."

"Cop smart?" Zane said, amused.

Asa nodded, grateful he was somehow managing to distract Zane. "Yeah. You know how to investigate. Ask questions."

"So do you."

"No, I know how to interrogate. I don't have your delicate touch. I'm all about getting the answers I want regardless of what's left of the subject once I do."

Zane was quiet for a long time, head resting against Asa's chest. "I want you to kill him," Zane said finally.

"I swear to you, I'll kill him, and then we'll find the others and I'll kill them, too. But one thing at a time. First, we torture Jerry, then we take out the game master. After that, we'll start worrying about finding the other handlers. Without the game master, the others will scurry off into hiding."

"I just want him to suffer. I need both of them to suffer. I need to see it with my own eyes."

Asa nodded. "I can do that for you, Lois. But none of us would blame you if you didn't want to watch."

"Was Noah there when they took out the men who hurt him? Was Lucas?" Zane asked.

Asa nodded. "Yes."

"Do you think they're stronger than me?"

Asa frowned. Relationships were so much more of a minefield than he'd ever imagined. One wrong word could lead to disaster. He wasn't used to having to watch his footing so much. "Of course not. I just don't want you to think this is some kind of test. Neither Noah or Lucas actively kill for us. There are plenty of things to do in this family that have nothing to do with picking up a weapon. Your contributions are going to be important, and even if they aren't, I'll still want you."

"When do we get this guy?" Zane asked, dropping a kiss over Asa's heart through his t-shirt. It was such a thoughtlessly sweet gesture that he couldn't help but reciprocate it by kissing the top of his head.

Asa squeezed him harder. He wanted to finish this shit so they could get on with their lives, whatever that looked like. But to do that, they needed to end this.

"Tonight, Lois. We go get him tonight. Let's get back in there and make a plan."

TWENTY-ONE

ZANE

Zane was coming out of his skin. They were almost to Atticus's and Jericho's murder cabin. The others were already there with Jerry. Asa had wanted to be involved in his capture, but Thomas didn't want amateurs involved in snatching Jerry off the street in broad daylight and Zane had refused to let Asa go alone. The compromise was neither of them go, instead meeting the others after they 'acquired the target,' as Thomas put it.

Asa was unsurprisingly calm, humming along to the music as they made the trek out to the woods. He said the only truly stressful thing about planning and executing a murder was ensuring an alibi was in place. There was no connection between Jerry and anybody in the Mulvaney family or Zane's family for that matter. Since there was no fear of reprisal with Jerry, there was no worry about forming an alibi, which meant Asa was easy-breezy like they were out for a Sunday drive.

"Are you sure they got him?" Zane asked for the

hundredth time since they got on the road.

Asa squeezed Zane's leg, giving him an amused glance. "Yes, Lois. I know this will shock you, but basement dwelling losers are surprisingly easy to catch. He's already been secured. They're just waiting for us."

"How long until we get there?" Zane asked, staring out the window as if he could gauge the distance by sight.

"We're not even five minutes out."

"Good."

Zane just wanted to get this over with. He'd been wanting vengeance since he'd realized what had been done to his brother, and after watching that video… Zane took a deep breath and let it out, willing his stomach not to rebel once more. He'd never realized how much his brother's death had eaten at him until the mere mention of his death had triggered his upchuck reflex.

"I know you want to be involved, but you can step out if it gets to be too much. Nobody would blame you."

Zane knew Asa was trying to be sweet. And it was sweet, but there was a war going on inside him. Part of him wanted to hear the man scream forever. The other half wanted him to die quickly so Zane could forget about him. But there were still answers needed.

Zane gave him a sharp look. "With what? Getting the information we need to make sure that nobody else dies because of this piece of shit? Yeah, I'll be fine."

"I promise you, I'll get whatever information I can from him before I kill him," Asa said, as if testing him.

Zane looked him in the eye. "I don't care if I'm vomiting

into a trash can. I'm not leaving."

"Lois... I don't know if you understand what you're saying. My brothers and I have no ability to feel remorse. Or guilt. Or empathy. When I torture somebody, I feel nothing. No matter how much they scream or cry or beg, it has no effect on me. You're not going to feel the same way."

"He stole my brother's grasp on reality, watched him wrap a noose around his neck, and then jerked off to the footage. His screams will be music to my ears."

Asa nodded. "Alright. You're right. He killed your brother. You're entitled to have first crack at him."

"And I get to decide how he dies," Zane muttered.

Asa turned onto the long winding drive to the cabin and parked outside. A white van and Jericho's Bronco were already there.

After they parked, Asa grabbed Zane's shirt and tugged him over the center console. "Give me a kiss, Lois."

Zane wasn't sure what he'd expected. Asa had two modes. Quick, almost chaste pecks on the lips and soul searing, scorchingly hot, near pornographic tongue kisses. This was neither. He cupped Zane's face, slanting their lips together in a slow slide, his tongue teasing but never truly deepening the kiss.

There was a hard rap at the window, causing Zane to jump, his gaze darting to the source of the sound. His mouth fell open when he saw Asa's image mirrored just outside the car window, his stomach plummeting into his shoes.

"Is that...?" Zane asked.

"Uh-huh," Asa said, sounding leery.

Zane stared up into Avi's unsmiling face. Their similarities were uncanny. Zane had seen plenty of identical twins in his day, and there was always something that separated them, that made one distinguishable from the other. But the only thing Zane could see was that Avi's left ear was slightly smaller than his right and Asa's right ear was slightly smaller. Mirror twins. Mirror twins who could communicate telepathically. Was he already saying something about Zane in Asa's head?

"Great. He already hates me, doesn't he?"

Asa's responding chuckle did little to quell Zane's already frazzled nerves. He couldn't tear his eyes away from Asa's twin. Avi was dressed in a pair of black cargo pants and a black henley. He wore surgical gloves on his hands. Zane looked over at Asa's almost identical outfit—minus the gloves—and frowned. "Do you guys always dress alike?"

"Not on purpose," Asa promised.

Avi opened Zane's door, offering a hand that Zane stared at for a long moment before taking, letting Avi help him from the car. "So, you're the reporter who stole my brother's...heart."

"Well, he kidnapped me. It seemed only fair," Zane murmured.

"Hurt him and—"

"Yeah, yeah, you'll rip my lungs out, cut out my tongue, castrate me. Trust me, I'm already terrified of you," Zane said, really wishing he could have saved this battle of wits for when he was better armed.

Avi eyed him suspiciously. "You don't look terrified."

Zane gave him a flat stare. "I'm screaming on the inside."

A slow, almost disturbing, smile spread across Avi's face before he looked at Asa. "I see it," he said mysteriously.

With that, he turned and walked towards the cabin, stopping at the door to say, "Well, are you coming?"

"You good?" Asa asked one last time.

Zane gave him an exasperated look. "Oh, my God. Stop asking me that."

Asa grinned. "After you, Lois."

Once inside the door, all bravado left him in one fell swoop when he saw the man who'd murdered his brother. Inside, Avi, Jericho, and Atticus had taken the man and strapped him, naked, to the large wooden table. They'd kept his glasses on. He appeared to be unconscious.

"He's not dead, is he?" Zane asked, looking from Avi to Jericho.

Atticus crossed his arms, expression grim. "No. But I just want you to know I'm burning this table."

Jericho rolled his eyes. "Relax, Freckles. I'll just sand it down and it will be good as new. We don't have to throw the whole table away because we tortured one guy on it. Besides, I'm sentimental about that table."

Atticus flushed but said nothing.

"Wake him up," Asa said.

Jericho pulled a small white packet from his pocket and snapped it open under Jerry's nose. He lurched violently, glasses going askew as he realized he was unable to move more than an inch or two with the thick leather straps around his ankles, chest, and midsection. "What the fuck?

What's going on? Who are you people?"

Asa ignored the man's sputtering, frowning at Atticus. "What are you doing here, anyway? I thought you didn't do the dirty work anymore."

Atticus looked at Zane.

"I asked him to be here," Zane said.

Zane had meant to tell Asa that he'd stolen his burner phone and texted Atticus. But Asa had decided Zane needed a distraction. And, well, Asa was very good at distracting Zane. So good that Zane forgot to care about text chains and stolen phones.

"Hello?" Jerry yelled, like he was worried they couldn't see or hear him.

"You did? Why?" Asa asked.

Zane glanced at Jerry, already desperately struggling against his bindings. "I don't know how to torture somebody, but I imagine it takes some skill to not kill them too quickly, right?"

"What? Torture? Me? What are you talking about? Whatever you think I've done, you've got the wrong guy," Jerry wailed.

"We'll get to you in a minute," Jericho said, waving a hand vaguely.

Asa was still looking at Zane, betrayed. "And you thought *he* was the best one for the job? He doesn't even like torturing people."

"I'm a fucking doctor," Atticus said sulkily.

Zane shrugged at Asa. "He *is* a fucking doctor."

Asa huffed a harsh breath out through his nose, then

nodded. "Yeah, okay. It's your show, Lois. You pick the cast."

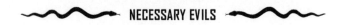

On the crude wooden counter, there was an array of sharp tools ranging from knives to surgical instruments. Zane picked up what looked like sharpened tweezers. "Jerry, did you ever play Operation as a kid?" he asked, running the dull end of the tool across his chest.

"W-What?" he sputtered.

Zane felt this strange sense of calm wash over him. "Operation. The game. Remember how you'd have the naked guy on the table and little red pinchers, and you'd have to carefully pull each of the man's organs out. But if you touched the sides—" Zane made a sound like a buzzer, making Jerry jump. "The patient died."

"I was excellent at that game," Atticus said.

Jericho kissed the side of Atticus's head. "Of course, you were, Freckles."

"Not me," Zane said, letting the sharpened tweezers sit just above the thick strap across Jerry's chest. "I sucked at it. But my brother, Gage, was amazing."

Jerry had tears streaming down his cheeks, but Zane found he truly didn't give a fuck about his tears, real or fake.

"Do you remember my brother?"

"No. What? No. Why would I know your brother?" Jerry asked.

Zane dug the sharpened tweezers into the man's doughy chest, then opened them, concentrating on the way his flesh parted. "That's a lie, Jerry. My brother played your game."

"What ga—"

Zane twisted the tiny tweezers, burrowing them deeper

while Jerry screamed. "We have your DVD collection, you sick fuck. But if you want me to grab the scalpel, we can see if my skills have improved since first grade. Up to you."

Jerry's chest was heaving, blood following the planes of his body to drip on the table, earning a miserable look from Atticus. Still, Jerry shook his head. "I don't know what you're talking about."

Zane sighed. "Have it your way." He placed the tweezers down on the counter and picked up a larger scalpel. "Atticus, if I were to slice him open here,"—he indicated a spot on the man's bloated belly—"would I kill him?"

"No, there's plenty of padding before you nick the intestines," Atticus said, bored. "But if you decide to eviscerate him, I beg of you, do it outside. Once the intestines fall out, they're almost impossible to put back in."

Zane shrugged. "I'll try to keep everything where it belongs."

He placed the scalpel against Jerry's skin, but before he could even move the blade, Jerry screamed, "Wait! Wait. I admit it. I knew your brother. I knew him. Okay?"

Part of Zane was disappointed Jerry was so easy to break. "Why?"

"Why what?" Jerry asked.

"Why did you do that to him? To them? To anybody?" Zane pressed, shaking his head.

"Because they deserved it," Jerry said, spit flying. "They have everything, and they just whine and bitch about how hard their lives are. They only have what they do because they have an advantage over me."

"Intelligence?" Atticus asked.

Avi pointed at Jerry. "Basic hygiene?"

"Sports prowess?" Jericho asked.

"Looks. It was all about their looks. That's all anybody cares about. I had the smarts to get into any school but they discriminated against me because I wasn't a Chad."

"A Chad?" Jericho asked.

"Incel talk for popular guy," Avi said.

Zane could feel his blood boiling. "My brother was valedictorian, had a million extracurriculars, and could have gotten a sports scholarship if he didn't get the academic one. My brother's admission had nothing to do with his looks. You're delusional."

Jerry sneered. "That's what all guys who look like you say. You don't want to admit it's not just chicks who have the upper hand because they're hot."

Zane dropped the scalpel and punched Jerry in the face, knocking off his glasses, letting himself enjoy the crunching cartilage and the blood exploding from his nose. He liked it so much, he did it again and again. He didn't even realize he'd done much damage until Asa was pulling him off of Jerry.

"Easy, Lois. We can't question him if you cave in his face," Asa said, holding onto him until he quit struggling.

"Make him tell us about the game master," Zane snarled. "If I get near him again, I'll fucking kill him, and he doesn't deserve a quick death."

Those not strapped to a table closed in around Jerry, looking down at his beaten face.

"What do you say, Jerry? Care to answer our questions, or should I get out the blindfold and show you how we play Operation?" Asa asked.

"The blindfold is for us, not you," Avi said casually. "Just in case that affects your decision at all."

"If I say anything to you, he'll kill me," Jerry whined.

"Read the room, Jerry. We're not here to tell you about our lord and savior, John Wick," Avi said, thumping him on the forehead. "We're gonna kill you."

"What?" Jerry gasped, as if he'd somehow convinced himself there was a way out of the situation.

"Yeah, Jerry. You're not walking out of here," Asa added. "Your death is a done deal. How many limbs you have when we kill you...well, that depends on you."

"Like my brother said, he's a doctor. You'd be shocked at how many appendages you can lose before your system starts shutting down."

Jericho reached into a bag at his feet and pulled out a tiny canister. No, a torch. A mini blowtorch. He fired it up, letting the flame explode dangerously close to Jerry's face. "Especially when we keep cauterizing the wounds."

"You ever been burned by a blowtorch, Jerry?" Avi asked. "It's my brother, August's, second favorite tool for torture. It can melt the skin right off. Smells kind of like barbeque."

"Oh, God," Jerry whispered.

"God can't help you now, Jerry. Tell us what you know about the game master."

Avi took the torch from Jericho and brought it close enough for the skin on Jerry's shoulder to blister. He gave a bloodcurdling scream, then said, "Okay! Okay. Okay. I'll tell you what I know."

Avi killed the torch. "Well, we're waiting."

"He's not local. He lives on some fucking island out in the middle of nowhere. When the game ends, the winners get invited to his private island. He doesn't tell us his name, and I don't know if he even lives there, but I think he does because his security system is fucking bananas. The highest of high-end gadgets."

"The winners?"

"Five players, five kills. The winners get a week on the island."

"That's it?" Zane asked. "My brother was tortured and killed so you could sip fucking fruity drinks on a goddamn beach? This wasn't even for money?"

Jerry snorted. "Money? No. This is for bragging rights, pride. Do you know how many years the military trains men to do what we do? We're elite. We can change people's realities. Make them think or do anything we want. We owned them. They were our slaves."

"Who is he?" Zane asked through gritted teeth.

"We don't use names."

"If you're so fucking smart, I guarantee you've figured it out. Who the fuck is he?" Zane asked again. "Tell me or I let them burn you alive."

"Okay. His name is Frederick Deetz," Jerry said, voice panicked.

"What? That can't be right," Atticus said.

Jerry nodded. "Oh, it is. It took some sleuthing, but it's

definitely him."

"Who is this guy?" Asa asked, still holding onto Zane.

"He owns Gecko Games," Atticus answered.

"The video game company?" Avi asked.

"Yeah, he and Dad have been in the same room more than once. He doesn't live on an island, but he definitely has enough money to own one. This one might almost be too easy," Atticus said, sounding disappointed.

"I don't care as long as they're all dead. I want the handlers, too," Zane growled.

"I can't give you those. I don't know them. I figured out Deetz because I had free range of his house. The others simply went by code names."

"Does he have a staff on that island? Security?" Asa asked.

"He did when we were there, but I don't know about any other times," Jerry said. "That's the truth. These players come from all over the globe. Russia, China…literally everywhere. You can shut down the game, but you're never going to find the other players. It's just not possible to track them all down."

"Do you believe him?" Zane asked Asa, his heart squeezing like it was in a vise.

"I do," Asa said. "But we can keep going until you're satisfied."

"It's just not fair that he gets to die quickly when he tortured my brother for weeks," Zane muttered, voice shredded.

"We don't have to kill him quickly," Atticus said, like he was discussing the weather.

"What do you mean?" Zane asked, looking from him to

Asa and back again.

"As long as he has fluids, we can keep him alive for weeks," Atticus clarified.

"It's not safe to have him stashed out here," Jericho retorted.

Atticus shrugged. "Not above ground, maybe. An extra large pine box, a six-foot deep hole, some IV tubing, and a trip out here daily to change the bag, and we can keep him alive for anywhere from twenty days to two months depending on how long it takes him to starve to death."

"What? That wasn't the deal!" Jerry shouted. "You can't be serious."

"How will you know when he's dead?" Zane asked, mulling the idea over.

Would it make him a horrible person? Did he care? Wasn't this an eye for an eye? He tortured Gage for a month. Why shouldn't Jerry experience the same level of horror?

Atticus gave that same bored shrug. "I'll know for sure about a week after I stop the fluids, so really, the choice is yours. You can decide what day he finally dies. Until then, he can lie around underground with nothing but the insects and his thoughts while he slowly rots."

"You wouldn't mind?" Zane asked Atticus.

"One of us is always out here anyways," he said. "Besides, you're family."

Zane's heart felt like it would explode in that moment. He looked to Asa, who nodded. "It's your choice, Lois. I can't make it for you."

Avi stepped forward. "If he'd done this to my brother, I'd

put a dive mask on him and stake him to the bottom of the lake so he could be eaten alive. You're a lot nicer than me."

For some reason, that was all Zane needed to hear. "Do it. Fuck him."

Jerry's screams rattled around the cabin until Jericho injected him with something that knocked him out. "Transports are easier when they can't fight back."

"Come on, Lois. Let's go home. We'll figure out how to deal with the game master tomorrow."

"What home are you going to?" Avi asked.

"The city. Are you coming?"

Avi shook his head. "Can't. I got a work thing with Felix and he'll shoot me if I miss it." Both Jericho and Asa stared at Avi for a long moment. "What? I said it's a work thing."

"You own the company," Asa reminded him.

"Maybe. But he kind of owns me," Avi said. "He just doesn't know it yet."

"Oh, he does," Jericho muttered with a snort.

"See you at home," Asa said, leading Zane out the door. "Are you sure you're okay, Lois?"

Zane wanted to say he was fine, but he wasn't. He turned and threw his arms around Asa. "I'm not fine. I'm not fine at all."

"What do you need?" Asa asked.

Zane looked up at him, eyes pleading. "I need you to make me forget everything but you."

Asa gave a stilted nod. "I can do that."

TWENTY-TWO

ASA

Everybody but Archer and Aiden were in attendance for the meeting that convened the following morning. Asa left the seat to his left empty for Avi—like he always did—putting Zane to his right so there would be no weirdness. When Avi entered, he zeroed in on the empty seat immediately but ignored it for the chair on Zane's right, plopping himself down and pulling it closer so Zane was tightly sandwiched between them.

Asa wasn't sure if Avi was attempting to intimidate Zane or bond with him. Zane didn't seem sure either. He eyed Avi warily, especially when he gave Zane a wide grin, patting him on the top of the head, flattening his curls. Zane looked to Asa for clarification but there was none to give. Avi had locked their mind-meld tight, keeping his thoughts of Zane under wraps.

Asa gave Avi a hard stare, but he just leaned back in his seat, rocking it with more force than necessary, causing it to bump Zane's chair with a rhythmic thumping sound that made Asa roll his eyes. Avi was clearly handling the situation like the adult he was.

Calliope started the meeting without any pleasantries. "Here's what we know about Frederick 'Freddie' Deetz. Owner of Gecko Games, eccentric weirdo, dresses like Willy Wonka and Michael Jackson had a poorly styled love child. There have been numerous rumors about sexual harassment, and several women have been quietly paid off. The fact that nobody picked up on what a potential problem this guy is would almost be funny if it wasn't so sad."

A picture appeared on the screen. The man was younger than Asa had imagined he'd be—no more than forty at most. In the picture, he wore a purple suit with a yellow shirt and had a slicked back, almost pompadour-like, hairstyle going. Calliope was right. This dude was suspicious looking.

"One of his company's most popular games, *Voyeur*, allows the player to play as either the hero or the villain. As the hero, you have to survive the villain's psychological torture. As the villain, you have to make choices that you think would cause the most trauma to the hero. Like the movie *Saw*, but you can decide whether you're one of the victims or Jigsaw himself."

"Jesus," Zane muttered.

"Do we have any proof he's involved in these games, though?" Thomas asked.

Calliope sighed. "No. Unfortunately not. His business computer was easily hackable, but there was nothing there. His home system is locked down tight, which leads me to believe that he keeps the goods at home where he can relive his greatest hits."

"Great. We have nothing," Zane muttered.

"Well, yes," Calliope agreed. "But I have an idea. It's a little bit crazy."

"We have a man rotting alive in a box on a property owned by my family," Thomas managed. "I think we've moved past a little crazy. What's your plan?"

"How fast can you guys get to Malibu?" Calliope countered.

Thomas waved a hand. "I can have a jet on standby. We can be there in a few hours if need be. Why?"

"Freddie might surround himself with armed guards on his creepy little island fortress, but in California, he has a minor security detail and a top-notch alarm system. It shouldn't be hard for a full team to breach his walls."

"Why does it sound like there's a but coming?" Atticus asked.

Adam snickered. "But coming," he repeated, earning a glare from August and a slap from Noah.

"*But,*" Calliope said, "when I drew up the plans for his house on the water, I noticed he also has a panic room, and if he manages to get in there, we've lost him and there's a good chance he virtually wipes his system so we can't ever find the evidence we need."

"What are you proposing, Calliope?"

"A leap of faith," she said with a sigh. "Freddie's drawing a lot of power into his beachfront mansion, and I'm pretty sure that means he runs the game from that system. If that's the case—and if you truly believe Jerry wasn't lying—then I think I can lure him into chasing me down a wormhole. If he tries to hack my system, I can back-hack him, get access to everything and get the dirt we need to not only prove what he did but get evidence needed to expose him."

"Well, that sounds ideal," Jericho said, sounding like he was also waiting to hear the flaw in the plan.

Calliope sighed. "But once I do that, he'll know we're onto him and he'll run. Or worse, he'll successfully hack me and find something on my computer he should never see and try to blackmail his way out of trouble."

"Yeah, that sounds like more than a leap of faith," Lucas said. "That sounds like a suicide mission."

"This is where the leap comes in," Calliope said. "Our only option is to simultaneously go after him. I distract him with the hack, while you get past security and take him out in whatever manner you see fit. But this has to be precise. Strategic. If either of us are off, it could ruin everything."

Thomas looked at Asa and Zane. "How sure are you that he's the guy?"

Asa looked at Zane, who said, "I don't think Jerry would have lied about this."

Asa nodded. "He doesn't seem like the type to take a secret to the grave. Once he knew he was dead either way, he sang like a canary."

"Can we do this with only five, Calliope?" Asa asked.

"Aiden can meet you there," Thomas said. "He's close and in-between assignments."

They all looked at Thomas for a long moment. He rarely brought up Aiden, but when he did, there was a sharpness to his tone, like he wanted to cut off any chance of one of them finally asking what the fuck had happened between the two of them to cause this level of tension.

"Six of us, then," Asa amended.

"Seven," Zane said. "I want to go."

"Yeah, no. You can't go," Asa fired back, and when Zane opened his mouth to argue, Asa held up his hand. "That's not up for negotiation. I can't focus if I have to worry about you getting shot."

"You can't just say, 'you're not going,' like I'm some kind of 1950s housewife," Zane snapped. "You're not…the boss of me," he finished, flushing.

"This has nothing to do with who's in charge of who," Asa countered. "This has to do with training. Do you know how to use a gun? A knife? Do you have any kind of combat skill needed that I don't know about?"

Zane's face fell. "No."

"Hold that thought," Calliope said. Blueprints appeared on the screen as well as what looked like satellite footage. "Strategically, it would seem like breaching the home from the water would be ideal, but the entire backside of his home is glass, so you'd have to go in completely under the radar. That means going in Seal-style with dive equipment and keeping a boat anchored out of sight. It means no guns. This has to be a completely silent attack."

"If he hears us coming, won't he just run to his little panic room?" Asa asked. "He can't possibly care about hacking you enough to risk death."

"This guy is a narcissist. He's going to be so pissed that I even dared to try to hack him that he won't be able to resist showing off how superior his skills are. Believe me, I know the type. I just have to keep him busy. Let him think he's winning, but while he's chasing me, I'm leading him right where I want him to go. Once you have him, I'll have his computer system."

"What if there's nothing there?" Zane asked. "We can't just let him go. What do we do?"

"We get the confession out of him the old-fashioned way and then we put him down and make peace with the fact that we might not be able to expose him for the monster he is," August said.

"Fuck that," Zane growled. "The world needs to know. Those families need to know."

"One crisis at a time," Calliope said. "Anybody know how to drive a boat?"

"I do," Lucas said, earning a surprised look from August. "What? I spent my summers fishing with my grandfather. Believe me, he made sure I knew how to do all of the manly things."

"Okay, so Lucas drives the boat. Zane, you can stay on the boat with Lucas. Once the target is acquired, you can be there for the justice part of it. Okay?" Calliope asked.

"Can I go?" Noah chimed in.

"I need you on the monitors, but we can set them up remotely on the boat. This has to go down at exactly the same time and someone is going to have to walk the guys through step by step. And that someone is you."

Noah nodded. "When is this going down?"

"Thomas?" Calliope chirped.

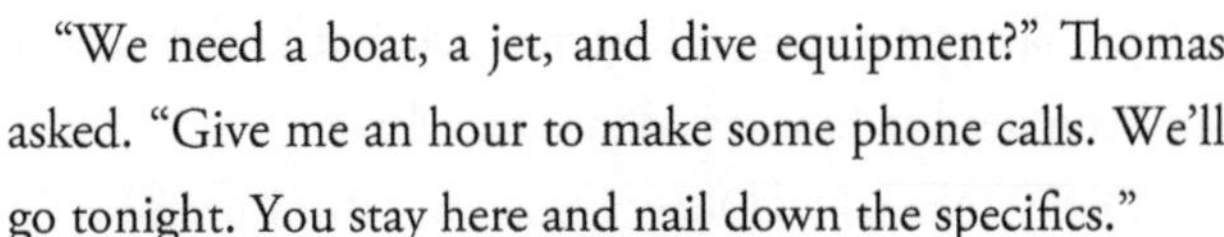

"We need a boat, a jet, and dive equipment?" Thomas asked. "Give me an hour to make some phone calls. We'll go tonight. You stay here and nail down the specifics."

They killed the lights on the boat about half a mile from Freddie's Malibu mansion. Zane and Noah were below deck, ensuring that the monitors were set up. The team on the ground would have cameras so Noah could monitor in real time with satellite footage as well as keep tabs on Calliope.

Asa found Zane sitting on the table, chewing his nails down to the quick.

"I don't like this," Zane said, shaking his head. "What if you get hurt? What if he calls the cops and you go to jail?"

"Then you can bake me a cake with a nail file in it. Okay?" Asa teased, earning a glare from Zane.

"That's not funny."

"It's a little funny," Asa said, chucking Zane under the chin. "Seriously, Lois. We've done this hundreds of times. This is going to be easy."

"I feel like you're fucking lying," Zane said, wrapping his arms awkwardly around Asa, who was decked out in his dive gear.

"I never lie to you, Lois. That's why we work."

"I love you," Zane blurted.

"Wow, you really *do* think I'm going to die. Have a little faith, Lois."

"I'm serious. I love you. I know it doesn't make sense and

it's too fast and you can't love me back, but I need to say it and you need to hear it just in case. Okay?"

"Okay," Asa said. "Okay. I hear you. But I promise I'm coming back. And I'm bringing that piece of shit with me, so you can decide exactly what you want to do with him. Be creative."

Zane continued to cling to him until Calliope's voice came over the comms. "Everything is in place. Noah, are you good to go?"

Noah flipped on half a dozen switches, and the monitors blazed to life. "I'm ready, yeah."

"Everybody in the water," Calliope said. "I want a last minute systems check."

"I'll be back, Lois. I promise."

Zane reluctantly let Asa go, chewing on his lip as he watched him leave. Above deck, August, Adam, Avi, Aiden, and Jericho were checking each other's gear before putting their rebreather masks on and giving a thumbs up, falling backwards off the boat into the chilly water, each carrying an underwater propulsion system.

Asa was the last in the water. Underneath, they did a final check, ensuring everything was ready. There were no guns to worry about, just the two knives strapped to Asa's thighs. The trip from the boat to the shore went quickly with the propulsion pulling them along.

"We're in position," Asa said.

TWENTY-THREE

ZANE

"Well then, here goes nothing," Calliope said.

Zane watched on the monitor as Calliope pulled up the link she'd used to try to join the game. His stomach lurched as the old school graphic popped up asking if she wanted to play the game. She clicked the yes button. The cursor flashed for a solid five minutes. Then, just like last time, the **GAME OVER** warning appeared and the screen went blank.

"Shit," Noah muttered. "What if he doesn't bite?"

"Be patient," Calliope warned.

Minutes dripped by, Zane's skin crawling with each second, until finally words appeared in block letters on the screen.

I TOLD YOU. GAME'S OVER.

Calliope clicked the blinking cursor, typing: **I know who you are.**

NO YOU DON'T.

Calliope didn't hesitate before typing back: **Sure I do, Freddie.**

"That should get him scrambling. Now, I just need to make a very obvious attempt to breach his system." Zane listened to Calliope's furious typing. "That ought to do it."

ARE YOU TRYING TO HACK ME?

Calliope cackled maniacally, typing: **Trying? Who's going to stop me?**

"Okay, go," she hissed.

Noah spun his chair to the other two monitors, pushing a few buttons. Zane could only watch as the satellite images appeared, seemingly refreshing every thirty seconds. Noah wore a headset that made him look a little like he should be working the window at an In & Out Burger, but his commands were short and to the point.

"Hold. There are two security guys standing at nine o'clock. Looks like they're bullshitting."

The others stayed submerged while Calliope continued to bait Freddie. "Yeah, that's right you fuck-wad, come and get me."

"The two guards are separating," Noah said. "One is retreating around the east side of the property. The other is staying put. Wait for my signal, then be ready to pounce."

When the guard turned his back, Noah said, "Go, now. Take him down."

Zane's heart stopped as Asa emerged from the water in one fluid motion, catching the man from behind and slitting his throat without effort before dragging him back into the water.

"One down," Jericho said.

"You're good to go," Noah directed.

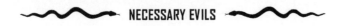

Zane paced as they walked from the sea, stashing their dive equipment on the shore beneath some plants. They all wore cameras, but Zane only cared about one: Asa's.

DO YOU REALLY THINK YOU'RE GOOD ENOUGH TO HACK ME? ME? YOU'RE A FUCKING AMATEUR.

Calliope scoffed but didn't respond to his message, focused on whatever it was she was doing that had lines of code flashing across the screen at a dizzying rate. "That's it. Come on. Just a little fucking more, you dumb motherfucker."

"Do you kiss your mother with that mouth?" Noah murmured into the comms.

"My mother's dead," Calliope shot back.

"Another guard at twelve o'clock, standing in the alcove behind the decorative wall. He's got an assault rifle and a side arm."

August motioned for the others to stay, then crept up to the wall with its Moroccan inspired cutouts, pulling a wicked-looking blade from a sheath on his leg and sending it through one of the gaps. "Guard two is done."

"Oh, what's that? That's right, it's me kicking in your backdoor, but you go ahead and keep searching," Calliope muttered to herself.

"You're free to breach the perimeter," Noah said.

Zane swallowed hard as he watched the glass doors part and the six of them enter the well-lit mansion, fanning out in formation. Noah shrunk the screen with the satellite image and enhanced the blueprints of Freddie's house.

"Jericho and Adam, take out the two guards just outside

the front door," Noah commanded. "Avi and Asa, find the panic room in the back of the master closet and cut off his access. Aiden and August, clear the downstairs and close off the exits."

Zane couldn't breathe. He couldn't think. He turned to the monitor where Calliope was locked in a virtual battle.

ARE YOU IN MY HOUSE?

"I'm everywhere," Calliope said out loud.

The wail of a security alarm came to life, echoing throughout the house and through the comms, causing everybody to wince. "We're made," Noah said, stating the obvious.

"Guards in the front are down," Jericho responded, "but if we don't cancel that alarm, there's going to be sirens in five minutes or less."

"Panic room is sealed," Asa added, pulling the master closet door shut and jamming something into the lock. "Where is this son of a bitch?"

"Not downstairs. It's cleared," somebody said, probably Aiden.

"Hah! I'm in!" Calliope screamed, triumphant.

Zane tried to keep eyes on Asa's camera but there was so much going on. People were running, images blurring. Zane dragged his gaze back to Asa's camera just as he rounded a corner into an empty hallway. He glanced quickly behind him, and when he looked again, he was face to face with Freddie and a shotgun that looked comically large to Zane's fear-soaked brain.

Zane sucked in a deep breath, but before he could let out the panicked sound building within his lungs, Avi was there, bringing down what looked like a ceramic pot on Freddie's head. Zane's knees gave way just as Freddie's did, only Freddie crumpled to the floor while Zane fell into the seat positioned beside him.

"We've acquired the target. Have Lucas come get us," Asa reported.

"Home stretch now," Noah said with a supportive smile at Zane. "It does get easier, I swear. There have been a few near misses but also hundreds of perfect scores. They really do know what they're doing."

Zane nodded, stomach lurching as Lucas put the boat into gear and stepped on the gas, the engine roaring.

"I canceled the alarm and gave them the passcode. We should have more than enough time to get us out on the water," Calliope said. "I've started downloading his files, but I won't know if we have what we're looking for until I sort through it all."

Freddie definitely didn't look like much in person. The shotgun he'd held was normal-sized. Rather, it was the man himself who was small, almost diminutive, especially in his too tight tank top and silky wide-legged pants. They'd tied his hands behind his back and dumped him on deck, making sure they were far out to sea before anyone tried to rouse him.

It took an hour for Freddie to wake enough to fully understand the gravity of his situation. Much to Zane's dismay, he seemed to find it funny, squinting at them in the darkness, mocking their wetsuits.

"Who are you losers? Did they send second string Navy SEALS after me? I hope you aren't trying to ransom me for money or anything. It's all tied up in crypto," he said with a weirdly high-pitched laugh.

"No, we're the men sent to kill you," Asa responded, tone bored. "We just wanted you awake in case you have any last words. It was the least we could do."

Freddie rolled his eyes. "Just put a bullet in my head and be done with it."

"Sounds good to me," Jericho said.

"The world is going to mourn me and all of my charity work."

"This guy's a fucking tool," Adam muttered.

"The world knows you as the guy who pays off his sexual assault victims." Noah sneered.

"Alleged," Freddie retorted with another high-pitched laugh.

Zane's heart twisted. Gage had died for this? Because of this man? "The world is going to know you for what you are. A sick, twisted narcissist who kills people for sport."

That brought Freddie up short, but only for a moment, then he was laughing once more. "You'll never prove that."

"Our analyst is going through your system with a fine-tooth comb. Sure you're as squeaky clean as you think?" Noah asked.

Freddie shrugged, his face growing pinched. "Whatever. It's all a game. This is all a game. None of this is real. You're all sheep."

Zane stumbled back, his words sinking in. "Jesus. You really believe that? Are you really this fucking delusional?"

Freddie looked at Zane like he was pathetic. "Delusional? Do you know how many of the world's greatest minds believe none of this is real? That this is just an elaborate game and the only way to win is to unplug?"

"As one of the world's greatest minds," August said, "I can assure you, they, like you, are fucking stupid."

"Your friend, Jerry, is currently rotting underground, slowly starving to death, so I'm sure he's hoping you're right," Asa said. "Maybe when he dies in a couple of weeks, after writhing in pain, you two can compare notes on the other side."

Freddie shook his head, like he mourned the loss. "Jerry was a master game player, but he got too involved. He got off on it. He didn't understand how truly transcendent my game was. I was freeing people. I was their fucking savior. When they were dying, it was me they were praying to, me they thanked for freeing them."

"Holy fuck, please, can we just kill this guy?" Adam asked.

Asa turned to Zane, blocking him from Freddie. "We're not going to get any remorse or apologies out of him, Lois," he murmured, putting an arm around him. "I think we need to just…put him down. How do you want to do it?"

Zane's blood boiled as Freddie began to whistle a jaunty tune like he was on a Caribbean cruise. "Painfully. Slowly. I want to know he died screaming." He looked at the others. "I'm open to suggestions. This is your area of expertise, not mine."

Avi looked at Asa, eyes widening, grinning like a kid on Christmas morning. "Oh, please. Oh, please. Oh, please. Can we? Can we, Asa?"

Zane looked between the two of them. "Can we, what?"

Avi looked at Zane with a maniacal glee that would have chilled him to the bone if he hadn't seen that same expression mirrored often on Asa's face. A face he loved. "What do you know about keelhauling?"

"Keelhauling? Like what pirates used to do?" Zane asked.

"It was actually made popular by the British Royal Navy," August said conversationally, dropping an arm around Lucas's shoulders.

"What's keelhauling, exactly?" Noah asked.

Avi turned wild eyes on Noah. "Basically, you tie a rope to your victim, weigh him down just enough to reach the keel, then drag him beneath the boat from one end to the other, slowly letting the barnacles tear him to pieces. It's like waterboarding meets death by a thousand cuts. Only at the end of our keelhauling, he'll meet with a fast moving blade and become chum for some hungry sharks."

Noah wrinkled his nose. "Gross. Sounds messy."

"Sounds time consuming, and we promised to be home before the girls wake up for their three o'clock feeding," Lucas said to August.

August glanced at his watch. "It's barely nine-thirty. We can keelhaul this guy and still have the jet back in time for their feeding. I promise."

Lucas sighed. "Okay, if that's what Zane wants, I'm fine

with it."

"Fuck, yes," Avi cheered. "Please, Zane? Zaney? Zaniac? If you want him to die slowly and painfully, let's keelhaul him. You get what you want and I get to scratch another thing off my bucket list."

Zane watched as a little bit of Freddie's false bravado slipped. "Yeah. Do it."

Avi whooped, lifting Zane up and spinning him in a circle. "Yes. You fucking rock. Tell me where I can find the rope and anchor on this bitch."

When Zane was on his feet again, he dropped onto the padded seat that ran along the back of the boat. He didn't participate in the prep, didn't care about anything, really. Suddenly, he was just…tired. He wanted this to all be over so he could go home with Asa and sleep in their bed.

Freddie did die. Zane didn't know if he was screaming when the blades took him, but he felt some satisfaction in watching the ocean water run red beneath the glow of the boat lights when he finally met his demise. Once they made certain he was dead, the others brought out booze and clanked bottles together to celebrate a successful mission.

Zane just sat out on the deck, watching the dark waters and the lights on the shore getting closer and closer.

"You okay, Lois?" Asa asked, sitting beside him.

Zane turned, resting his back against Asa's chest, some of the ache disappearing as Asa wrapped his arms around him. "I'm okay."

"The worst is over. Now, you get to do what you do best. Write. You get to tell the world the story. Your way. You get to decide how they remember Freddie Deetz."

Zane could feel tears leaking down his cheeks, but he didn't care. "I thought I'd feel better when everybody was dead…or at least taken care of. But Gage is still gone. And now, he doesn't even talk to me anymore."

"Maybe you gave him the peace he needed to move on?" Asa suggested.

"Or maybe he was never there in the first place and my mental illness is resolving," Zane muttered.

"You don't know that. My brother and I can communicate without words. Lucas can see the past just by touching an object. Who's to say what's real or not. Your brother would be super fucking proud of you."

"But now, I'm just…alone. My mother's a nightmare, my father is dissociating, and now, Gage is gone. My whole family is obliterated."

"I know it's not the same thing, but you have a ton of family, better family. Family who might not all be able to love you but who will fucking die to protect you. Who will go to bat for you. Who will do everything in the world to make sure you succeed."

"I know."

"I got you, Lois. No matter what. We all do."

Zane nodded, burrowing deeper into Asa's arms. "I know. Tell me you love me. Even if you don't mean it. I just need to hear it."

Asa's hands threaded through Zane's curls, and then he was gently turning his head so he could look him in the eye. "I do love you, Lois. In whatever ways I can. I do.

Believe that."

"I do," Zane said.

"Good. Are you willing to say those words again in about six months in front of hundreds of people we barely know?"

Zane blinked at him. "What?"

"I'm asking you to marry me, Lois."

Zane's pulse skyrocketed. "Oh."

"Oh?" Asa said, looking flummoxed enough to make Zane laugh.

"Yeah. I mean, yes. Yes. Yes, I will marry you."

Asa let out a big breath that was swept away by the wind. "Way to give a guy a heart attack."

Zane smiled, then suddenly couldn't stop smiling. Maybe Asa was right. Maybe Gage had moved onto a better place. He'd still talk to him, even if he didn't talk back. The Mulvaneys were loud and crazy and certifiably insane, but they were a real family and that was what Zane had wanted his whole life. A real family and a man who loved him.

Now, he had both.

EPILOGUE

ASA

"Oh, fuck. That's it. God, your mouth should be illegal," Asa grunted, listening to Zane gag and sputter as he worked himself deeper into his throat. "Fuck, I've missed this. I can't believe you made me wait twenty-four hours to see you."

Zane moaned, long and low, sending vibrations shivering over him.

"I'm going to come," Asa warned, his head hitting the wall, eyes rolling as Zane's throat convulsed and he swallowed every drop.

As soon as he gathered himself, he pulled Zane up, undoing his pants and plunging his hand into his underwear, eyes widening when his hand found a sticky mess. "Did you come untouched, Lois? God, you're so fucking perfect. Do you love sucking me off that much?"

Zane buried his face in Asa's white shirt. "Shut up. It's our wedding day. I was already keyed up. Just seeing you in that tux had me hard, and when you dragged me in here, I knew I wouldn't last more than a minute or so."

"So fucking hot," Asa whispered, wiping at a drop of cum on Zane's lip.

"Do you think they're looking for us yet?" Zane said, looking at his watch.

Asa shrugged. "I don't think it matters. It's not like they can start without us."

"Are you sure you want to do this?" Zane asked, his gaze suddenly trepidatious.

Asa frowned, tugging Zane's hair back. "What? Where's this coming from? Have you ever known me to do a single thing I don't want to do? Ever?"

Zane shook his head. "I mean, to say our....courtship was a whirlwind would be an understatement. Our relationship was based on sex and blackmail. Everything just sort of happened so fast. I don't want you to feel like your dad forced you to, like, take one for the team."

Asa smirked at him and brushed his thumbs across Zane's cheekbones. "Are you drunk, Lois? Did you start pre-gaming without me? Because the only time you start doubting us—or me—is when you've been drinking."

Zane sighed, his voice hesitant. "I'm sober. I just don't want you to regret this."

Asa tilted his head. "What would I regret? We have an amazing life. We have mind-blowing sex. We're young. We're hot. We're rich." He kissed his forehead. "I found the one man on the planet who doesn't mind that I'm a murderer and, more importantly, that my brother will be living with us forever. We're a fucking power couple, Lois. Your YouTube channel is killing it. My firm is as successful as it's always been. Seriously, what's to regret?"

"All of those things are true, but none of them have anything to do with…feelings."

Asa's brows knitted together. "I tell you I love you all the time."

"Yeah, but you tell me you love Swiss Cake Rolls with the same level of fervor," Zane reminded him.

"Duh, because I do. A man can love more than one thing. It doesn't negate the other." Zane leveled a flat stare at him. "Okay, like, *if* I had to choose between you and a box of Little Debbie's, I'd definitely choose you. But you both hit just right," he said with a grin, giving Zane a deep kiss.

Zane slapped his shoulder. "Come on, Asa. Be serious. I know psychopaths can't love. Is what we have enough to keep you happy forever?"

Asa sighed. "Are you asking if I feel that weird goopy feeling when I look at you that people talk about in romance novels? If so, the answer is no. I don't have the ability to feel that. But whenever you walk into a room, I feel grateful you're mine. I feel calmer knowing you're there, where I can see you, protect you…" He kissed Zane's lips softly. "Do dirty, dirty things to you whenever I want."

Zane opened his mouth to speak, but Asa pinched his lips shut.

"I know people who'd give anything to have what we have. I've killed for you. I would die for you. I will put your wants and needs above mine forever because I want you to be happy. Is that love? Because when you're not around, I feel like there's…a splinter under my ribcage, and it only goes away when I see your face. That's enough for me. Is it enough for you?"

Zane swallowed hard, tears rolling down his cheeks. "That's enough."

Asa felt the knot in his chest loosen. "Good. I think we need to get cleaned up, though, because I'm pretty sure we were supposed to be at the front of the church twenty minutes ago, not in the broom closet."

"I'm pretty sure people would call what we just did in here sacrilegious," Zane said, peeking out the door.

"Whatever. I'm an atheist." Asa shrugged, pushing Zane out the door and rushing him towards the room where they were supposed to be getting ready.

They opened the door to half a dozen disappointed faces and one smirking one. The smirk belonged to Avi. "I told you they were somewhere doing the dirty."

"We were not," Zane lied, face flushed with embarrassment.

Avi snickered. "Dude, my brother's jizz is on your cheek."

Zane whirled on Asa, eyes accusatory. "Oh, my God. Why didn't you say anything?"

"We were having a moment," Asa said, defensive.

Noah chuckled, taking a wet wipe to Zane's face. "Yeah, well, your dad's pissed. He was afraid you blew this off and eloped to Mexico or something."

"We were just getting a jumpstart on the honeymoon," Asa said with a shrug. "I didn't think a blowjob was going to be such a huge ordeal."

Adam shrugged. "Apparently, it is when there's a guest list of five hundred people and an ice sculpture melting in the reception hall."

Cricket breezed in, a baby on each hip. "There you are. Can we get this going? These two have to go down for their nap in thirty minutes, and if you think Beverly threw a fit, wait until you see these two meltdown."

Zane went rigid at the mention of his mother's name. "What about my mother?"

Cricket gave August and Lucas a bug-eyed look. "You didn't tell them?"

Noah's hands waved wildly. "Haven't exactly had time. Can't exactly have Zane showing up at the altar looking like the fluffer on a porn set. Yell at them."

"What about my mother?" Zane asked, allowing Noah to poke and prod at him in an attempt to make his clothes look less wrinkled.

Avi did the same to Asa, but mostly because he'd made the suits and wanted them to look perfect for the paparazzi.

"She tried to crash the event," Cricket said, shifting the babies.

Asa had no idea how she managed to look effortless while holding onto two squirming infants and wearing four-inch stilettos, but she did. He stepped away from Avi, knocking Noah's hands out of the way to cup Zane's face as he began to hyperventilate. "Babe, we knew this was coming. You said so yourself. It's fine. This is fine. Cricket said *tried* to crash. Tried. Right?"

He looked to the others for confirmation. They all nodded.

"They dragged her out of there like she was Archer after a

bender at the strip club," Jericho promised.

"It's true," Archer said from where he lounged in the corner, flask in hand.

"I told you she would ruin this for me," Zane whined, his voice taking on a slight edge of hysteria.

"No, she tried. But she failed. She will always fail. We've got your back. That's what family is for," Noah promised.

"I thought it was for a good cover story?" Zane said, a little bit of humor returning to his voice.

"That, too," Asa said.

"Anything good in my life, she tries to take," Zane muttered.

"And fails. She will always fail," Asa reiterated. He'd say it as many times as Zane needed to hear it.

Zane was right, though. Since Asa and Zane had gone public with their relationship, and then engagement, Beverly had done everything in her power to wedge herself into the family. Zane had almost given in to her guilt trips a dozen times, but Asa made sure he was the line Beverly had to cross to get to Zane and Asa would not budge.

Zane was finally happy. The handlers they'd found in Freddie's files were being dispatched slowly but surely. He and Asa were the definition of a power couple, like Asa had said. When Zane revealed evidence that Freddie Deetz had created a game that had cost dozens of people their lives—including his own brother's—his stock immediately rose. Within hours, he was juggling job offers from hundreds of papers and magazines.

When Freddie's body eventually washed up on the shore,

with evidence showing he'd been murdered, Zane took to his brand new YouTube channel to postulate about a possible vigilante taking revenge on the cruel and heartless monster, rocketing his views to a level that made him worthy of panels at Crime-Con and got him guest spots on a dozen talk shows.

Bev tried to make herself a part of it all. She tried to leverage Zane's guilt over Gage. She tried to get interviews. She even floated around a tell-all book where she vowed to tell all of Zane's secrets. As if Zane had secrets. Zane was perfect. Above reproach. His background was choirboy clean. Every single time Beverly tried to steal Zane's spotlight, Asa made sure the full weight of the Mulvaney name crushed whatever deal was in the works. But, somehow, she always broke Zane's heart.

"Guys, we really gotta go," Cricket said, nodding towards the doorway. "Money only buys so much grace with the Episcopalians."

"Okay, okay," Asa said, holding his hand out to Zane. "You ready, Lois?"

"Let's do this." Zane nodded, screwing a nervous smile onto his face.

Asa practically dragged Zane through the double doors at the back of the church, then up the aisle where more than a hundred people watched and whispered. When they reached the front, Asa gave the priest a smile. "Sorry, there was a…fire."

"A *what*?" the priest asked, horrified.

"A little one," Zane said, pinching his fingers together.

"No damage. Let's get started," he said, giving the crowd a smile that made them smile back.

Everybody loved Zane. As they took their places, the family split. Adam, August, Avi, Atticus, Archer, and even Aiden standing for Asa, and Noah, Lucas, Jericho, Felix, Thomas, and Zane's friend, Blake, standing for Zane.

When a sudden bout of energy hit Asa, he turned to look at Avi with wide eyes. His brother gave him a comically obvious thumbs-up, making the guests chuckle.

The music swelled, and Cricket pulled a little wagon up the aisle with the two smallest Mulvaneys decked out in white frilly dresses, taking a seat at the front.

"Dearly beloved, we are gathered here today to join these men together in holy matrimony." There was nothing holy about the things Asa wanted to spend the rest of his life doing to Zane, and the look he gave Zane made sure he understood that. Zane flushed, giving Asa that smile that made his dick hard.

Asa zoned out until Cricket hurried forward with the rings, handing one to each of them. Zane gave Asa a look that was part nervous excitement and part panic. Asa gripped his hand.

"Place the ring on his finger and repeat after me," the priest said. "I, Asa, take you, Zane, to be my lawfully wedded husband, to have and to hold, from this day forward, for better, for worse, for richer, for poorer, in sickness and in health, to love and to cherish, till death do us part."

Asa repeated the vows, goosebumps erupting along his skin as he slid the ring on Zane's finger.

The priest nodded, glancing down at his cards. "Zane, place the ring on Asa's finger and repeat after me. "I, Zane, take you, Asa, to be my wedded husband, to have and to hold, from this day forward, for better, for worse, for richer, for poorer, in sickness and in health, to love and—" The priest stumbled, frowning, startled eyes going from Asa to Zane. "Obey?"

Zane tilted his head, leveling a fake glare at Asa, who grinned at him. "What? It was worth a shot?"

Once more, the guests tittered.

Zane rolled his eyes and gave the priest a nod, letting him know he could continue.

"Till death do us part."

Zane shook his head, looking much more relaxed. "I, Zane, take you, Asa, to be my lawfully wedded husband, to have and to hold, from this day forward, for better, for worse, for richer, for poorer, in sickness and in health, to love *and to cherish*, till death do us part."

The ring felt cool against Asa's now overheated skin. The priest continued to talk about marriage and responsibility and then made each of them say, 'I do,' but Asa only cared about one thing.

"You may now kiss your husband."

So, he did, thoroughly and completely in front of friends, family, strangers, and paparazzi. He kissed him like nobody was watching. He kissed him like he could somehow kiss away all of Zane's fears and worries and doubts.

When he pulled back, Zane stumbled a little, cheeks flushed and gaze a little shocky. The crowd erupted in applause, but Zane stared at Asa like he was the only one in the room. Neither of them made any move to leave.

Avi leaned into their bubble. "You guys know you can't stay here, right? You've got a whole reception to stare at each other like that. Looks great for the cameras. Maybe you can even sneak in a quickie during the cocktail hour." When the priest cleared his throat, Avi winked at him. "Sorry, Padre."

Once they were firmly tucked into the back of the limo, Asa dragged Zane into his lap. "Still worried?"

"I wasn't worried," Zane hedged.

"You were definitely a little worried."

"It's you who should be worried," Zane teased. "We don't have a prenup."

Asa snorted. "The only way out of this family is with a bullet, Lois."

"Are you threatening me on our wedding day?" Zane asked, clutching fake pearls.

"Me? Never. We're forever, Lois. Even if I have to chase you down and remind you of that every night."

Zane snickered. "As if you don't chase me down almost every night as it is. Do you know how much makeup I have to wear when I record just to keep you out of the headlines?"

Asa kissed Zane's cheek, then bit his ear. "I can't help it. You bring out the beast in me."

Zane turned his head to find Asa's lips. "Well, I wouldn't let just anybody chase me through the woods at night."

Asa pushed the button on the partition between them and the driver. "Now, about that quickie."

DEAR READER,

Thank you so much for reading *Headcase,* Book 4 in my Necessary Evils series. I hope you loved reading this book as much as I loved writing it. Look for Avi's book, *Mad Man*, coming soon.

If you've read my books before, none of the content of this book will surprise you. My history as an RN has exposed me to many different things in my life, and people feeling suicidal is unfortunately common in that profession. If you or somebody you know is dealing with these impulses, you can find help at: **www.opencounseling.com/suicide-hotlines**.

I'm obsessed with writing about the psyche and exactly how both nature and nurture often play a part in who a person becomes. I spent years working as an RN in a psychiatric hospital, most of those years spent with children aged anywhere from five to eighteen. It took a big toll on me and my own mental health, which is why writing these characters has become my own form of therapy. While sociopathic bodyguards and megalomaniacal cult leaders are all works of fiction, my heroes and villains are all drawn from real people who I encountered in my time as a nurse.

The game depicted in *Headcase*, while fictional, is based on a real international game briefly mentioned in the book: The Blue Whale game that targeted children. There are many places to read about the game, but not much information is known about it, so the details mentioned in this story are of my own imagination.

As always, thank you so much for loving my boys and my books. I'm blown away by your support and super grateful you were willing to go along for this ride with me.

If you guys are really loving the books, please consider joining my Facebook reader group, **Onley's Oubliette**, and signing up for my newsletter on my website so you can stay up to date on freebies, release dates, teasers, and more. You can also always hit me up on my social media and find all my links at **fans.link/OnleyJames**. You can find me literally everywhere, so say hi. I love talking to readers.

Finally, if you did love this book, (or even if you didn't. Eek!) it would be amazing if you could take a minute to review it. Reviews are like gold for authors.

Thank you again for reading.

ABOUT THE AUTHOR

ONLEY JAMES is the pen name of YA author, Martina McAtee, who lives in Central Florida with her children, her pitbull, her weiner dog, and an ever-growing collection of shady looking cats. She splits her time between writing YA LGBT paranormal romances and writing adult m/m romances.

When not at her desk, you can find her mainlining Starbucks refreshers, whining about how much she has to do, and avoiding the things she has to do by binge-watching unhealthy amounts of television in one sitting. She loves ghost stories, true crime documentaries, obsessively scrolling social media, and writing kinky, snarky books about men who fall in love with other men.

Find her online at:

WWW.ONLEYJAMES.COM

Milton Keynes UK
Ingram Content Group UK Ltd.
UKHW011958160124
436144UK00001B/44